MASS HYSTERIA

Praise for Michael Patrick Hicks

MASS HYSTERIA

"Fun, horrible fun, from start to finish."
-      Horror Novel Reviews

"It's fast paced, action-packed, and bloody. Really, almost everything a horror gore-hound could want. ... Undeniably talented, Michael Patrick Hicks shows evidence of a rather deliciously depraved mind..."
-      SciFi & Scary

"Mass Hysteria was a brutal horror novel, which reminded me of the horror being written in the late 70's and, (all of the), 80's. Books like James Herbert's The Ratsor Guy N. Smith's The Night of the Crabs. There are a lot of similarities to those classics here-the fast paced action going from scene to scene-with many gory deaths and other sick events. In fact, I think Mass Hysteria beats out those books in its sheer horrific brutality."
-      Char's Horror Corner

"I'm telling you now, this book isn't for readers with weak stomachs. It is brutal in all the right ways."
-      Cedar Hollow Horror Reviews

"If you are an aficionado of author Richard Laymon, you undoubtedly will like this book. This is horror at its bloodiest, guttiest and most shocking."
-      Cheryl Stout, Amazon Top 500 Reviewer

LET GO

"*Let Go* is a poignant zombie story. ...an excellent addition to the zombie genre, a study not in bloodthirsty hordes but the internal struggles of one lonely, old man."
- Hunter Shea, author of *We Are Always Watching* and *Just Add Water*

"Emotionally charged, suspenseful and wonderfully written."
- David Spell, The Scary Reviews

"A visceral roller coaster ride [and an] excellent literary contribution to the zombie apocalypse genre."
- Daniel Arthur Smith, author of *Tales From The Canyons of the Damned*

REVOLVER

"*Revolver* by Michael Patrick Hicks, however, takes the 'shocking' gold medal. A classic example of social science fiction … most gripping."
- David Wailing, author of *Auto*

"*Revolver* is one of those stories that, once I got over the initial shock of the subject matter and the sheer vulgarity of the content, I immediately had to listen to it a second time. … with all the political turmoil, particularly the attitudes against women, that the world is being exposed to right now. I think this makes *Revolver* all the more terrifyingly plausible."
- Audiobook Reviewer

"A lot of what happens in this story resonates with what we see and what we read in our very lives today. *Revolver* is a great story, bristling with tension, unflinching with its

descriptions and thoughtful. I get the feeling that people who misunderstand this may need to perhaps take a long hard look at themselves in the mirror."
-    Adrian Shotbolt, The Grim Reader

"*Revolver* is a perfect short story/novella to read right now. The political extremists are gaining more and more power and they aren't easily ignored anymore. *Revolver* tells the story of what would happen if we let this extremism go too far. And wow was it good. ... *Revolver* is a big "what if" book that will leave you feeling raw and full of emotion."
-    Brian's Book Blog

CONSUMPTION

"*Consumption* is one of the most horrifically intriguing novellas that I've read for quite some time....a quite different tale of horror that resonates feelings of dread and shock, very well written, some great ideas and some darkness around the invention of various culinary delights."
-    Paul Nelson, *SCREAM Magazine*

"Your stomach will turn, your throat will restrict, and jaw will clench tighter than a bull's arsehole in fly season."
-    S. Elliot Brandis, author of *Young Slasher*

"...wonderfully macabre! Cleverly thought out, I was both disgusted and excited by this tale. This a MUST read for horror fans."
-    Great Book Escapes

Also by Michael Patrick Hicks

<u>DRMR Series</u>
Convergence (Book One)
Emergence (Book Two)
Preservation (A DRMR Short Story)

Extinction Cycle: From The Ashes (Kindle Worlds Novella)

Mass Hysteria

<u>Short Stories</u>
Consumption
Revolver
Let Go
Black Site

MASS HYSTERIA

MICHAEL PATRICK HICKS

HIGH FEVER BOOKS

MASS HYSTERIA

Copyright © 2017 by Michael Patrick Hicks

HIGH FEVER
BOOKS

High Fever Books
First Edition: August 2017

Edited by Shay VanZwoll
EV Proofreading
http://www.evproofreading.com

Cover artwork by Kealan Patrick Burke
http://www.elderlemondesign.com

CONSUMPTION

Copyright © 2014 by Michael Patrick Hicks

Edited by Carol Davis
A Better Look
http://caroldavisauthor.com/a-better-look-editing-services/

Printed in the United States of America

ISBN-13: 978-1-947570-00-9 (paperback)
ISBN-10: 1-947570-00-5 (paperback)
ISBN-10: 1-947570-01-3 (ebook)
ISBN-13: 978-1-947570-01-6 (ebook)

For Maureen and Ben.

And I will cause them to eat the flesh of their sons
and the flesh of their daughters, and everyone
shall eat the flesh of his friend in the siege and in
the desperation with which their enemies and
those who seek their lives shall drive them to
despair. (Jeremiah 19:9)

1

BUCKLEY scratched at the door, a shrill and nervous whine stuttering from his probing muzzle. His nose was flared as he sniffed at the thin gap between door and doorjamb, his nails scrabbling against the wooden trim.

"Jesus, Buck!" Melisa Delacourt said. "Calm down."
She had raised the volume on the television three times, but the damn dog just kept getting louder and louder, determined to outmatch the flat screen's audio. The news was reporting on last night's meteor shower and she wanted to hear about the rock that splashed down in the lake.

"Sky watchers have been in for a real treat these last three or four nights," the weatherman was saying. "A rare celestial event has been lighting up the skies in various parts of the world, but if you happened to be up late last night, you might have caught sight of a few shooting stars right in our own backyard. If you were asleep, though, no worries. A few of our night owls sent us these stunning videos, so let's have a look!"

The weatherman, a stocky fella who barely looked out of his teens, was replaced with shaky cellphone footage. The first couple of seconds were dark and blurry, but after a moment, the nighttime sky lit up with a brilliant streak cutting diagonally across the screen. The meteor was a little bitty one, but still—a meteor strike! Damn near in her own backyard, too!

"Another viewer caught site of this much larger meteor," the weatherman said, "and we've confirmed that it did indeed land out by the old McClellan farm." He continued to prattle on as another motion-sickness-inducing cellphone video showed a bright speck in the sky, one that rapidly grew bigger and brighter until it exploded in a flash of blindingly white light.

The video was intense, but Melisa paid the broadcaster no mind as he talked over the looped footage. Besides which, the fucking dog was barking so goddamn loudly she could hardly even hear the report. She knew the story wouldn't be very juicy, though – the farm, if one could even call the small caved-in house and toppled barn a farm, had been abandoned for ages. And since Melisa hardly ever went out onto the peninsula, she could care less what went on there. The lake, though, now that was exciting. Maybe one of the reporters would come by to interview her! She hoped it was that Carmichael fellow. He was tall, with a cast iron jaw and silver hair, handsome as the devil with icy blue eyes that sent a pleasant chill through her every time the camera zoomed in on him during one of his nightly reports. Melisa thought about doing her hair and make-up, just in case. If Carmichael did come out this way, she wanted to look her best.

Buckley though, he had other ideas and sounded to be in one hell of a tizzy.

Goddamnit, dog!

Slamming a rocks glass filled with tequila, she shoved off the couch and walked to the golden Lab. The dog looked at her, to the door, back at her. As she drew nearer, he began barking more urgently.

"I'm coming, I'm coming."

Dog's really gotta go, she thought. She'd never seen Buckley this agitated before, but brushed it off as an achingly full bladder. Poor thing waited too long, that's all.

As she drew nearer, Buckley let out a louder bark, the fur along his spine standing on end. A low, tremulous growl shook loose from deep inside his throat, and he took a step forward, baring his teeth.

"What's gotten into you, boy?"

This was weird behavior, but then again, Buckley was a bit of a weird dog. He'd take himself for walks. Put a leash on him and let him take hold of the loop in his teeth, and he was good to go. He'd wander all over the neighborhood, head held high and tail wagging, happy as can be. He'd also eaten an entire bag of mothballs. Only the once, and years ago at that, but she was convinced the chemicals had messed with his mind, making him even weirder. He was probably getting doggy dementia from it.

She reached the door, forcing Buckley to step back, and the growl grew deeper, louder. He barked once more, and— now growing annoyed with him—she told him to shush. He backed up, blocking the door, a rope of drool leaking from the side of his mouth.

"C'mon, you wanted out," she said. "Move."

Christ, he really was getting demented, she thought.

She had to lean across the dog to turn the deadbolt, but as soon as her arm was stretched out he moved fast. His jaw clamped down around her forearm, his guttural growls sending an odd vibration through her skin as he shook his head back and forth.

The teeth tore through her, bone deep, but the attack was so sudden and unexpected that the pain hadn't even set in. Shock flooded her immediately, and she screamed, "Buckley!"

Delacourt went to take a step back, her heel slipping on the entryway throw rug, and she fell hard on her ass, her arm twisting painfully, still gripped tightly in her dog's mouth.

Once she was down, he let go. And then, eighty-five

pounds of hard muscle and golden fur dropped atop her chest, his face in hers, jaws snapping.

Her pain receptors were firing with maddening frequency as her cheek was torn away, and she smacked at the dog's flanks, like punching a slab of beef and just as useless.

Her ears were filled with the noises of her own pain, of Buckley's grunting and growling and snapping. She smacked at his head, hard as a brick and twice as heavy. He nipped at her face again, her nose cutting open against his teeth.

Delacourt went to deliver another smack, but Buckley was fast. His jaws took off three of her fingers before her open palm could land again.

"Get off," she screamed, losing herself to the panic. Her feet fought for purchase beneath her, trying to push herself backward, but she was stuck under the weight of the dog, trapped between his four legs and snapping mouth.

The second she moved, his face lunged down into the meat of her throat. Teeth drove through flesh, crunching through the thick, rubbery vein and splashing crimson against his golden face. His snout burrowed deeper and when it came up, it was with a mouthful of throaty sinew.

Her fighting legs went limp, one bare foot collapsing to the floor, lifeless.

Buckley stood over her for a moment, watchful, waiting. Finally, a single, unenthusiastic wag of his tail and a small whine broke the stillness. He turned and went back to the door, clawing at the jamb and sticking his gory snout into the gap between the floor, whining again. Fighting with the door, his paws and face smeared his dead owner's blood across the white metal finish. His nails dug grooves into the trim, peeling away paint and wood.

🐾 🐾 🐾

Hector was a twelve-year-old, black and red-haired tortoiseshell cat with the most gorgeous green eyes. Despite the masculine name, Hector, who had been named such by a previous owner, was very much female.

For the last seven weeks, Declan and his wife, Kirsti, had done everything they could to keep Hector out of their newborn's crib. The stairs were gated at both the top and bottom, and the door to Sarah's room was closed each night when she was put to bed. Even the furniture had been arranged in such a way to make it impossible for Hector to get into the crib.

Somehow, the little terror always found a way into the room, where she snuggled up beside Sarah for warmth.

They were lucky the cat hadn't suffocated their baby girl, and Kirsti was in a state of near-constant paranoia, particularly at night. Declan, who had rescued Hector nearly a decade ago, was worried that he'd have to cave in to his wife's demands to get rid of the cat. He was torn, and hated that he had to choose at all.

The house was quiet and content for the moment, though. Kirsti had gone to the gym, once Declan had been able to convince her that it was okay for her to leave and have some time to herself.

"I got this," he had promised. "I need some daddy-daughter time."

With her out of the way for a little while, he'd brought Sarah onto the main floor and set her up on a bacterial-resistant, spongy play mat with some soft blocks and rattles that she could bat around during tummy time. His little girl could go nuts while, hopefully, his big girl took some time to prevent herself from going any more nuts than she already was.

Running hot water to warm her bottle, Declan caught a flash of movement from the corner of his eye as Hector peered around the corner.

"Hey, buddy," he said, using the same baby-voice he found himself talking to Sarah with.

Hector scratched her face against the corner of the wall, then slowly padded forward across the kitchen linoleum. Usually, the cat would veer toward him and rub up against his legs, but not today. She went straight through and into the dining room.

He watched her squat low, a few feet away from the living room and Sarah's play mat. "That's a good girl," he said.

At least the cat finally seemed to be adjusting to the newborn's presence. *It'd only taken a month*, he thought, somewhat ruefully.

Turning back to the sink, he tested the water and filled a small pot. Sarah's scream shook him and the pot flew from his hands, crashing to the floor and sending water everywhere. He bolted into the living room, unsure of what he was seeing.

There was a large bundle of writhing fur and flailing limbs, screaming and hissing, and…it took a moment for his brain to process it, but he was almost sure he saw blood.

He darted forward, his heart racing.

"Oh fuck," he screamed. "Fuck, fuck, fuck. No, no, Hector, get out of there!"

His hands were on the cat's backside a heartbeat later, but crossing the room had seemed like an eternity. Sarah's screaming was ear piercing as he hauled the cat away.

Hector's hind claws immediately found his arms and tore grooves up and down his wrists and forearms, the cat's limbs pinwheeling and grasping for purchase. He briefly thanked the stars that she was front-declawed as her forelimbs smacked at his face and she hissed and spit at him

He turned and threw her down, back into the dining room, and screamed, "Get!"

Sarah was crying, her face a bright strawberry red, and puncture marks from where the cat had bit her marked her arms and legs and chest. The little girl was only wearing a diaper, and Hector had clearly been in a careless frenzy.

What the fuck happened? he wondered. Declan's head was

spinning.

Hector darted past his feet, on a path for Sarah again.

"No!" he yelled, his reflexes astoundingly fast. He snatched her tail and dragged her back toward him, her claws making a clear trail in the carpet.

Hector let out a loud hiss, her ears pinned back tightly against her scalp, biting at him. She had strong jaws and razor-sharp teeth. It stung when she nipped at him, but this was far worse. This was no playful nip. The fucking cat was in full-on attack mode.

"What the fuck's gotten into you?" he shouted, but the cat replied only with shrill hisses.

Two strides to the backdoor. Declan flung it open angrily, holding the squirming cat to his chest while he worked the screen door lock, her nails digging into his chest and the cat biting at his face and neck. He threw open the door, then threw the cat outside, hauling the screen door shut again.

"Jesus Christ," he muttered, exhausted.

A thud landed against the glass behind him, and he turned to see Hector making a second pass, throwing herself at the door and smacking at it. She went up and down the porch steps, tail slunk low, eyes narrowed.

Declan shut the backdoor and bolted it, more out of habit than any particular worry toward the cat getting back inside.

"Oh, sweetie," he said, taking his screaming baby in his own bleeding arms, rocking her gently.

He needed to get these wounds clean, both hers and his. Kirsti was going to freak out, he knew.

How the fuck am I going to explain this to her?

The only thing he knew for certain was, Hector was a goner for sure. No way could he keep the cat after this.

Fuck.

🐾 🐾 🐾

The Delta Boeing 757 cut through the clear, blue skies over Falls Breath, Michigan, still gaining altitude following its departure from the Cherry Capital Airport in Traverse City, en route to Detroit.

The captain of the narrow-body, single aisle, twin-engine airliner was unable to see the unusually large flock of seagulls lifting off from the beaches of Grand Traverse Bay until it was too late. As the white gulls massed around the plane, he and the one hundred passengers quickly began to take notice.

Bird strikes were a common, and mostly insignificant, occurrence in air travel. Most involved the bird striking the edges of a wing, or the front of the nose cone, and caused little damage to the aircraft.

Flocks of birds, though…that could do some real damage.

In all his twenty-seven years of piloting, Captain Lucas Robertson had experienced plenty of bird strikes, but nothing like this. He squinted his eyes, unable to believe what he was seeing.

A flurry of small bodies—hundreds of them!—darkened the cabin in seconds and he could feel their assault on the Boeing.

Passengers began screaming as the gulls struck the windows, small bodies breaking against the glass.

The engines' intake sucked the gulls in, like a vacuum. Compressor blades broke apart under the assault of so many bodies and were turned into shrapnel.

Engine two failed first, and then engine one, both bursting into flames and trailing sooty black smoke.

The plane pushed through the dense flock, but there seemed to be no end in sight. Bodies slammed into the cabin windows, cracking the glass and then shattering it. A hail of broken glass rained down upon Robertson and his flight crew, the cabin depressurizing.

And the gulls kept coming, into the plane now, slamming into Robertson and his copilot, hundreds of flapping wings blinding him. The flying glass had cut him good and nicked the carotid artery in his neck. He tried to stop the bleeding with one hand, fighting off the birds with the other, but there were just too damn many of them for the two of them to ward off.

Sparks flew from the control panel as the birds dive-bombed the electronics, impaling themselves on the boards of switches and knobs and the flight sticks. The crew was in a panic, too busy fighting off the attacks to their bodies. Blood and feathers and bird remains—what they called snarge—was everywhere.

Feeling faint, Robertson caught of a flash of land outside the cabin window, the ground rushing up to meet them.

As suddenly as they had come, the seagulls vanished. Light flooded the cabin, too late.

The Boeing 757 crashed into the center of downtown Falls Breath at 2:08 p.m., barely ten minutes after liftoff. All one hundred and four souls aboard were lost, along with many more on the ground.

2

LAUREN Scott thought she was in love. Not that she knew much about love; even she would have to admit that if push came to shove.

Jacob Teller, though—he was something special. And he was twenty-one. A college man. And he could buy beer legally, which, at seventeen, Lauren was still far away from doing on her own. Not that her age had kept her away from beer.

Beer, in fact, had played an integral part in their meeting. Two months ago, Lauren was celebrating her friend's birthday at the beach and whiling away the night with a few bottles of brew around the bonfire. The turnout had been pretty good, about twenty of their friends and friends of friends, when all was said and done. Jacob, he was a friend of a friend.

He'd opened a bottle of Labatt for her, and when he passed the bottle over their fingers had brushed against one another. They started talking, and that was pretty much that. He gave her his phone number, and left the ball firmly in her court. She could call, or not. She liked that. So, two days later, during her lunch break, she called.

They'd seen each other nearly every day since. And last night…well, last night had been something special.

Driving along US 31, a pleasant ache burning deep in her core, she couldn't help but smile at the thoughts of the prior night.

Lying on a large blanket, the two had watched as meteors streaked the sky in the pre-dawn hours. They'd had the beach entirely to themselves, and it had been a clear night. There had been so many meteors it had been impossible to keep count. The sight was amazing, but watching Jacob's face light up with awe was the best, by far.

He was an astrophysics major, and an astronomy nut. His enthusiasm had been infectious, and it hadn't taken much prying to get her to agree to stay up with him on the sandy shore.

Wearing shorts and a Traverse City hoodie, she'd bundled up in a blanket and cuddled her man, exchanging kisses under the moon's glow and silvery streaks piercing the sky, a cooler of beer beside him.

"Look at that!" Jacob had shouted, excited, but too loud into her ear. His arms had been warm and secure, giving her a sense of not only assured security, but pure serenity. She followed the path his finger cut through the air, catching sight of a bright white light trailing down from the sky.

"Oh my god," she said, entranced. And a little bit afraid. The meteor was growing brighter as it streaked closer, piercing the night sky with a sudden dawn.

A loud sonic boom exploded overhead and the darkness returned, the space rock lost as her eyes readjusted. Momentarily blinded, she could hear the faint splash as the meteor hit the lake, way off in the distance.

"That was amazing!" She felt exhilarated, a shot of adrenaline lacing her blood. To see a meteor that close, to have it land so near, was both frightening and exciting and her heart shook as if she'd been on the most intense rollercoaster ever.

"There's more," he said. His mouth hung open in a wide,

smiling *O*. She laughed, with him of course, feeling giddy.

Thin bright contrails scarred the sky, none of them even close, and she followed the trajectory of each, counting more than a dozen of them. More lit up the sky, the rest far up above in the Earth's orbit.

They spent the early morning hours with their eyes cast to the heavens, until the meteor shower ended and all that was left was a faint silvery shimmer of stardust falling to the earth, lit aglow by moonlight.

After getting a few hours' sleep and a warm shower, she found herself missing him already.

She couldn't waste the daylight pining alone in her room, though, waiting to see him again. She pulled on shorts and a tank top over her bikini and hit the road, hoping to get some prime time on the sand. Maybe back at the spot she'd shared with Jacob earlier…

Her face was sore from the constant grin, but it was a good kind of soreness. She'd thought about taking the soft top off her old Wrangler and letting the warm breeze wash over her, but laziness had gotten the better of her.

The bay was calm and a vibrant green that turned a rich, deep blue out a ways, the sun glinting off the water and making it look almost like glass.

And then she saw the plane overhead, and the amorphous, shifting web of white and black that surrounded it, a tail of smoke belching from its dead engines as it went into a dive.

What the fuck? she thought, her mind struggling to make sense of what she was seeing.

She turned her attention back to the road in time to see the cars in front of her slowing. She slammed on the brake, the car behind her sounding its horn.

Everyone had stopped, it seemed, to look at the sight overhead.

Long black scabs marred the clear, blue sky.

"Oh my god," she said breathlessly.

The plane streaked down, lower and lower, and then—

An explosion erupted from the outskirts of downtown, across the bay, as fire bloomed across the skyline.

Jacob!

Jacob was downtown, working at one of the coffee shops that lined Michigan Avenue. A coffee shop on the bay.

"Oh my god," she said again.

She had to get down there, had to get out of this traffic snarl. None of the cars were moving in either the northbound or southbound lanes, and all the drivers were on their cell phones. A few had even gotten out of their cars and were standing in the middle of the street, eyes wide and turned toward the center of Falls Breath.

Without even thinking, she turned the wheel hard to the right and nudged the gas pedal, putting the Jeep on the shoulder and half-bumping onto the grassy incline beyond. She didn't care, though, and gunned it down to the stoplight, where she hoped the traffic was thinner and she could get back over.

She stayed on the shoulder, running the red light, and cut off a van making a left across the intersection and into the lane she barged her way into.

US 31 was lined here with houses and businesses on opposite sides, trees and hotels, obstructing the view of the water and downtown. Traffic was moving now that the distraction was largely hidden, save for the rising columns of smoke.

She pressed forward, weaving in between slower vehicles, her heart racing at her own recklessness. In her rearview she saw flashing lights, the noise of roaring sirens piercing her worry.

Fuck!

She slowed and pulled to the shoulder again, but the police cruiser shot on by. And then another, and a third. Behind the sheriff department's units was a massive fire truck, and it rumbled past, shaking the frame of her Jeep. Wasting no time, she darted back onto the road and into the wake of the fast-moving authorities. More angry horns sounded at her brash driving, but she didn't care in the least.

She had to get downtown.

She *had to*.

The trees grew thicker as the highway twisted through the woods, a metal crossing bridging the nature trail cut across the stretch of road. She caught a flash of movement and turned her head, surprised to see a woman running up the steps, her boyfriend following and casting fearful looks over his shoulder.

Lauren slowed, even more surprised to see deer chasing the couple. A large buck plowed forward, head down, his antlers pointing forward as he charged the fleeing man. The man twisted around once more, stumbling, right as the eight-point buck ran him through.

Foot off the pedal, she gasped, unable to believe what she was seeing.

The buck reared back, pulling gory antlers loose, and the man dropped to the ground, bleeding profusely. Two other smaller bucks charged over him, pursuing the woman up the steps to the bridge. The large one danced around the fallen man, raining a flurry of blows upon him and biting at his face. The man tried to get an arm up between him and the deer, but the buck knocked it aside, going for the man's head and throat again.

This is insane, she thought, the Jeep rolling slowly. She had to pull the wheel to keep from going off the road, but she couldn't take her eyes off the weirdness playing out before her. She looked from the road, back to the woods, and—

The buck was watching her. Intently. Staring her down.

And then it charged.

Lauren didn't need to think this time. She mashed the gas pedal to the floor and the Wrangler jolted forward, its engine roaring with the sudden burst of RPMs.

The buck gave chase, but the Jeep was moving too fast for it to keep up. She let out of a long, deep breath.

A doe darted out from the woods, right in front of her. Impossible to avoid.

Lauren screamed as the front end of her vehicle crumpled and the doe slammed into the windshield, its head crashing through the glass beside her as the airbag exploded in her face.

The Wrangler veered sharply off the road, colliding with a thick tree, and stilled. The engine ticked a final time, steam pouring out from beneath the crumpled hood.

Lauren twisted her face and saw a still black eye. She slumped forward against the airbag, the darkness surrounding her, swallowing her as her eyes pinched shut.

3

DEPUTY Matthew Scott recognized the Wrangler that blew through the red light and nearly crashed into a minivan as the one belonging to his daughter, Lauren.

"What the fuck is she doing, Hex?" he asked his partner, a black and tan German shepherd sitting in the back of the Grand Traverse County Sheriff Department's Ford Interceptor SUV.

Hex, of course, had no answers but whined an awful lot, which was unusual for the sixty-pound import from Poland with Czech bloodlines.

Scott would need to have a stern talking to with Lauren later. Another one. She was driving like a complete maniac, but there wasn't time to deal with her right now. If a Boeing hadn't just crashed into the middle of downtown, he'd have pulled her ass over and thrown her in lockup overnight for this stupid stunt. He just had to hope she wasn't stupid, or reckless enough to get herself killed.

With lights and sirens going, traffic parted. There were a few stragglers, and some who outright ignored the warning of this train of emergency vehicles, but the sensible ones that pulled off to the shoulder created a large enough path that the going wasn't too rough.

Hex's nails grated against the wire mesh installed across the driver's side rear window. The Havis canine transport system installed in place of the SUV's back seats did not provide much room for pacing, but Hex made do. His nostrils occasionally flared as he pressed his snout against the diamond-pattern grid of air holes and sniffed at Scott in the driver's seat.

"Calm down, buddy, we'll be there soon. You'll be able to get out and stretch in a minute."

Hex was normally very calm and placid, unless called into action to run down a fleeing perp or focused on searching for a missing person. Although the sudden anxiety was odd, Scott wasn't worried.

US 31 cut through the sparsely populated commercial area, where Walgreens and a Speedway sat aside a mini-golf course, and wended away from the bay through the preserved wetlands. A few walkers were taking advantage of the sun and cutting their way along the nature trail, and Hex caught sight of them. He began barking, the wire mesh practically denting his snout.

"Hex! *Platz!*"

The command, German for "sit" went unheeded. The dog continued barking until he lost sight of the walkers, and then he went back to pressing his face against the air holes between him and Scott.

"*Pfui!*" Bad dog!

Normally, Hex looked sheepish when he was called a bad dog, but it had no effect on him this time. Scott shook his head and tried to ignore the anxious behavior. Whatever was wrong with him, Scott understood that Hex at least had no other way of communicating it, and he knew that Hex wasn't deliberately trying to be provocative. Maybe he just had to go to the bathroom something awful and this was his way of letting Scott know.

He took a deep breath and assured his dog again. "We'll be there in a minute, buddy. Just hang tight and try to relax, okay?"

The woods on either side fell away to small cabin lots and a resurgence of hotels and motels with neon vacancy lights lit up. The highway bent back toward the bay and civilization, the train of emergency vehicles slowing to a halt.

"Jesus," Scott said, his eyes wide to absorb the madness before him.

Downtown was covered in smoke and ash, fires raging across the storefronts, motionless, smoldering bodies everywhere. Sitting in the midst of devastated buildings was the airplane, its nose cone buried in the collapsed remains of what had, only moments earlier, been an Italian restaurant, a litter of bricks and burning furniture from the store opposite surrounding the tubular body. Dense black roiling coils of smoke blotted out so much of the strip that it was hard to tell exactly how bad the damage was, but he could easily make out the burning buildings closer to the intersection. The firemen were working fast to get their hoses rigged up to the hydrants, and EMTs were rushing in to collect the closest of the wounded, but already he could tell there were more bodies than emergency workers. More survivors were coming out of the pitch, faces covered with filthy, ashy shirts, looking like they'd just been freed from a coal mine, smoke curling off their bodies. Suddenly, another body jolted out of the blackness, a human torch covered in flames head to toe and swerving drunkenly across the street, colliding with another survivor and taking them both to the ground, the fire spreading to consume that hapless soul.

"Jesus," he said again.

He put the vehicle in reverse, and blocked off the oncoming traffic lane. Shay Hendrix did the same in her patrol car, cutting off the opposite lane of US 31. They were going to have to start directing traffic and routing it through the parking lot of the marina and back onto the southbound lanes.

Hex was going wild in his cage, spittle dotting his lips

and webbing across the bottom of his jaw.

Outside, Scott could feel the heat of the flames boiling off the air even though he was a good distance away. Horns were honking, from both the upset motorists and alarms that had been jolted by the crash and set off in the nearby parking lots.

Hendrix was already waving drivers into the marina. Hopefully they understood to turn around. This was going to be a nightmare.

The first order of business was to set up a command center, which Scott would have to coordinate until Sheriff Alex Tremblay arrived on scene. The media would soon be having a field day, and, honestly, he was a bit surprised that none of the reporters from the local networks or papers had arrived yet. It was only a matter of time, of course. In the meantime, Tremblay was probably busying buttering up the mayor. Hopefully he found time to put in requests for support from the surrounding communities' police and fire departments. Hopefully a request for some overtime, too.

Leaning back inside the SUV, he grabbed Hex's leash from the center console and turned to open the rear door. Before it was even open wide enough, Hex shoved his way through, panting heavily and barking, teeth bared. The dog stopped to growl at Scott, taking small steps forward.

They'd been partners for six years, and he'd never seen the shepherd behave like this. Never. On top of that, this was the absolute worst time for such sudden disobedience. They had to get a perimeter established and get these people out of here to make room for more EMS.

"*Platz*, Hex," he tried again, but that seemed to only incite the dog further.

Scott held his hand out, the universal sign for "stop". "*Ruhig.*" Quiet.

Hand out, he stepped forward, but rather than step back or sit, Hex also stepped forward, growling.

"*Nein. Sitz!*"

Hex darted forward, his teeth burying into the inside of

Scott's outstretched arm.

"Nein! Aus! Aus!" Scott yelled. No! Let go! Let go!

Hendrix caught sight of the commotion and ran into the street, toward Scott. Horns were blaring, and drivers stared out of the windows open-mouthed. A few opened their doors and went to stand, but Hendrix waved them back inside.

"Stay in your car!" she screamed.

Blood was pouring down Scott's arm and Hex was latched on good, driving his squat, muscular body forward and putting Scott on his ass. Scott's face was burning red, teeth gritted in pain. He'd stopped shouting commands at the dog but something had Hex riled up good.

Hendrix knew enough not to try and intervene with a dog gone rabid. Her training kicked in, and she pulled her gun free, her heart hammering. She took aim and fired.

Hex released Scott's arm and scrabbled away, falling to the side as his back legs gave out. His side was a bloody mess, the fur matted. He tried to get back toward Scott, his front paws scrabbling against the asphalt, growling and growling, pink bubbles popping from the corners of his snout. His black eyes were beady and evil looking, Scott noticed. There was no other way to explain it. Somehow the devil had gotten into his dog.

Hendrix's shot had gone high, hitting Hex in the spine. She was careful not to get too close as she put a second bullet through his head.

Scott sat there cradling his arm against his stomach, his eyes puffy with tears.

She grabbed her radio and spoke the words of every police officers' nightmare: "Dispatch, we have an officer down," she said. "Repeat: officer down."

4

LAUREN woke slowly, her eyelids heavy and gummy. Her entire head throbbed in a way that went beyond a mere headache, feeling utterly wrecked and bruised.

One eye was stuck shut, and when she palmed at it there was a sticky substance coating the skin. She rubbed harder until the lid sprung free and she blinked several times, trying to focus. Looking at her hand, she saw blood. A syrupy warmth crept down the side of her face.

After a very long moment, she began to recall what had happened, where she was, and the confusion began to evaporate. She looked to her right and let out a brief, startled scream, the black eyes of a doe staring lifelessly at her. Her heart knocked against her ribs as she drew in a calming breath.

The doe's thick neck was bent awkwardly and her body obstructed most of the windshield. Lauren remembered hitting the deer, hitting the tree. White radiator steam boiled out from beneath the crumpled hood.

She moved slowly, her entire torso a knot of bruised agony. The airbag had gone off and was now deflated, probably the reason her face felt so puffy and painful. Even something as simple as unbuckling her seatbelt took tremendous effort and she winced at the pain in her neck and shoulders with a short hiss.

The car rocked with a thud against the driver's side window.

She turned her head, ignoring the agony, and saw the buck. His antlers were spotted in gore. He jostled the car again, banging the side of his face against the driver's side window, nostrils flaring as it snorted and briefly steaming the glass.

Then he reared on his hind legs and kicked. The glass spider webbed around the center of impact. Lauren swallowed her scream, her mind barely processing what was happening.

"Oh shit, oh shit," she said, scrambling for the seatbelt release. The shoulder strap was locked in place, keeping her torso pressed into the seatback. She closed her eyes and took a deep, calming breath, the car shaking against another impact. In the still quiet between thudding attacks, she could hear the safety glass cracking again, like breaking ice.

She grabbed the shoulder strap and forced herself to relax as she worked the harness loose, unlocking it, and then thumbed the release. The seatbelt retracted with a whispery noise, the metal male connector clanking against the interior window.

The buck was pacing and snorting, watching her all the while, preparing for another attack of the driver's side window.

The doe's head was slumped over the dashboard, shards of broken safety glass stuck in its matted, blood-encrusted hair and strewn across the passenger seat and floor. The way the deer had come through the windshield didn't leave much room for her to escape. The dead body took up too much room and didn't leave her with enough space to climb over the center console and out the passenger door.

The buck was readying to strike again, and she knew this would be the final blow. The window was barely holding together, and one more strike would make her deer food. She was surprised he hadn't ripped through the soft top of the Jeep already.

She had to get out of the Wrangler, but there was no way she'd be able to slip past the buck, either.

She slipped her hand between the door and the seat, reaching for the seat back release and pulled it all the way up, leaning into the back and pressing it down. She ignored the flaring sparks of pain that lit up her neck and spine and pushed herself back, just as the glass exploded and showered down upon her bare legs. A hoof banged into her knee and she let out another surprised shout, kicking herself across the seat back, tumbling onto the bench seating behind her.

The buck's head was reaching into the vehicle, but his antlers prevented him from getting very far in, nipping at her and snorting angrily, a hot gust of fetid breath warming her ankle.

This cannot be happening, she thought, breathing raggedly and taking a brief moment to recoup from the exertion.

The buck retracted its large head and glared at her through the rear driver's side window. Then he slammed his face against the glass.

"Here we go again," she said, forcing herself to sit up.

She pushed open the passenger door. It stopped, leaving only a scant few inches of space. A tree was blocking it from opening any further.

"Son of a bitch," she said. Adrenaline was coursing through her, her flight reflexes kicked up to eleven. She wanted to run, and to just keep on running. She didn't care how badly that would hurt, how much her sore ribs would ache. She needed to get out of here.

And panicking isn't going to help, she chided herself.

She pulled the door shut as the buck kicked both front hooves into the opposite window. The glass cracked.

She chided herself for being stupid as she realized there was a way out of this. She was too jazzed and afraid to think straight, but she saw her answer well enough and began rolling the window down with the manual hand crank. The Wrangler was an older model, and she'd not been bothered by the lack of power windows, never thinking their absence might one day save her life. Turning the crank took damn near forever, though, what felt like hours and days, and the buck struck again.

Once the window was down, she shoved herself through head first, landing in a mat of dirt and old, dead leaves. Still feeling dazed from the crash, she slowly made it to her feet.

The buck was still on the other side of the vehicle, grunting angrily. When the Wrangler had crashed, its back end had slid, catching against another tree. If the deer was going to come after her, it would have to go around the front, and she wasn't sure how long it would take for him to realize that.

Which meant she was still a very viable target, she realized. Getting out of the car had only been a small step in getting away from the crazed buck. She wasn't out of the woods yet, she knew, and rather literally at that.

She pushed deeper into the trees but kept sight of US 31, treading lightly so as not to attract attention but also to maintain a more comfortable pace. Running would be too loud with the floor of the woods covered in so much detritus and rotting vegetation, and too painful on her taxed and whiplashed body.

The buck was making plenty of noise, though, attacking the Wrangler. Hopefully the ruined remains of her Jeep would keep him distracted, although she kept checking her surroundings to make sure he wasn't giving chase, or that she wasn't being followed by anything else.

There was clearly something wrong with the deer. That wasn't difficult to surmise, but she had no idea what had made them go crazy. Usually deer spooked easily, but these guys? She'd never even heard of something like this. She had heard of deer attacking, even seen a few YouTube videos, which she recalled heartily laughing at with her girlfriends, but, Jesus, not like this. This was fucking insane.

She wondered what had happened to the woman, the one she'd seen running across the bridge over 31, whose partner had been gutted and stomped to death. She hazily recalled two other deer going after her, and tried desperately not to think of the awful outcome. Those deer had been rabid, too, like the buck. Had they all eaten something they shouldn't have, or been attacked by something or infected with a virus?

Jacob would know. Or at least maybe have some kind of insight. She had to get to him.

Her feet crunched through the dry leaves, the world slightly off-kilter. Her head was pounding, her pulse a steady, aching drumbeat in her ears. She kept one arm out to support herself against the trees, as if she were passing herself between the thick trunks.

A rustling to the right, from deeper in the woods, made her pause, a quick flash of movement making her jump. Something small and fast darted beneath a leaf, a rapid skittering of tiny feet giving chase.

A chipmunk bolted into view and stopped, small beady black eyes looking at her briefly before studying the ground, its nose puckering as it sniffed with intent. Another chipmunk broke cover and popped out from under the leaves, too slow.

The small critters fought viciously, their bodies rolling through the leaves and muck. One was clearly larger and fought viciously.

Lauren stood stock still, open-mouthed, horrified at what she saw. A trail of blood stretched across the woodland floor, leading to an unmoving mound of fur, close enough that she could make out the torn fur and deep lacerations.

The larger chipmunk wriggled loose from beneath the small dead body and stared at it for a long, hard minute. It moved cautiously and then launched itself at the body once more, its claws digging into the dead one's belly, tearing it open to stick its face into the gap.

Her eyes refused to close, and she was too afraid to move. There was a mixture of disquiet, disgust, and morbid curiosity at the sight of this alpha chipmunk's cheeks bulging out with harvested guts.

Move, idiot, she thought. *Get the fuck out of here!*

Deer. Chipmunks. *What the fuck is happening?*

Her head swam in a confused and funky miasma, but she had to move. She wasn't safe here.

Cautiously, she raised one foot, intent on taking a slow and quiet step forward and away from the rabid animal. But the movement—or whatever minimal sounds she might have made—was enough to catch the animal's attention. Those little beady black eyes latched onto her instantly.

The chipmunk watched her with deliberate intent, challenging her. A small pink thread hung from its mouth, its whole face covered in gore.

She set her foot down, the leaves crackling under foot, the woods quiet enough that she could hear the squelch of damp soil beneath the soles of her sandals.

The chipmunk darted at her and she kicked out at it. She missed, but it was enough to make it pause and reconsider its line of attack. The animal took small herky-jerky lurches toward her, but Lauren wasn't about to wait and see what it would do next. She was moving, as fast as she could.

Pain wracked her body, but adrenaline compelled her forward. Four years of track, of running in freezing rain and through charley horses and horrible periods that lit her belly on fire with cramps, kept her running determinedly through the aches as she cut a line between the trees toward the road.

Her sandal sank into mud and stuck. She tripped and fell forward, the road in sight. A light, furry weight scrambled up her leg, over her butt, onto her back, sharp claws stitching fresh pinpricks of stabbing pain in a jagged, vertical line up her body.

She rolled over, kicking the sandal free, hoping to crush the chipmunk beneath her but the damn thing was freaking fast. It moved across her neck, onto her shoulder, and up the side of her face where she swatted at it. The damn thing was in her hair.

She found her footing again, standing up as she ran her hands through her hair. Barefoot, she began running again, trying to shoo the creature out of her long, brunette locks.

"Ow!" *Fucking thing bit me!*

She flung her hair out, the rodent hopping into her hand and scrabbling down her arm, but she kept running, running, running. Almost to the road.

The chipmunk's claws dug into her neck as it climbed, darting past her groping fingers.

Her foot hit the rocky rise of the shoulder right as the furry little fucker bit her cheek. Its small attack gave her just enough time to grab it, wrapping it tight in her first. It writhed against her palm, taking small chunks of skin out of her hand, scratching and biting at her.

She reeled back her arm, like she did in her old softball pitching days, and threw the damnable creature into the road—

And into the path of an oncoming Saturn.

The small thud of the chipmunk striking the windshield sent a small shiver of satisfaction through her. She hadn't even noticed the car, but damn if the timing hadn't been fucking perfect! She couldn't help but laugh, on the verge of hysteria.

"Hey! Hey, wait!" she yelled, waving her arms at the open-mouthed driver and rushing after the vehicle's brake lights. At least he was slowing down. The car looked familiar, too.

The heat trapped in the asphalt burned through her muddy soles, and as she approached the vehicle she got a clearer look at the driver. And yep, just as she thought, it was Declan Carver, who lived at the other end of their subdivision, leaning across the center console to open the passenger door for her.

"Lauren?" He seemed surprised.

"Hi, Dec."

She fell into the seat with a groan and a relieved sigh. Declan stared at her, his mouth still open, looking utterly lost. Then Sarah's crying caught her attention. She'd babysat the infant once before, for a couple hours. There were small bandages on the baby, her face marked in at least a dozen spots, and on her arms and legs. Everywhere, really.

As Lauren looked toward the backseat, her spine screaming bloody murder, she caught movement on the side of the road.

The massive buck was striding down the center of US 31, heading directly toward them.

"Oh, shit," she said.

"What is going on, Lauren? Is that your Wrangler back there?"

"Just drive, man. Go!"

Dec check the rearview mirror, saw the horror in the teenager's face, and clearly realized now was not the time to argue. He put the car back in drive and gunned the accelerator.

"What happened to Sarah?" she asked.

"About what happened to you, from the looks of things."

As Lauren looked at him—really studied him—she saw that he, too, had been bleeding.

Eyes on the mirror again, he saw the buck chasing after them, but the car outpaced the deer easily enough. Once they were around the curve, the deer was out of sight entirely.

"What's going on?" he asked again. "Do you have any idea? What is happening here?"

Instead of answering, Lauren only stared blankly ahead. Tears spilled from her puffy eyes, and the sobbing began. She hid her face in her hands and spent a long while crying.

5

HECTOR stood on his hind legs, pawing furiously at the storm door. Whenever Dec looked toward her, the cat hissed and yelled. The cat was working itself up into such a stir that she was foaming at the mouth.

Dec's first thought was rabies. He quickly dismissed that, though, because Hector was not an outdoor cat. In fact, Dec was fairly certain this was the first time Hector had been outside of the house at all, not counting trips to the veterinarian, but even then Hector was always put in a carrier.

How the hell could a timid, little, indoor lap cat get rabies?

Then again, Hector wasn't all that timid anymore. And, from the looks of her, if she jumped in his lap right now it might only be to bite his face off.

"Oh, stop it, Hector!"

The cat met his stare and held it, eyes made bigger from the dilation as if she were hunting. She let out another loud peal of noise, and then began ramming her head into the door. Not headbutting it, like she would against Dec's elbow when she wanted to be pet, but actually smashing the flat of her skull into the glass pane, over and over, trying to push her way through the solid door.

Sarah was crying in his arms and he tried to shush her, making loud, breathy whooshing noises in her ear. Sometimes that helped, mimicking the noises of the womb. His baby girl was completely distraught, though, and screamed all the louder, her face empurpled. Nothing was working—not the white noise, not her pacifier nor her favorite burp rag that she clung to as if it were a life preserver, and certainly not cuddles. Small Band-Aids covered her chubby body from where the cat's teeth and claws had sunk into her, and she kept on roaring, pausing only to catch her breath before resuming her loud assault on her father's eardrums.

Dec's mind turned, again, to rabies.

"I don't believe this," he said.

And now I'm talking to myself.

Where the fuck is Kirsti?

Why the hell did she pick today *to need a time-out?*

The dull thudding noises of a cat's head against the glass door had compelled Dec to open the primary door, and now he wished he'd never bothered. Since opening the door, the cat had only gotten more out of control and crazy. Red smears streaked the base of the glass door, clumps of hair matted in the gore. Hector's head was wet, fur pasted down to her scalp between her reared-back ears.

THUD.

THUD.

THUD.

Sarah continued to cry in his ear, refusing to calm.

His arms were getting fatigued and jittery from lightly bouncing her while whooshing in her ear. She just kept crying, on and on and on, and the cat kept striking the door with paws and head, on and on and on.

Hector leaped off the porch and ran down the backyard a ways. Dec breathed a small sigh of relief, telling Sarah over and over, "It's okay, baby, it's okay."

Then, he saw the saw fast-moving ball of fur racing toward the door, leaping up the porch steps and—

THUD!

—into the glass with enough force to split the skin across her skull. The cat fell, dazed, and he saw a flash of bone from where the flesh and fur had unzipped. Hector rose slowly, blinking and shaking her head, sending a spray of spittle into the air. A large, natty clump of fur was glued to the window by a thick, dripping splotch of blood. As Hector stared at him, Dec saw that one of the cat's emerald eyes bulged half out of its socket, the bone around it pulverized so that side of her face slumped brokenly.

Hector paced unsteadily across the patio, staring down Dec and Sarah. Hissing at them. He could hear her growls through the door. Foam pooled around her jaws, thick white drops hitting the pink stones.

The screeching and hissing grew louder and louder.

But that wasn't quite right, he realized.

Not louder per se, but with more depth and resonance, more volume than a single cat could produce alone. While the treble and pitch wavered, the noise itself was continuous.

A flash of movement darted from around the corner of the house, and he saw the second cat emerge. Then a third and a fourth.

Five. Six. Seven.

A dozen.

As if all of the neighborhood cats had gotten loose and converged on his home, rallying alongside Hector and vying for space at the top of the stone risers, demanding to be let in, pawing and clawing and crashing into the glass door.

"Son of a bitch!"

Dec slammed the back door shut once again, locking it, leaning against it for a breather, trying to soothe Sarah all the while. He could still hear the cats screaming and hissing, saw them rushing back and forth along the backyard patio through the dining room windows.

"This is insane," he said. "This is so fucking stupid."

Not in front of the kid, Kirsti's voice mentally chided him. She worried that Sarah would adopt Dec's potty mouth, and that her first word be of the four-letter variety rather than *momma* or *dada*.

In the kitchen, he fumbled single-handedly for his phone, yanking it free of the charging cord and finding his wife's contact info on the favorites screen. Instead of even getting a dial tone, it skipped straight to her voicemail.

"Hey, hon, hi. It's me. Uh, look, something's come up here. The uh"—*how in the hell do I even explain this?*—"the cat, Hector, flipped out. She bit Sarah up pretty good, and I'm taking her to the doctor's now, just in case. I don't know what's gotten into the cat. Rabies, maybe? I don't know. Anyway, call me."

Oh, for fuck's sake. Why did I mention rabies? Kirsti's going to flip the fuck out. "Shit."

After disconnecting, just to cover all the bases, he fired her off a quick text.

TAKING SARAH TO ER. CALL ME. 911!

"Okay, sweetie, let's go."

He kissed Sarah's red, tear-streaked cheek, cradling her close to his chest as he wriggled his feet into his sneakers, not bothering to lace them. Phone in his pocket, he shouldered the diaper bag, stuffed with diapers, cloths, and a spare outfit or two in case Sarah blew out her diaper or spit up or drooled enough to soak her top. He made it to the garage door before realizing he should take a bottle for her. It could be a while before she got her next feeding, and if she was upset now, he could only imagine how much worse she'd be later.

"And I need the fucking car seat," he muttered to himself. "Stupid."

Get a grip, dummy! Slow down and think.

After getting Sarah buckled in and trying unsuccessfully to curb her crying with another pacifier, this one attached to a small stuffed giraffe, he took stock of things, forcing his mind to clear. Car seat, diaper bag, bottles, car keys, wallet, phone.

He hurried into the garage, striking the garage door control with his free palm. His car was in the driveway, because he'd planned on mowing the yard and needed the room to get the mower out of the back of the garage.

Dec was hyper-aware of the noise of the garage door rolling upward, and he could hear the racket the cats were making. He ducked under the still-rising door, intent on getting to the car as fast as possible, and smacked his forehead against the cobwebbed lip of the door.

"Shit!"

Two steps out of the garage and he caught movement from the corner of his eye. A sleek, black cat darted toward him, rushing between his legs, nearly tripping him. The animal circled back and he kicked out at it, hearing the rushing of the other cats approaching, the pads of their paws hitting the concrete drive.

Soon, he was surrounded by them. A sea of writhing furballs heaved around his feet, biting his shins and calves, tugging at his untied shoelaces. Claws lashed at his skin.

He stepped forward, his feet catching on another darting cat. Balance lost, he twisted and fell, his reflexes putting Sarah's safety first. His back hit the ground, the car seat slamming into his chest, and soon enough the cats were on top of him. Sarah's cries grew even louder, and the car seat wobbled with the shifting weight of his squirming baby and frenzied cats. Half a dozen felines were swarming over both of them, nipping and biting and clawing.

He used his free arm to swat at them, screaming at them all the while. The shoulder strap of the diaper bag caught in the crook of his elbow and he slipped his arm free, grabbing the bag's handle and using it as a sort of shield, swiping at the cats with it.

After what felt like forever, he was able to get his feet under him. He grabbed a cat by the scruff of its neck, hauling it out of the car seat and away from his daughter, his heart breaking at the fresh scratches on her face, and threw it as hard as he could. Then he swung the diaper bag again, its wide arc giving the cats second thoughts. The animals were still circling, occasionally darting toward him and under the bag, but they were wary of his reach. *The diaper bag is a game changer*, he thought, somewhat proudly.

Sarah's face was bleeding, the skin around her eyes red and puffy from pain and tears.

The sight of his wounded daughter was enough to rekindle his anger and he lashed out at the cats again, kicking, swinging the bag, screaming like a maniac.

The heel of his sneaker caught one tortoiseshell cat square in the nose, and he stomped on the back of another cat, then kicked a calico under the ribs and lifted the damn thing right off the ground.

Dec made it to the back door of the Saturn and piled in, swinging the door shut on a cat trying to storm through the opening after him.

"Jesus fuck," he said, the car seat heavy on his lap.

Sarah was crying, more scared than ever, and blood dotted her face, his hands and arms, and stained his shirt. She cried and cried and cried.

Eventually, Dec cried as well, sobbing in the backseat with his daughter held close, her grip tight against his index finger.

"Okay," he said to himself, several minutes later. He swiped at the wetness across his cheeks, trying to compose himself. "Okay, okay." *Deep breath, long exhale.* "We can do this."

He was so fucking scared. His brain wasn't firing right, wasn't working at all. Shit.

He maneuvered the car seat into the base, heard the reassuring click as it slotted into place.

Those fucking cats were still out there, crying loudly, swatting at the door.

They know we're in here, he thought. And they wanted in badly.

Not going to happen.

He double-checked the restraint harness securing his daughter, then clambered across the center console, pulling himself between the two front seats and falling into the driver's seat, fighting to get his leg past the wheel and into the footwell.

He was fucking exhausted, breathing heavily, his whole body fatigued and shaky, a muscle-deep ache from head to toe. He let loose a bark of laughter, which threatened to turn into uncontrollable sobbing. He covered his sweaty face with his sweaty palms, ran his hair back with his fingers, and tried to square himself. He wasn't a fucking action hero, and he felt absolutely crazed, panicked.

He punched the remote to close the garage door. Fished the keys loose from his pocket, which nearly sent the phone tumbling out and to the floor.

The key went in the ignition, and he watched in the mirrors as the cats scrambled around his vehicle, hitting the gas pedal and making the engine roar.

"All right, you little fuckers."

A dim part of his mind wondered if he'd truly and finally gone off the deep end.

He threw the Saturn into drive and hit the gas pedal, feeling a rewarding crunch through the frame as his rear wheels thudded over something furry. He gunned the car into reverse, backing up to the end of the drive, then threw the car back into drive and slammed the gas pedal down. The engine growled like an angry beast, the needle on the RPMs jumping high, and he aimed his two-ton missile toward the crowd of felines running toward him.

He felt the car jostle over their bodies, quickly slamming onto the brake before he crashed through the garage.

Breathing ragged, adrenaline coursing through him, white knuckles gripping the steering wheel hard. Sarah screaming her head off. He had to get control of himself. He couldn't lose it. Not now.

In the rearview mirrors, long streaks of gore stretched

down the drive. Matted fur, small bodies broken open, burst apart beneath the car's tires. Long bloody streaks bearing his car's tire treads left purple and whitish-blue entrails pulped along the length of the drive. Plenty more cats were still moving, though, and clearly agitated as they darted toward the car.

Just leave, he thought, but heard Kirsti's voice in his mind. *There's nothing you can do about this. Just leave.*

He fought to control his breathing, closed his eyes, and tried to calm his mind and body. Slowly, he reached down to the shifter and put the car into reverse again, rolling down the driveway with a greater sense of peace, less like a maniac.

Just leave, Kirsti said, and she was right.

⁂ ⁂ ⁂

"And that's it," Dec said to Lauren. "That's what happened to us."

The teenager shuddered, her eyes glistening with pooled tears. She brushed them aside with the back of her hand, blinking to clear her vision. She snorted back her runny nose, a gloopy, wet, crinkling noise.

"Son of a bitch," she said.

Dec couldn't help but laugh. "Yeah, that about says it all, doesn't it?"

Deer, cats, and apparently chipmunks. He shook his head, trying to clear out the crazy thoughts all this shit stirred together in his mind.

"Do you have any idea what could do this?" he asked.

"I don't know. I was thinking…a virus, maybe?"

"Like rabies? That's what I thought, too."

"But all this?" she said, waving out her window at the surrounding woods and the world beyond. "I don't think rabies works like that. This is like, I don't know, *an epidemic*."

The words put a hitch in his chest and he drew a deep

breath, trying to loosen the knots there. Maybe she was onto something, though. How else could the entire animal kingdom go bat-shit insane all at once like that? If it wasn't rabies, then it was clearly something much, much worse.

He dug his phone from his pocket and woke it with a tap to the home button. No messages, no missed calls. No Kirsti. He tried calling her again, but couldn't get through. The call jumped straight to voicemail again. Frustrated, he hung up.

"What the hell?" Dec said suddenly, sitting up straighter. Lauren leaned forward, practically pressing her face to the windshield.

US 31 bled into the heart of downtown, and ahead, through the traffic, he saw flashing lights and the source of the thick black columns of smoke.

Even with the windows up and the AC on, he could hear the screams of beachgoers and the loud pops of gunfire.

"Can you see?" he asked. "What's happening up there?"

Lauren's face went white and her mouth fell open. She looked at him, as if she were going to explain, then shut her mouth and undid her seat belt.

"Hey, wait!" he tried, but it was no use.

She threw the door open and darted out of the car, slamming the door shut behind her.

All Dec could do was watch her rush into the traffic jam, darting between the stilled cars and drawing the gazes of frustrated motorists stuck there with him.

"Son of a bitch," he said, slamming an open hand against the steering wheel, as Lauren was lost in the murky haze consuming downtown.

6

DEPUTY Scott was propped up against the front wheel of his patrol vehicle, gritting his teeth against the pain and watching the blood leak out of Hex, pooling on the ground and spreading. Hendrix had pulled a first aid kit from the trunk of her car and was busy wrapping Scott's forearm in gauze.

The air around them was thick and sticky. Whatever progress the firefighters were making was slow, ungainly.

Strands of Hendrix's auburn hair had pulled free and hung across her forehead in a messy fashion. Her bold green eyes met his with a grimace. "You're going to need stitches."

Scott nodded.

"I'm so sorry," she said again. She'd apologized profusely multiple times, but the words landed with hollow thuds.

He simply nodded, his mouth dry and eyes burning— from tears, from smoke, from loss. What the hell could he say, really? He'd just lost a member of his family, watched him gunned down in the street. Hex had gone savage, inexplicably crazed, and Shay did what she had to do. He understood that, but it didn't make the pain any less prominent.

From where he sat, he had a clear line of sight across US 31 and to the beach across the way. What he had taken for raucous behavior from the college kids, or worse, tourists, resolved into a different scene.

He sat up straighter, leaning forward. Hendrix took it for an improper signal and leaned away, saying, "Woah there, bud," as if he were trying for a kiss. But then he was up and shoving away from her.

"Where are you going?"

She saw it as well.

A young bikini-topped redhead on rollerblades, was jetting along the sidewalk with her mutt. A thick, muscle-bound Rottweiler who quickly turned tail, ripping his leash out of her hand and pulling her off balance. Toppled and dazed, the dog leapt atop her, savaging her bare skin as teeth and claw sank into her naked midriff, her white frayed shorts stained red. She screamed and tried to fight, distracting the dog from her mauled guts long enough for the crazed animal to sink its fangs into her throat. The Rottweiler's head shook viciously, blood spraying from between its jaws as it tore away a thick chunk of meat. The girl fell back, dead before her skull crashed onto the pavement, and the dog returned to his original focus. Scott stared in open-mouthed shock as the Rottweiler's muzzle disappeared into the hole of the woman's belly.

All across the greenery fronting Bay Beach, pandemonium erupted. Dog walkers tried to tame their animals, opening themselves up to attack, or inadvertently loosening their hold on the animals, leaving them to attack others. A pit bull broke free, making a beeline for a baby stroller, the mother screaming and unable to do anything to stop it. A Labrador barreling into a team of volleyballers, jumping on the bare back of a college-aged man and sinking its teeth into the man's scalp, clawing at his shoulders and neck.

Even the ducks and gulls were rebelling against the

natural order, presenting a united front against the beachgoers and park walkers. A mallard dove at one woman's head, webbed feet and furiously flapping wings beating at her face. The seagulls dive-bombed and gouged bare skin.

Scott watched as an angry robin leapt at a small boy's head, thrashing him with its wings. Feathers flew, and through the fog of the attack he caught a spray of gore, heard the child's inhuman wail, and saw the bird's head retract with an eyeball caught in its beak. It flew away, leaving the kid to kneel in the sand, an empty crater in his face, the tissue pulped and inflamed, mouth open in a breathless, prolonged cry of agony.

He yelled to the other officers that were trying to get traffic unsnarled and turned around, waving them toward the park. "Get those people out of there!"

Tires screeched as another siren approached and bumped off the sidewalk and back onto US 31. The sheriff department's second K-9 unit arriving on scene. Scott was ahead of Hendrix, torn on which way to go. Thankfully, she heard the noise and darted back to the SUV as it ground to a halt. She was waving her arm in the air, shouting at the officer.

"Keep your dog contained! Keep him contained!"

There was too much cacophony, and Deputy Barrents opened the door. Jupiter, already plainly agitated, leapt free, jaws snapping.

Scott saw the geyser of arterial blood as Jupiter clamped down on his partner's neck, and rushed toward the scene.

Gun in hand, he strode up alongside Hendrix, and both officers raised their weapons and fired. His stomach tugged painfully, as if it were attached to a barbed cord that had just been yanked hard to the side of his belly.

Barrents screamed, his heels kicking uselessly at the ground. One hand was pressed to his neck, blood welling between his fingers, his face deathly pale. A crimson pool spread around his head, staining the road in a growing sheet of blood. Even as Hendrix rushed for the first aid kit in Barrents's vehicle, Scott knew it was too late. The deputy was bleeding out, and fast.

Never in his entire career had Scott felt so surrounded and indecisive, so torn and drained. The deputies were trying to get people out of the park and off the beach, but their attackers were unrelenting and far too numerous. There was a mess of gore, feathers, and fur. Dead birds and dead dogs littered the park, and the officers' uniforms were tattered, shredded, their exposed skin scratched all to hell.

A Rottweiler—maybe even the same one that had torn apart the rollerblading girl—bounded toward him, mouth frothing. His jowls shook crazily as it ran. Without even thinking, Scott leveled his gun and pulled the trigger, killing the stubby-tailed mutt instantly. The dog collapsed at his feet, nearly cartwheeling over its own head.

"Dad?"

He turned, and there was Lauren. Barefoot and bloody, a number of scratches marring her skin, her hair a ratty nest, brown hair shooting up at odd angles.

His stomach did that funny lurch thing again, and then an amassing shadow fell across his daughter as a flock of blackbirds honed in on her, squawking angrily.

"Get down!"

7

LAUREN was flanked by her father and Deputy Hendrix, their bodies partially shielding her as they broke into a run.

Blackbirds swarmed them, wings beating violently against their bodies, talons tearing at their flesh. She kept moving forward, lost in the maelstrom of feathers and flashes of snapping yellow beaks. A hundred sharp jabs darted across her back, her arms and legs, and she kept her hands raised to protect her face.

Scott's grip tightened around her upper arm, pulling her.

A gunshot rang out close to her ear and she could smell the smoky discharge through the stink of the birds. The attack lessened, ever so briefly, and then the blackbirds resumed their assault with renewed vigor.

Feathers stuck to her skin. Small pricks jabbed at her belly as beaks and claws dug into her stomach and nipped her through the tank top, the birds swirling between her legs and scoring her thighs and calves. She tried waving them off with one hand, but that was even more useless than Hendrix's gun. All it earned her were bit fingers and a slashed palm.

They were in her hair, talons poking at her scalp, beaks

jabbing into her skull. She could feel blood welling and matting her locks to her head, a fresh current of gore pasting it to the sides of her face.

"Get off!" she screamed, panic rising in her. If not for her father, she'd be completely lost in the swirling, unending black vortex. The birds encircling her, blotted out the sun, leaving only a world of darkness and poking, prodding pain.

Scott pulled her in a different direction, the noise of her bare heels slapping the ground lost in the shrill screams of the birds' squawking.

She caught a flash of pale movement as Hendrix tried to shoo them away from her own face, Scott doing the same.

Scott yanked Lauren's arm again, hard this time, as if frightened.

She wasn't ready for it and she fell, the concrete skinning her knees and palms. She hit hard, the air knocked out of her. The birds seized the opening, battering her immediately and pecking at her back through the thin cotton fabric of her shirt.

Hands pushed through the squirming mass, fighting to grab for her and hoist her back to her feet, pulling her away from the assaulting flock.

"No!" she yelled.

Angry barking broke through the birds' shrieking and she saw, through a flash of flapping wings, a pair of pit bulls charging toward them, their muzzles caked in gore.

"Oh shit," she said, hating the high-pitched whine in her tone.

We're dead. We're fucking dead.

Wings smacked her face, stinging her like a thousand paper cuts, and then—

Clarity.

The birds swarmed the dogs, encircling them with a fury of swift-moving viciousness. Barks and yelps and snapping sounds filled the air. A cry of pain rang out from one of the mutts, but she had no time to take in the scene as the predators fought over their claims to the three humans.

Her knees burned as she ran, her whole body aching and sticky. She kept close to Scott, Hendrix nearly right on top of her as they rushed toward his patrol car.

Scott pulled open the passenger door, then shoved Lauren inside, who scooted across the seat to make room for Hendrix. The seat leather stuck to her skin, her whole body sticky with blood and bird shit, errant feathers clinging to her. Then Scott piled into the driver's seat, slamming the key into the ignition but not starting it just yet. He looked through the window, taking in the scene around them.

Outside the SUV, Lauren realized how badly life around them had degenerated.

The birds had blinded the pit bulls and were savagely gouging away at their flanks and faces, but the dogs were still putting up a good fight, snatching birds from the thick morass surrounding them.

Across the way, other dogs fed on the remains of the humans they had managed to bring down. A rich coffee-colored Labrador tore into the belly of an overweight woman wearing a one-piece bathing suit; she'd clearly run up from the beach, her feet coated in thick clumps of sand. The Lab tore free a stringy rope of innards, jaws snapping.

A number of dogs lay dead, the street covered in a detritus of still birds and ducks and geese, the beach stained a dark, ruddy red that bordered on black.

Gunshots cut through the air. A large swan felled one of the deputies, close enough to the SUV that Lauren heard his surprised shout over the cacophony. When he screamed, his open mouth invited the long beak of the swan to enter and Lauren had to turn away, but not quickly enough. The scream was cut short, but the sight of the man's tongue being ripped from his mouth stained her vision.

Ahead, fires raged through downtown, but there were no sign of the firefighters. The truck was abandoned, its hose left limp in the street, trickling water. Fire feasted on the structures lining either side of the street, devouring the bookstore, a coffee shop, one of the many tourist-oriented t-shirt companies, and stores carrying handcrafted goods, flames licking at the marquee of the theater.

The movie theater had special Friday midnight revivals, and this week they were scheduled to show *Jaws* to help kick off their summer movie season. She and Jacob had planned on going. Had planned, in fact, on making those Friday showings their "thing". The calendar that had been released was marked up with a host of classics, from *Ghoul* to *Critters I* and *II*, and *Big Trouble in Little China*, which had become one of her all-time favorites after her father introduced her to it. That flick was one of his favorites, and she had fond memories of rainy Saturdays curled up on the couch with him beside her, watching Kurt Russell make an ass out of himself. No more *Jaws*, and she felt the tears welling as her throat burned, thinking, *No more Jacob either.* Thinking that, yes, she really did love him, and she didn't care if she was too young to know anything about love at all, but damn it she *knew.*

"It looks like the apocalypse out there," Hendrix said, echoing Lauren's own thoughts.

Scott looked at the women, his eyes soft as he took a deep breath. Then, he turned the ignition and got the SUV turned around.

Lauren noticed how oddly quiet it was without Hex, but her body and mind could only take so much heartache, and she felt awfully numb right now.

The stalled traffic had transformed into abandoned cars as drivers gave up trying to free their way from the snarl and grew panicked by the suddenly violent animals around them. A smattering of confused drivers still remained, their knuckles white from the death grip they maintained on the steering wheel, eyes wide in shock and panic and disbelief, not knowing at all what to do or where to go.

"Wait, stop," she said, putting her arm on her father's hand.

She waved to the driver of the Saturn, still sitting where she had left it. Christ, that felt like hours ago. Days ago. A week. She motioned for Dec to join them.

"Open the back door," she said.

She saw a faint glimmer of recognition in Scott's eyes. He rolled down the window, and Dec did the same, their faces parallel.

"Howdy, neighbor," Dec said.

Scott couldn't help but grin. "Get in, man. You'll be sitting out here all day otherwise. There's no getting through."

"What happened?" Dec asked, getting out and going to the back of his car to free Sarah from the car seat.

"It's a long story," Scott said. "There's no seat there, sorry. Hope you don't mind taking the floor."

Dec pushed Sarah's carrier ahead of himself, then sat beside her. The canine bed wasn't meant for human ride-alongs, but Dec wasn't complaining.

"Thanks for stopping," he said. "I need to get Sarah to the hospital."

"Not through downtown, you won't. It's a disaster."

Dec's face scrunched up in confusion. "The hospital?"

"Downtown," Scott said. "It's gone. Everything's burning, out of control. Everything's gone tits up." He shot an apologetic look at his daughter and Deputy Hendrix, cheeks burning, and mouthed a quiet, "Sorry."

Lauren twisted in her seat, at least as much as she could. There wasn't a lot of room to maneuver. She checked on the baby and Dec through the air holes separating the front cabin from the canine bed. "She's quieted down."

"Wore herself out. Eventually cried herself to sleep."

Lauren nodded, suddenly feeling ashamed for ditching them on the highway. Maybe she should have stayed, or told him to come with, to bring Sarah, but…no. That could have been an even bigger disaster. Sarah would have been bird food, so maybe temporarily ditching them had been the best choice.

Hendrix tried radioing dispatch, but there was no response. Frustrated, she gave up.

"What are we going to do?" she asked.

Scott scratched at his face, globs of bird shit and streaks of blood smeared down his forearm, crusting the hair along his arm and hand. "We're getting Dec and Sarah to the ER. After that…I don't know."

8

THE Emergency Room receiving area was packed—the seating area outside triage was filled to capacity, turning the area into standing room only. The check-in desk was slowly working through the line of people, but the staff were stretched to their limit.

Scott had taken them on a circuitous route to the hospital, avoiding downtown by cutting through the residential areas and taking a parallel path that brought them to the rear parking lot. Traffic had still been plentiful as people worked their way off US 31 or Michigan Avenue, or aimed to avoid both altogether.

Triage was a mass of confusion, moaning, and swearing. People had their arms wrapped in soiled t-shirts or towels, hunched forward and groaning, some of them pale, others clutching their bellies with their faces scrunched in a perpetual wince. There were seeping wounds and the stink of burned flesh.

Having worked the area as a deputy for more than twenty years, Scott recognized a number of faces.

There was Fred McCaskill, who had the bison farm up

on the peninsula. A couple dozen day laborers who worked the vineyards, cherry orchards, and apple farms along Old Mission Peninsula, each bore signs of an attack, with long stretches of skin gouged open. Scott wondered if maybe the hawks or owls had gotten to them since they didn't seem to have bite marks. A lot of their injuries looked more like what Lauren had suffered from the blackbirds.

Derrick Thompson, a veterinarian, and Shirley Fields, who manned the front desk and scheduled appointments for him, both bore signs of an animal mauling. Their faces were scratched, and he had a thick towel wrapped tightly around his forearm, gauze around his leg, and a bandage on his neck that looked to be the least of his troubles. Fields wasn't much better off.

Familiar faces, a lot of them, even if he didn't know all their names. Enough, too, that he didn't recognize and chalked up as tourists.

"We should have somebody look at your arm," Hendrix said.

"Sarah's the priority here. Lauren, too."

"You need stitches."

"I'll be fine," he said.

"Dad, you should listen to her."

He scowled at his daughter, knowing both women were right but damned if he wanted to sit around in a hospital waiting all day to be seen. The place was packed tighter than a sardine can, and he was getting antsy at being so thoroughly surrounded. Scott didn't like crowds, but he'd never thought of himself as claustrophobic before. Maybe just more of a homebody. But as all these bodies jostled around him, he realized that he couldn't stand here much longer. He needed to escape, get out, get some fresh air—anything. If he stayed, it wouldn't be long before they were buried under all these people.

"Stay here with them," he told Hendrix. "I need to get ahold of dispatch."

His throat was tight and forcing the words out had been

difficult. A cold sweat brewed atop his forehead as he pushed his way through the crowd and back to the security desk near the entrance. This area was less congested and he felt himself relax slightly.

"Use your phone?" he asked the hospital guard.

"You're welcome to try. Lines are jammed. No calls getting in or out."

Scott nodded, but dialed the direct line to the dispatch center anyway.

"I'm sorry. Your call cannot be completed at this time," a recorded voice told him. He scowled at the intercept message, hung up, and dialed again.

Still nothing.

He checked his cell phone again, but there was no change there, either. The display still showed a No Network symbol.

"Your cell phone working?" he asked.

The guard shook his head. "Nah, man. All the phone are down, looks like. The way this place is hopping, the grid's probably overloaded. What the hell's going on out there?"

Scott snorted out a humorless laugh, unsure how to explain it. Plane crash, animals gone berserk and attacking anything and everyone. How do you even begin to relay that?

"A Boeing went down along the main drag," he said, keeping it simple. "You guys are going to have your hands full for a while."

The population of the region was low enough that this lone hospital was the primary care facility. There were a handful of doctors' offices, urgent care centers, and walk-in clinics, but for emergencies this was the one and only. Clearly it wasn't going to be enough, the way things were heading.

Pushing his way back through the crowd, he found that their group had barely moved. Lauren was looking at her iPhone, impatiently checking it every few seconds.

"Lines are down," he said. "Mine's useless, too."

Hendrix checked her cell, confirming that she, too, had a No Network error.

Scott put his arm around Lauren's shoulder, pulling her close. She leaned into the hug and squeezed his middle. After a minute, she broke away to check her phone once more. She looked utterly defeated.

"Maybe we should go check on Mom," she said. The suggestion was offered softly, tentatively, as if she regretted the words but felt compelled to say them nonetheless.

"You need to get checked out," he said.

"I'm fine, Dad, really."

"Your mom's okay," he said.

"How do you know?"

He let out a windy exhale and shrugged. "I don't," he said. "I just figure she's all right."

"We don't know that, though. After what's been happening today…"

On any other day, Lauren would never have mentioned her mother, let alone make her the focus of conversation. Like his daughter, Scott was not in any great hurry to see, or even discuss, Melisa, but both were bound by some weird sense of necessity.

"We'll get you looked at first, then go check on her," he said.

"I think we need to get over there now, Dad. Before things get any worse."

He noticed how she was holding one arm, her hand closed around her bicep to cover the small circular scars that dotted the skin, hiding the cigarette burns that her so-called mother had inflicted upon her years ago.

"The doctor should look at you."

"I told you, I'm fine. It's just a few scratches. C'mon. And you said it yourself, Sarah's the top priority here. I'm not."

Having his words flung back at him by his own daughter like that stung him deeply, a real sucker punch. He hadn't meant to make it sound like he was putting another family above his own, but there was a certain bite to Lauren's words that he couldn't ignore.

"I didn't mean—"

"I know," she said.

"You can go," Dec said. "We're good here. Thanks for getting us here."

"I'll stay with them," Hendrix volunteered. "Make sure they get seen."

Scott let out another deep breath, feeling cornered again—this time by his own people, even with the crush of strangers pressing against him.

"All right, fine," he said. "But I'm bringing you back here after. You probably need a rabies shot or something."

Lauren nodded, but her face remained implacable.

"Do you think Buckley is okay?" she asked.

Rather than answer, Scott put his arm around his daughter's shoulders again, helping lead her through the crowds. Her phone was gripped tightly in one hand, and he caught her checking again as she stumbled through the mess of injured people.

Kids and their phones, he thought.

9

MELISA Delacourt had been a shitty mother.

As the years passed, Lauren stayed in touch with her less and less. Melisa had been apparently fine with the transition, as she never made even one attempt to reach out to her daughter or make amends for the past.

When she was younger, the visits were always supervised, either by her father and held in neutral public grounds, or conducted in the lobby of the police station within sight of the desk sergeant.

She had been very young when Melisa and her father divorced, and one of her earliest memories was of Dad explaining to her the cause for their separation.

"Mommy's very sick," he'd said.

Lauren had no reason to question this, and her immature mind had little reason to explore the subject with any depth or logic. At only three years old, she'd understood what it meant to be sick—coughing, runny nose, a fever—and those things always made her miserable. Whenever she got sick, she just wanted to curl up on the sofa and be left alone. So when Mommy left to go be by herself, Lauren understood only that Mommy must have been really, really sick.

Not until many years later did she learn the truth, when she started putting the pieces together on her own. Eventually, she'd had a heart-to-heart with her father, and as she was old enough and mature enough to understand the realities of the situation, Matthew Scott finally came clean to her.

Sitting at the kitchen table, he explained how one night, only a few months after Lauren's birth, he'd come home from his shift to find Melisa in their apartment dining room stoned and cutting herself. He hadn't gone into exquisite detail, but her imagination filled in the blanks nicely. She could imagine a young Melisa with manic, drug-shot eyes taking a kitchen knife to her forearm and carving slits in her flesh from wrist to elbow.

"Melisa was committed for a little while after that, and spent about three weeks in psychiatric care," Scott had explained.

"I still loved her, though, you know? I wasn't ready to give up on her. She just had some problems, and the doctors worked with her for a while to get her on a good medication schedule to help her screw her head back on right. And she was fine for a while," he continued.

For a little more than a year and a half, things between Matthew and Melisa went well. Well enough that when their marriage began to deteriorate, he was able to turn a blind eye to it for a while. Until she became moody and took up smoking again, a habit she had broken after finding out she was pregnant and had kept at bay for the better part of two years.

"She started drinking and quit taking her medicine. We were fighting more and more, and she lied to me about it— about quitting the meds, I mean. I started counting the pills in her prescription bottle and…"

At that point, he'd rubbed his knuckles into his eyes and drank a glass of water. Lauren had been surprised at the amount of care and longing in his voice as she recognized that he was reopening very old wounds for her. As much as she admired her father, she could not understand for the life of her how he could be so choked up over the abusive crazy woman that she knew as her mother.

When he saw her absentmindedly massaging the scars on her arm with her fingertips, he'd sobered up and his eyes went clear, if still distant. "I don't know how long she'd been off her medication, but things started to crystalize for me. She started wearing long-sleeved shirts all the time. Even in the summer, she wore long-sleeved t-shirts. I was stupid, you know? I didn't think much of it at first, not until she started slipping.

"It'd been mostly a good year up to that, kinda like old times. I thought maybe we had started to resettle into a groove, gotten used to this new state of being. And I thought she was just paying you more attention, being more attendant, being a better mother. But she kept slipping, and I started to realize that what she was doing, really, was shielding you from me. Hiding you behind herself so I couldn't see what was happening.

"I was working extra hours, trying to pull in as much OT as possible. It was good money, and we needed it, so I was missing an awful lot at home. And I know that's not an excuse but—"

"It's not your fault, Dad."

He shrugged. "It's one thing to hear you say that, and another thing entirely for me to believe it. And it's something that your mom always used against me when we fought. My not being home was a weapon she could use against me, and damn it if it didn't work. And in some ways she was right. I *wasn't* home, I wasn't seeing what was happening. To her. To you. I just didn't see it. But I started putting the pieces together, slower than I should have. I wanted to give her the benefit of the doubt, though…you know?"

Lauren had reached across the table, putting her hand atop her father's and giving him a gentle, encouraging squeeze.

"I'd left work early, got another guy to cover for me. Melisa was giving you a bath, and the water was running so she didn't hear me come in. I could see what was happening—what was about to happen—in the mirror as I got near, but still, there I was telling myself I was only being paranoid, trying to trick myself into believing everything would be okay. And I knew I was lying to myself, too. Fuck's sake, I could see you right there in the mirror and I could see all these tiny red marks on your body and it all clicked. Melisa had her sleeves pushed up so they wouldn't get wet, and there were scabs all over her arms.

"She had a cigarette in her mouth. She was smoking and giving you a bath," he said, unable to hide the exasperation at his ex-wife. "She was blowing smoke right in your eyes and you started to cry. That's when she took the cigarette from her mouth, and I knew she was going to burn you. If I hadn't grabbed her wrist right then…"

Lauren nodded. Many of the cigarette burns that marred her body were small scars, diminished with age and they'd grown barely noticeable as she grew. A few, like the cluster on her upper arms, were more readily apparent, even if she had no direct memory of how they had occurred.

"I had to shove her aside and get you out of there, back into your crib, soaking wet and screaming your little head off. I arrested your mom that night, and the next morning I filed for divorce while she was put back into psychiatric care."

After the Child Protective Services and police investigations, and the ensuing court proceedings, Melisa was found guilty of child endangerment, willful negligence, and assault and battery, convicted and sentenced to three years at a women's correctional facility. Upon her release, she petitioned to be allowed supervised visits, which the court granted. Matthew had not objected, still believing there was some small measure of hope for normalcy and that Lauren deserved a chance to know her mother.

Most of the time, Melisa skipped out on the visits, and Lauren and her father would spend hours together at the park making the best of the time they had together. He'd push her on the swings, take her for ice cream after. Those were good times, she thought, the memories dim and distant. Other times Melisa would show, barely lucid or exhausted from her prescribed pills. Eventually, as the years wore on, she stopped trying altogether and Lauren was left, out of some misguided sense of familial obligation, to carry the weight of salvaging their relationship. That burden grew too heavy eventually, and she began to show the same disinterest in continuing things. As she got older, she made friends, went to school, and—more recently—got a part-time job. Whatever mom-sized hole was in her life had been filled with other interests. Still, she couldn't help but wonder what it was like to have that sort of happy balance. Of her small group of close friends, she was the only that came from a "broken" home. There were never any freshly baked, made from scratch, cookies in her home, although her dad was pretty good with the oven, and she had learned how to cook pretty well from the age of twelve.

When she suggested that they go check up on Melisa, it wasn't out of any sense of loyalty or compassion for the woman. Instead, there was an odd sense of obligation and maybe even a degree of one-upmanship and a perverse display of moral superiority. A way to demonstrate to the woman how much better Lauren Scott was without her, despite Melisa's best efforts.

You couldn't even bother to call, but look at me. Look at us. We came out here to just make sure your pathetic, sorry ass was safe and sound. Even though you didn't give a single shit about either of us. So suck on that, bitch.

"You expecting a call?" Scott asked.

His gaze flickered between her and the road ahead of them. She glanced down at her phone again, then slipped it into her pocket.

"No," she said. Then shrugged, as if bored.

Please, Jacob, if you're out there, please call me. Please.

⚜ ⚜ ⚜

Hex hadn't been a dog easy to rile and often sat quietly in the compartment behind Scott. That said, the dog had carried a certain weight and made his presence known. The dog's absence was unsettling, and despite knowing that Hex was dead, Scott still expected to hear the sound of his breathing, or snoring, or the shifting of his frame within the back of the SUV. Instead, the sterile quiet was painfully noticeable.

Scott fought back the tears of grief and tried his damnedest to ignore the burning iron ball that had settled in his belly. Hex was gone. His friend, his partner, a fellow officer, and—most importantly—a family member. He had no trouble admitting that Hex was his little fur baby, and with the shepherd gone, and so violently, Scott was fighting a rising tide of emotion. There was no time to mourn, though.

Casting his eyes at Lauren, he saw she was fiddling with her phone again, even though both of them knew damn well that it was dead to the world.

Who is she expecting to call? he wondered. Maybe one of her friends, maybe Crystal. She was a good kid. He tried hard to think of the names of her other girlfriends, but couldn't dredge them up. Or work, but he wasn't sure if she was expected at Best Buy today or not. She certainly hadn't been in a hurry to get to her job when he saw her cut off that minivan earlier in the day, and even though she loved the beach he hoped she wasn't that reckless just to catch some rays.

Driving like a mad woman, fidgeting with her phone, showing up downtown. What was she hiding?

"You expecting a call?"

"No," she said, giving the phone one last look before sliding it into the hip pocket of her jean shorts.

Her eyes did not rise to meet his, though, and he knew for sure that she was keeping a secret.

Hell, though, he couldn't blame her, he supposed. With his work schedule of six months on days and six months on nights, he'd missed half of her life, at least. Those night shifts were killer. He'd sleep in the day, while she was at school, and by the time she got home he'd be getting ready to leave for work. When his off-days rotated in, they still only had a handful of hours before she was off to bed to start her next day, or, if on weekends, when he was lucky enough to have a weekend off with her, she'd be off to go hang with her friends. Day shifts were a little better, and made being a family easier, but Lauren still had a life of her own. A life that he wasn't as integral to as he'd once been.

Somehow, in the blink of an eye, she'd grown from being this tiny little baby into an adult, or close to anyway.

His fingers curled tighter around the steering wheel, knuckles whitening. He'd never felt the wall between them as clearly as he did right now. She was keeping secrets, and his cop's mind raced over the possibilities.

He'd missed out on enough of her life. He'd been blind to Melisa's behaviors for so long, and by the time he'd glommed onto that, his daughter had been burned. What was Lauren hiding? Drugs? He thought not, but maybe she was just into the lightweight stuff. Could she be trying to get ahold of a dealer to score a joint, something to help cut through the day's edge? She never behaved like a tweaker, and her skin wasn't marred with track marks. Maybe a boy? He wasn't overly thrilled with the idea of his little girl dating, but he knew she was mature enough to handle it. Still, things happened…

Was she seeing somebody? And if she were, was that really so bad?

No, he decided, it wasn't the worst thing in the world. How long had it been going on, and why hadn't she told him? That last question was the one that nagged at him.

He thought about all the times she'd checked her phone today and decided that, yes, it probably had to do with a boy.

"How long have you been seeing him?" he asked.

"Who?"

He glanced at her. After a moment she met his gaze, but there was that tell again.

"The boy you're worrying over. The one you keep expecting to call, or hoping that you'll get a signal so you can call him."

Slowly, her eyes softened and she stared into the footwell for a moment, pushing back loose strands of hair behind her ears.

"His name is Jacob. We've been seeing each other for two—almost three—months now."

"You like him, then."

"I do."

"So what's the big secret then?" he asked.

Lauren sighed. "I don't know," she said. "I mean, I meant to tell you, like, a while ago. But somehow it just didn't happen. You were busy with work, or I was, or with homework or whatever. And then somehow it just became a secret. And then I thought I couldn't tell you, because then you'd be mad that I hadn't told you earlier, which meant I couldn't tell you at all, and…it's stupid."

"It's okay," he said. "I'm not mad."

"You sure?"

"How old is he?"

"Um," she said. "He's a little older than me."

Now he did look at her, hard and full on. "How much older?"

"He's twenty-one."

"Jesus, Lauren."

"He's a good guy, Dad. I swear. Don't freak out. Please?"

For whatever reason, Scott couldn't help but laugh.

"What?" she asked, her face crossed with worry.

"You remember when you were six? You found this old painting pole in the garage, and you were twirling it around in the living room and—"

"—and I broke that lamp Grandma gave us."

"And you met me at the door before I could get into the house and you stopped me. You told me, 'Don't freak out. Please?'"

He laughed, wiping away a tear that had been threatening to boil over. He thought that, maybe, that one was a small bit of joy, of relief.

"I wanted to be Donatello," she said.

He laughed again, remembering his young daughter's obsession with the *Teenage Mutant Ninja Turtles*. He'd had to buy her a cheap purple t-shirt so she could cut it up and make a mask.

"And it wasn't a painting pole," she said. "It was a friggin' bo staff!"

She was laughing now, too, and the sound of it glued the fractures of his heart together.

"I was pretty kick-ass with it, if I recall right."

Slowly, the laughter trailed off and both were plunged back into silence.

"I'm sorry about Hex," she said, suddenly somber and swiping at tears of her own.

"Me too, baby. Me too."

"Do you think, whatever all this is, that it got Buckley, too?"

Scott took his time answering. Based on what he'd seen over the course of the last few hours, there was definitely cause for concern in the case of Buckley, and a part of him figured that the dog was already—what? Possessed? Infected?

"I don't know, Lauren," he said, rather than admit his fears. "I hope not."

Shortly after, the two lapsing into silence once again, he made the turn into Melisa's subdivision, then turned left into her driveway a few blocks later.

※ ※ ※

Melisa's neighborhood was oddly quiet. Her car sat in the driveway, a rusted old heap that hadn't seen the inside of a carwash in as long as Lauren could remember. The vehicle was covered in mud and bird crap, but Scott pressed his palm against the hood.

"Hasn't been run lately," he said.

Looking at the excrement coating the car, Lauren shivered and wondered where all the birds had gone. Then again, maybe their absence was for the better.

"Stay close to me," Scott said.

She nodded and shadowed her father's movements.

The lawn was overgrown and the hedges lining the front of the house had gone wild ages ago. The front porch was nearly hidden in an archway of reaching limbs from the shrubbery and as they passed through, the brambles caught on their skin, tugging at the sleeves of Scott's uniform.

The overgrown bushes had also obscured the living room's front picture window. The glass was stained from Buckley's wet nose, and she could make out the impressions all along the sill and higher up, from when the dog stood on the back of the sofa. More troubling, though, was the long streak of red, and the various misshapen blobs marring the window.

"Dad?" she said, pointing.

He had seen it and simply nodded, his hand resting on the butt of his firearm holstered at his hip.

Their steps were cautious, so as to avoid making the boards of the porch squeak as they approached the front door.

Lauren jumped as Buckley slammed into the front window, inches from her face, and began barking furiously.

His face pressed to the glass, he spread more gore across the pane, leaving bright red streaks as he darted along the couch, going back and forth, raising hell and staring her down.

At the sight of the dog, Lauren's heart collapsed. Whatever was happening, not even Buckley had been spared. The dog had always been good to her and loved people, wagging his tail hard enough that he nearly shook himself right off his hind legs, even for perfect strangers.

This dog before her wasn't Buckley. Any traces of the dog she had once known were gone, obliterated.

His thick skull smashed into the glass again with a dull, meaty thud. The warning was clear enough.

Buckley's face was coated in grime and clumps of—well, Lauren was certain she didn't want to know, swallowing down the rising bile. Thick trails of mucus and foam leaked from his face, his golden fur nappy and glossy with a wetness that stained him nearly black.

Scott edged his way between her and the window, trying to see past the dog and into the house. Buckley wasn't having any of that, though, and he followed Scott's movement with violent determination, obscuring the view with his blocky head and torso, dragging more long red marks and frothy globs of spittle across the stained glass.

"Can you see anything?"

"No," Scott said, his voice soft. He pulled the keys to the SUV from his pocket and handed them over to his daughter. "Go wait in the car. If I'm not back in a few minutes, get out of here. Go back to the hospital and stay with Hendrix. You got it?"

Lauren nodded numbly, his words tearing open a void inside of her and she bit her lip, hoping to avoid examining her father's threat of dying. Of being killed by Buckley. She couldn't face that. She couldn't lose him, not him, not on top of having lost so much already.

She knew Melisa was dead, and that Buckley had killed her. There was no other way that particular story could have ended. Suddenly, taking her father's keys and turning tail, she felt those spiky tendrils of guilt stab at her heart and soul. She'd come out here to one-up her own mother, driven by a selfish desire to prove herself the better woman, the one standing on the peak of the moral high ground, but all she'd found was more death, more savagery. And now her father was talking about dying, telling her that he might not be coming back.

Her legs numbly carried her back to the SUV, and she looked back once to see her father watching her, making sure that she complied and folded herself into the passenger seat. Not the driver's seat, because he was going to make it, he was going to come back, and he was going to drive them away from here.

Closing the door, she pulled on her seatbelt, more out of muscle memory and reflexive action than any conscious thought. Scott looked back at the house, at Buckley, then descended the porch steps and moved around the side of the house. He banged on the siding as he went, to lure the dog into following, she guessed—and tried not to worry about him attracting other threats in the process. She lost sight of him as he turned into the backyard, her heart knocking against her ribcage.

Moments later, she heard the loud report of a gunshot, and then an eerie stillness. After several long, agonizing moments that felt like forever, Scott reappeared, following the driveway back to his vehicle, his eyes vacant. He opened the driver's side door and climbed in, resting his head against the headrest, eyes closed.

"Did you go inside?"

He nodded.

"Mom?"

He shook his head, then turned to look at her. The sorrow in his eyes was obvious, but she thought it was more for her sake than Melisa's.

"And Buckley?" she asked, although she knew well enough that he wouldn't have fired his gun if it hadn't been to eliminate the threat of the dog.

"He won't hurt anyone else."

After starting the vehicle, he fiddled with the radio, cycling through the AM and FM bands but getting mostly static.

"What are you doing?" she asked.

"Somebody has to know something about what's happening. I was hoping for maybe a news station or something."

Lauren looked back toward the house. "We could try the TV in there."

Scott paused, then shut off the radio. "I tried that already. None of the stations are coming through. It's all dead."

Lauren swallowed audibly, but said nothing. She merely watched as Scott turned his attention to the police radio mounted on the dash, scanning for an active frequency. Although the volume was loud enough, he still kept his head cocked, as if concentrating, listening for any kind of tell that somebody was out there and broadcasting.

The numbers grew as he turned through the dial, and then there was a squelching break in the signal, the faintest impression of a voice. He leaned in closer, nudging the dial.

"—people need to stay inside," a voice said. "Again, this is Jeff Miller, broadcasting from the Grand Traverse University campus in Falls Breath. It appears that solar storms are causing severe magnetic disruption, making cell phones, GPS, and radio and television broadcasts impossible in our region. There have also been a number of reports of animal attacks, and I'm getting word of a plane crash downtown, so please, stay indoors. Stay in your home. Do not go outside.

"If you can hear me, I say again, do not go outside. Keep by your radio and we'll provide updates as soon as we can. Jacob Teller, from the GTU Astronomical Association, will be joining me in a bit to give us the lowdown on what's happening overhead, so just sit tight."

Lauren shot up in her seat at the mention of Jacob.

Scott noticed and said, "Is that your Jacob?"

She nodded, open-mouthed. Wanting to believe, but torn between not wanting to get her hopes up.

"We have to go there. Can we go there?"

He unclipped his radio from his shoulder and raised Hendrix. "What's happening on your end?"

"Nothing new," she said. "I'm still at the hospital, but feeling pretty damn useless. Sarah's looking to be a pretty low priority. There's all kinds of injuries ahead of her, plenty of more severe cases."

He had been worried about that, but as long as they were indoors they were safe, and that outweighed everything else. "I'm heading over to the university. I think there might be someone with some answers over there. If Dec and his girl are all situated now, I need you to get over to the mayor's office and brief them on what's happening. Find Tremblay first. We need support, whatever we can get."

Scott had almost forgotten about Tremblay entirely. The sheriff had been radio silent the entire day, which was strange in and of itself. He hadn't even tried to coordinate his officers, and there'd been no sign of backup anywhere. Scott's patrol vehicle seemed to be the only sign of an official response on the streets at all anymore.

"I'll radio in once I have news," Hendrix said, a quirky pep in her voice. She must have been happy to finally be doing something, after waiting in the crowded ER.

"All right," Scott said, pulling the shifter into Drive.

"Let's go meet this Jacob of yours."

10

THE last time Scott had set foot on the Grand Traverse University campus, it had been to break up a rowdy frat party. There had been a lot of underage drinking, which led to a fistfight between several of the boys from two rival fraternities. That had been maybe a year ago, but Scott knew the campus well from his own time there as a student many years prior.

The campus hadn't changed much in the intervening years between student and officer, with one exception. Blood now stained broad stretches of the campus's grounds, and a number of still bodies lay scattered in the grass, the parking lots, and on the sidewalks. It was like a scene straight out of a war movie, a total massacre that he had trouble processing. Wind jostled the open car doors, their drivers collapsed nearby, having failed to make it to the safe interior of their cars.

"Oh, god," Lauren said, turning her face away, eyes scrunched tightly.

When Scott glanced out her window, he caught sight of what had disturbed her. Somebody had made it inside their car, but a fox had been a hair quicker. The animal stood on

67

its hind legs and nibbled at the dead student's face.

"Any idea where your boyfriend might be?"

"I did a campus tour last month. They showed us where the clubs are located in the University Center. It's down there," she said, pointing to the right. "Radio club's on the third floor."

He nodded, aware of the UC's location. Not much had changed at all, and the University Center was still situated along Lake Shore Drive, right on the bay.

Wary of what might be out there, he pulled the patrol car up to the circular drive outside the main entrance, ignoring the No Parking signs placed every few feet along the curb. He doubted the bus would be pulling through here on its route to drop off anyone.

"We're going to make a run for it," he told Lauren, looking out the windows for signs of predators nearby. "Hurry up and get inside. Okay? On three, then."

He did a count, and threw his door open when he hit three, then slammed it shut. Lauren was already ahead of him, nearing the automatic doors while he cleared the curb and rushed up behind her.

The doors refused to part, but there was a regular door alongside it. He reached for it, and found that the door was locked. He tugged again, uselessly, the door rattling as the deadbolt struck and rattled its frame.

"Damn it!"

From the trees lining the courtyard, he heard a low rumble and turned in time to see the branches sway. Looking back toward the car, he saw four dogs amble into view from around the side of the UC, their heads slunk low and wolf-like, their lips rising to reveal sharp, pointed teeth.

"Lauren, run."

She darted left, and Scott followed, pulling his firearm free. The pack of dogs gave chase, and the air filled with the cacophony of their barking as their paws slapped concrete.

Scott turned to fire, leveling his weapon at the nearest dog—a yapping corgi covered in blood, with clumps of black-spotted gore glued to its tiny, disproportionate body. The bullet obliterated its head, turning its last yap into a high-pitched squeal that stopped suddenly.

From the parking lot, an Alaskan malamute scrabbled free from under the shade of a Taurus, on a direct path for Lauren. A Catahoula mix, a pit bull terrier, and a border collie were gaining on Scott.

"Get around the side," he yelled. "Go toward the bay, there's a rear entrance."

Running, he leveled the gun forward, aiming on the malamute—a beautiful breed, black and white, with a big, fluffy upturned tail. The dog was enormous, and, if he had to guess, was at least eighty pounds. The dog was gorgeous and he hated to put it down, but it was the dog or his daughter, and there was simply no contest.

His finger tightened on the trigger.

And then he was falling as a thick, heavy weight slammed into him. The collie hit hard and rolled off, but the wind was knocked clear out of Scott's lungs. The gun had fired, exploding a hole in the sidewalk a few feet in front of him.

The collie was on top of him, biting into his back, tearing at the shirt fabric.

Pain lanced through his calf as the pit bull sank its teeth into him, and he couldn't help but scream.

Miraculously, the gun was still in hand, and he shot the pit bull point blank. The gunfire was loud enough to hurt the collie's sensitive ears, and the dog whined and leapt away from him. He knew better than to second-guess the small opening that had been provided for him, and he leveled the gun on the collie, pulling the trigger just as the Catahoula latched onto his forearm, the same arm Hex had dug into earlier.

The collie's right eye burst, the bullet tearing his ear and collapsing the side of its face.

The Catahoula's teeth was tearing through the gauze, through the skin on his arm, and he coldcocked the mutt with the butt of his gun.

Lauren delivered a quick kick to the side of the animal's head, right as the malamute leaped onto her back and tackled her.

Scott was able to raise his gun and fire at the Catahoula, his arm blazing from the reopened injuries and brand new lacerations.

Lauren's screams sounded over the blast, and he turned toward the malamute, wishing now that he'd been able to kill the dog when he'd had the chance.

Another thick body leaped into the fray, and Scott saw a flash of wood and heard the sickening crunch of bone breaking apart. The malamute was still, and the batter kicked the dog off Lauren.

She moaned and twisted, forced herself into a sitting position.

The man, dressed in crimson-stained white pants and a white jersey, his legs covered in thick white pads, offered her an open hand, which she took.

Scott realized that the man's weapon wasn't a baseball bat, as he'd first thought, but the long, oar-shaped paddle of a cricket bat.

"C'mon, you need to get inside," the sportsman said, his voice oddly familiar.

He darted ahead of them, back toward the main entrance where they'd come from only moments ago. He pulled the door open without any problem, waving them inside. Once Scott and Lauren cleared the doorway, he slammed the door shut and threw the deadbolt.

"Jeff Miller," he said, extending his hand to Scott.

They shook, and Scott said, "The guy from the radio."

"Yes, sir. One and the same."

Lauren let out a noisy gasp and then brushed past him quickly. He saw her dart toward another man and fling her arms around his neck.

"And that must be Jacob," Scott said.

After a moment, she released the red-faced man, allowing him to get some air, and turned toward her father with a proper degree of bashfulness and a look he recognized as mild humiliation. He'd never seen her so jazzed to see somebody, not even him, but he recognized the expression. She usually wore it when she was caught doing something unexpected or out of character, even though she'd really done nothing wrong. She had every right to be happy, and Jacob clearly had her under some kind of spell. Scott couldn't help but smile, an odd feeling of levity crawling over him, as he reached toward Jacob with an open hand. Then he put his arm around his little girl and gave her a fierce hug, grateful that she was still safe and sound, and that maybe there was a chance for her to keep on having a happy life with a man she loved.

"How much do you guys know about what's happening out there?" he asked.

Jeff and Jacob exchanged a look, silently deciding who would go first. Jeff ran a red-slicked hand through his hair, unconcerned about his mussed style or the stained strands. He absently tapped the cricket bat against the side of his padded shin guard, deciding what to say.

"Enough to know something is very, very wrong," Jeff said. "C'mon, let's go upstairs. If Jacob is right, this could get a bit complicated."

Then, as if that were its cue, the building's lights flickered and died. There was enough daylight to see by, but the loss of power was an ominous portent nonetheless.

"And it's clearly getting worse," Jeff said.

"What is?" Scott asked, wanting answers immediately.

"Come on," Jeff said, tilting his head toward the stairs.

Somewhere between their entrance and the climb to the third floor, Scott noticed that Lauren and Jacob's hands had become intertwined.

"I thought you were working at the coffee shop," she said.

"Dr. Havish called, asked me to come down here and monitor the observatory. So, I ended up calling off for my shift and got one of the girls to cover for me."

He gulped as the repercussion of his words sank in, hitting him hard. "Which, I guess, means I effectively killed her."

"Don't go down that road, son," Scott said. "It's not your fault, and you had no way of knowing."

Jacob laughed, but it lacked humor and warmth. "There's the rub, right? I guess I kind of did know. At least in a way."

"What do you mean?"

They approached the door to the radio club and passed into the broadcast room, the door clicking shut behind them. The UC felt hollow and empty, and Scott couldn't help but notice the complete absence of students, staff, and faculty. He supposed everyone was either hiding in their dorm rooms, or had managed to evacuate the campus safely. The parking lots outside were hardly empty, but they definitely weren't as full as they should have been.

"Take a seat," Jeff said, waving them to a well-worn and stained sofa.

Scott and Lauren obliged, sinking into cushions so badly used their asses nearly hit the floor.

A laptop sat open near the radio equipment, its screen black. The switchboards and radio controls were all dark, as well. The tape and digital audio recorders, cassette decks, CD players, digital clock display, and on-air warning light— all dead.

"Well, I'd hoped to give you a little audio-video demo, but that's out the window," Jeff said.

"I'm fine with a verbal summary," Scott replied impatiently.

Jacob fell into a chair, sliding it closer to the couch, the wheel casters squeaking badly.

"You know about the meteor showers that have been happening over these last days?" He asked the officer.

Scott nodded.

"We had a few comets hit our atmosphere, a few right over our heads even. Literally," he said, looking at Lauren, who nodded. "You could see them burning up in the sky above. Most probably disintegrated, but a few touched down, some too small to do any real physical damage. I'm sure you could find a few small craters out in the woods today, but probably not too many. There's at least one in the bay. A big one, though, landed on the old McClellan farm."

Scott nodded again. The farm was little more than the remains of ramshackle buildings. The walls of the house had collapsed ages ago, leaving what little was left of the roof to sit atop the mess of lumber and get grown over with grass. Most of the barn was still standing, although the roof had caved in right in the middle, obliterating a large chunk of the west-facing wall. A meteor wasn't bound to hurt the property all that much.

Jacob stood and began pacing the room while he spoke.

"There's been an increase in objects hitting Earth's atmosphere over the last few years, but with all the budget cuts and a lack of decent funding for NASA, nobody really pays much attention to it, unless something big gets through, like the asteroid that splashed down in Russia a few years ago. Now, that one, nobody ever saw that coming. Everyone was focused on another asteroid called 2012 DA14, which had absolutely no danger of hitting Earth. But this other asteroid, nobody ever knew it was on its way. It was coming at us from the direction of the sun, and we were completely blindsided by it.

"So, these last few nights, we were all caught up in the meteor shower, thinking it's just any other celestial event, perfectly normal, perfectly harmless. But there was shit out there we couldn't see, stuff we didn't even know about it, coming at us from an entirely different direction."

"A double-whammy," Jeff said.

"Okay," Scott said, "but what does that have to do with this? You're saying the animals are freaking out over space rocks?"

Jacob's lips twisted into a grimace. "Yes and no. This is

all completely hypothetical, but I think it's possible, and it's the best I've got. Did either of you watch the news this morning?"

Both Scott and Lauren shook their heads.

"An asteroid hit Russia, a big one. Bigger than the Tunguska event of 1908, which, in case you didn't know, was fucking huge…like bigger than the nuke we dropped on Hiroshima in World War II. And there have been a few others, too. Some big, some small. None as big as the one that splashed into Russia, but big enough.

"The Russian blast was enough to disrupt cellular communications over most of the world. This power loss now, that's because of the asteroids pummeling us. When these suckers hit, there's a huge release of thermal and electromagnetic energy. Basically, we've been hit with a bunch of big EMP bombs all day, with more and more of these shockwaves pummeling our planet. We're looking at a sort of cascading effect."

A noisy ripping halted Jacob's speech for a moment as Jeff undid the Velcro straps of his batting pads.

Scott was confused, still trying to wrap his mind around all this. Comets and meteors and asteroids and EMP pulses. This was all crazy.

Before he could open his mouth, Jacob held up a hand and hurried on.

"But that's only part of what's happening here. It's not just comets, okay? These rocks, they're like little petri dishes of bacteria. When the Philae lander touched down on a comet, we learned all kinds of stuff about these rocks within hours. The surface was rich with organic material, which means there was organic life on the damn thing…probably still is under all the ice."

"You're saying this is some kind of alien invasion?" Scott said.

Jacob laughed. "if you want to look at it that way, sure. I guess it is. I was thinking more of an outbreak than an invasion. These rocks have been hitting earth for the last few days, breaking apart or crash landing, and spreading bacteria all through the atmosphere, hitting our lakes and oceans, some coming down right in the middle of a city, like in Russia today. Or in the bay or out at McClellan's."

"And infecting the animals?" Lauren said.

Jacob nodded, slowly, less enthusiastic than he'd been during his pseudo-lecture. "I think so, yes. And with amazing rapidity, at that. Whatever this bug is, the way it just moves through hosts, it's seriously unlike anything else on Earth."

"And you think this is happening everywhere?" Scott added.

Jeff propped himself onto the desk, swinging his legs. "Over the ham radio, we were hearing from people about animal attacks. Before the phones and internet went down, there was stuff on Twitter and Facebook. Crazy stuff. And then, I guess, it finally caught up with us."

"Not just caught up," Jacob corrected him. "Overtook."

"Does the ham radio still work?" Lauren asked.

"It wasn't in a Faraday cage," Jacob said. "So, no. The EMP shockwave would have killed it, too, along with the power grid, our computers, phones, everything."

After a moment of silence, Jeff moved around to the opposite side of the studio, to a cooler tucked under the desk by the operator's station. He pulled free a twelve-pack of Miller Lite and began distributing cans to everyone. Once he had a brew in hand, he clinked his can against the others with false cheer.

"Welcome to the end of the world as we know it."

11

SHAY Hendrix maneuvered through traffic, en route to Government Plaza. Thankfully it was in the opposite direction of the decimated downtown, north of the hospital where she had left Dec and Sarah, in what had once been Old Downtown.

Driving was slow going, the streets jammed with stranded vehicles. Many of the stalled cars were still occupied and trapped between unmoving, deserted autos, drivers and passengers sitting inside and plainly worried. They waved for her to stop, and she felt guilty as she rolled past, trying not to watch as they slammed their hands against the windows in anger.

Then there were the bodies. Too many bodies. Corpses dotted the shoulder, or had simply fallen in the middle of the street. These she tried to go around, but one particularly dense stretch of road had made that impossible. Slowly, her car crept over the dead stretched across the shoulder, and she tried to ignore the awful thumps her tires made as she rolled over the bodies, the car slightly raising and then lowering as she passed. She tried not to make eye contact with the people still in the vehicles beside her, pounding on the windows, their muted screams managing to find her. Tried not to think about the skulls popping under the weight of her police cruiser, meat sacks exploding with a bony crunch as if she were running over a full pop bottle instead of murdered people. She had to close her eyes for a moment as she caught sight of the Realtor who helped her buy a house, just before the woman's body cracked under her tires.

Pop, pop, crunch, crunch.

Too many similar sightings worked her nerves raw and she wiped away a tear as she realized she was driving through the apocalypse. She understood the frustration of those few remaining drivers and trapped families as they frantically waved to get her attention, their eyes wide in desperate pleas. She couldn't stop and help them though, no matter how badly she wanted to. She saw what they didn't, or maybe what they simply didn't want to. On either side of the road, lining the shoulder and tucked away in the tree line beyond, black watchful eyes tracked her.

A sigh of relief escape her as she crossed into Old Downtown.

A product of a bygone era, the area was quiet, its storefronts smaller and always less bustling than their more expensive counterparts along the newer strip. This was where the locals came to shop when they wanted to avoid the tourists that flocked to the main drag, and its land-locked nature and the absence of beachside views or easy access to the lake made it an urban oasis.

Even miles away from the decimated strip of the newer downtown area, she could see the columns of black smoke darkening the sky, could still smell the putrid rank of burning insulation and human flesh and scorched metal.

Her patrol car died suddenly outside the squat, weather-beaten library. Her car coasted briefly, until she pumped the brakes and brought it to a halt. The library's windows went dark. So, too, did the buildings on either side of it, and across the street from her.

The Grand Traverse County Sheriff Department. City Hall. Little Tot's Daycare. All dark.

She put the car in park, turned off the vehicle, and tried to restart it. Nothing. Tried again. Still nothing. Putting it all together, she knew it wasn't a dead battery or any kind of internal malfunction.

Whatever was happening to the world around her, it just got that much worse.

She stared out the windows, turning her head to get the full one-eighty, checking her mirrors to see what, if anything, was happening on her six. The coast was clear.

She pulled her phone free and saw that it, too, was dead. The phone wasn't merely lost in the No Service oubliette, but dead-dead. She pocketed it, then checked her surroundings once again, looking for those eyes watching her as she watched for them.

City Hall was five blocks away, straight ahead. That was where Old Downtown ended, with a roundabout that fed back onto Averly Street in the opposite direction. Old, large conifers encircled the seat of local government, the building oddly modern in comparison to the surrounding relics, and a full story taller than anything else in the vicinity.

I can do this, she thought. *Easily.*

Another glance at her surroundings. No animals. No people.

Plenty of blood, though. Like US 31 and everywhere else she had seen, the streets were slick with it, the sidewalks stained in ruddy darkness. Mangled bodies dotting the landscape, torn apart, clothes rent, limbs gnawed on, and organs spilled.

That wasn't going to be her, though. Of that, she was bound and determined.

Her heart knocked loudly in her chest cavity, not merely thudding, but booming and banging, ready to punch through her breastbone and leap free of her body by sheer force of will and unstoppable momentum.

Sweat-slick fingers pulled the door handle and she

shoved her way out, running as soon as her boots hit the ground. A mental tally ran through her head as she ran.

Five blocks.

Four blocks.

The noise of her hammering heart was loud in her ears, the breathy whooshing of her aspiration an echo in her skull.

Her countdown barely hit *three blocks* when the sound of barking crashed into the air and the padded thuds of gray wolf feet slapping asphalt gave chase.

She couldn't outrun them, she knew. There was no way. Going over the cars would be fruitless, since the beasts could make the jump just as easily, if not better than she could, and it would only slow her down in the end. She kept her eyes forward, kept her legs pumping.

Run, you bitch! Just fucking run!

Sunlight glinted off glass overhead and a thunderous boom sounded over the wolves' noises. A painful sounding yelp rang out, too close, and then a dull thud as an animal hit the ground. She didn't look back, just kept running.

Two blocks.

More gunfire, more yelps, and—she hoped—more dead wild dogs.

The shooter was on the second floor of City Hall, dead ahead. She couldn't make out who it was, but she was grateful as all hell for their support. His aim—at least she thought it was a he—had been true and had given the wolves a little something to think about. Barking sounded behind her, but fainter, enough to ease her mind as she realized they were no longer pursuing her.

She gave a quick glance back to confirm, and sure enough the pack left standing—four of them—were stock still in the road, their teeth bared but otherwise unmoving. One decided to take his chances and bolted forward. Another crack of gunfire ended the chase, and Shay found herself considerably more grateful. The wolves looked to their fallen comrade, the anger clear in their eyes as they snarled and shouted at her.

One block.

She ran down the middle of the circular drive fronting City Hall, trampling over the mound of fresh flowers at its center, and bounded up the stairs to the glass doors. She grabbed for the handle, barely registering the tacky slipperiness of the metal bar, and pulled.

Locked.

"Motherfucker!"

She turned back to see the three wolves cautiously stepping forward.

"Come on," she whispered, waiting for the booming gunshots to ring out from overhead and cut them down.

"Come on, come on."

Sweat lined her forehead and her legs burned. Moving ever so slowly, she reached for her gun and slid it from its holster, never taking her eyes off the wild dogs. She knew well enough to avoid making eye contact with them, lest it spur them on even further. The last thing she wanted was to challenge a rabid wolf.

Why wasn't he shooting? she wondered. Why wasn't he opening the door? Where was he? Her body slipped into a shooter's stance, holding the gun in both hands, one leg in front of the other.

A metal snick rang loudly in her ears and she turned as the door opened.

A greasy hand reached out quickly, snatching her hair, and pulled her back into the darkness of City Hall.

          ✔ ✔ ✔

Dec's head throbbed from the noisy buzzing of the packed emergency room. Those places where he'd been bitten and scratched burned and itched with an annoying tenacity.

The growing crowd was making him uncomfortable, and his personal space was routinely trampled upon as people nudged, bumped, and shoved past, knocking into his knees, shoving their asses right into his face, and one had even elbowed him in the forehead.

The hum of activity was a hornet's nest of thrumming, angry warnings, the chattering of nervous conversation and painful moans piercing his ears, drilling right into the middle of his brain, digging, digging, digging, the veins in his temples pumping mightily, beating against his skull, hammering away with baleful punching sting and twists.

And the people.

Jesus Christ, the people.

The television had mollified most, and even Dec had been able to escape into the news coverage that reported the same stories over and over. Whatever exuberance there'd been over last night's sky show was buried under reports of the Russians breaking their cease-fire and invading Chechnya. Gaza erupted in flames as open season was mutually declared between Israel and Palestine, the two sides trading suicide bombings for blitzkrieg runs, tit-for-tat. Eventually, the twenty-four hour news network caught wind of animal attacks breaking out across the nation, across the world in fact, and briefly reported on that before interrupting with the news that now Lebanon and Egypt had joined in against Israel in defense of the Palestinians.

What the fuck is going on? he had wondered. The whole world had picked a hell of a time to go crazy.

An hour ago, the power cut out completely. He couldn't see the panic of the nurses, but he could hear their faint, hushed worries. His smart watch and Android were dead. The TV winked out, along with the lights, but thankfully there was enough daylight filtering in from the windows to see by. When power did not come back on soon enough, people became antsy. Antsier still as more bodies found their way to the ER, cramming into the already overcrowded pillbox of a waiting room.

Conversations grew strained as voices snapped. People turned red-faced with tension, their cheeks burning hot enough to fry an egg. Quarters tightened so that he couldn't even stretch out his legs, and his arms were held tightly to his chest cradling Sarah, trying to shush her screeching wailing. The room had grown into standing room only hours ago, and proceeded to get worse from there. Trapped body heat raised the temperature to what felt like more than one hundred degrees.

Sweat beaded his forehead. His shirt was soaked, massive dark rings staining his armpits and neck, gluing the fabric to his wet torso.

And, on top of all that, he had a fucking kid's song stuck in his head on an unending loop. Sarah's play mat loudly sang *Itsy Bitsy Spider*, *This Old Man*, and *Heads, Shoulders, Knees and Toes*. This last song was what had taken up permanent residence in his mind, the shrill, too-loud electronic noise playing over and over and fucking over.

Sarah had been crying for at least an hour. He tried feeding her again, uncomfortably contorting himself to reach the bag stationed between his legs. Digging around, he found the bottle and—

The god damn fucking thing popped right out of his hand, propelled away by the slick of sweat coating his palms.

He wanted to scream, felt the roar building in his chest, torn between venting his anger and giving up completely and breaking down in a flood of tears. His eyes stung and he squeezed them shut.

Why couldn't anything go right? he wondered. Why could nothing ever go his way, just this fucking once?

He watched with a sad mixture of resentment and desperation as the bottle rolled across the ground and settled against a pair of Converse sneakers.

He half-rose from the chair, holding Sarah close, as he reached toward the bottle. His fingers found empty air, the bottle just out of reach. He knew if he stood, he would lose the chair immediately. He had already seen that happen to a few others, and a fistfight had nearly broken out over the trespass. The security guard that had broken up the intense argument won a broken nose and a hell of a shiner around one eye for his trouble.

"Hey, excuse me," he said, trying to get the attention of the kid across from him. "Could you please?"

The teen looked at him, dazed, face pale and coated in a wet sheen. He held his stomach in both arms, bent over in a rictus of pain. Eventually, he leaned down and grabbed the bottle from between his feet. He stared at the foreign object with a look of both confusion and concern, his eyes bobbing between Dec's outstretched hand and the bottle of breast milk. Then he nodded, and handed over the bottle. Just as the plastic hit Dec's open palm, the man bent to the side and vomited between his legs and those of his neighbor, splashing them both with his upchucked sickness.

Sarah screamed and howled, and Dec tried to ignore the rotting stench of whatever it was that had come out of the man, wanting to get away from all of this, from all of these people, but he couldn't. He and Sarah were trapped. He was literally wedged into his seat, a bloated man on his right and a heifer of a woman on his left, their excess fat spilling over the wooden armrests and crowding him. Both stank of blood and sweat.

He poked the nipple of the bottle between Sarah's lips, but she pulled away, unleashing a fresh bout of screams. She whipped her head side to side, her chubby little arms smacking at his face in protest. He had already checked her diaper and found it clean. He tried the bottle again, knowing that forcing it on her was futile, but sometimes if he just got the nipple in her mouth she'd realize what was being offered and settle down. She jerked away, her open hand slapping his cheek while she redoubled her crying fit with new energy.

Aw, fuck it, he thought. He decided she must be as uncomfortable as he was, and his own agitation was probably helping to fuel hers. She was too hot, bothered by too much noise, and probably still hurting from Hector's crazy assault.

He went back to shushing her, bouncing her lightly in his arms, blowing a loud feathery noise into her ears to mimic the noise of the womb she had spent so many months inside. All of his usual tricks failed miserably, to the point that she took yet another swat at him, as she buried her face in his neck. He spoke to her in a calm and reassuring voice, telling her, "It's okay, sweetie, it's okay."

She probably knew he was lying.

"How much longer do we gotta fucking sit here?" somebody bellowed. Dec couldn't see who, the complainant lost to the crowd. But he heard him well enough.

"Huh? Fucking somebody answer me! I've been fucking mauled! When do I get to see a fucking doctor?" he screamed.

The buzz, chattering, and clacking of hushed conversations and angry intonations ground to a halt. Heads turned toward the shouting voice, but Dec still couldn't see the man.

An uncomfortable stillness settled over the ER waiting room, a brief moment of thick tension that threatened to turn into something worse. Even Sarah seemed to quiet, drawing a fresh breath in that moment of hushed silence. Somebody snorted, a tittering sort of laugh, and the tension popped.

Slowly, conversations resumed.

Sarah wailed again. The buzzing built up, gaining a good head of steam, and the painful thuds echoing inside Dec's skull struck and struck and struck again, giving a bloody, knotty tempo to the kids' song still clattering around in there.

The pale, greasy looking teen across from him moaned again, clutching his belly, kneading at the surface of his taught stomach with the fingers of both hands. Dec noticed that the boy's hands were wrapped in stained strips of fabric, which looked to have been torn off his sleeves, the frayed strings of fabric jutting out across his bare shoulders. His knees were scraped raw, his shin covered in raw, oozing bite marks. Dec could see the yellow fat globules beneath the skin, torn wide open at the side of the boy's calf and on his forearm.

The teen groaned again, sticking his head between his knees and heaved dryly. He worked up a thick loogie and hawked it between his Converse sneaks, the gob of mucus spattering into the puddle of vomit he had loosed upon the floor several minutes earlier.

Head still tucked low, the teenager looked up at Dec with bloodshot eyes, spit hanging in a thick, webby string from his lower lip. "Would you shut that fucking kid up?"

Dec's face burned, his mind racing with a thousand awful thoughts, Sarah's body the only thing keeping his hands from coiling into fists. "I'm sorry," was all he said, but he was too tired and far too fucking annoyed to try faking remorse.

"You're sorry, huh?" the kid said—and really, he was only a kid, Dec realized, checking his anger, probably not even old enough to drive.

He felt ashamed at having wanted to throttle this boy, and he leaned back in his chair to put more distance between them.

"You're fucking sorry all right," the kid said, mustering up a heaping measure of scorn that went well beyond his years.

"Look, kid, we're all in a spot here. Just chill out."

The kid laughed. Chill out. Yeah, that was a joke, all right. It was fucking sweltering in here.

Dec adjusted Sarah, transferring her head from one shoulder to the other, and shushing into her ear. That only riled her up even further, her chubby little arms and legs flailing at him, tiny little fingers pressing against his cheeks, trying to push his face away.

"It's okay, sweetie, just a few more minutes," he said. "It's—"

Pain flared in his face as his nose shattered. He hadn't even seen the kid move. The boy had darted out of his chair, shirt stained with a half-moon of vomit, spit, and sweat, and launched forward, slamming his knuckles right into Dec's face. Dec's head snapped back, his skull thudding into the wall.

Another punch, then another, and again.

He was only dimly aware of the boy's other hand grabbing for Sarah, fingers twisting around the back of her shirt and pulling, the strained noise of the fabric groaning under the threat of tearing.

"No, wait," Dec said, the taste of iron and copper in his mouth. His front teeth were loose.

A fat arm swung at the kid, shoving the boy aside, and Dec wrapped Sarah up in both his arms, his own pain forgotten. He'd been saved, thank Christ or Allah or Vishnu or whoever the fuck, but he'd been saved.

The heifer was on her feet, too, going after the boy, and Dec was suddenly sorry that he had ever thought her a heifer. No, she was a fucking goddess! She'd saved Sarah! She swung a thick ham-sized fist at the boy, knocking him square on his ass.

Go, lady! He wanted to cheer to her on, scream her name in victory.

She fell upon the boy, pinning him to the ground, throttling his face. Those ham-hock hands turned into ground beef as the skin of her knuckles shredded against the boy's teeth. There was a wet, grisly popping noise as her fist blew past the teeth and wedged into his mouth, his jaw forcibly pried open around her thick, wobbly, sweat-shined wrist.

She tore her hand away, the boy's tongue flapping uselessly in her grip. Broken teeth studded the back of her hand. She flung the tongue aside and grabbed his lower jaw in one hand, the fingers of her other hand stabbing into the boy's nostrils as if his head were a bowling bowl, and savagely pulled in opposite directions. A wet tearing sound, along with the boy's squealing, rose over the noisy madness around them, and then the woman held up a deflated flap of skin in victory. As she moved, Dec saw blood pouring profusely from the boy's face. The teen's nose was missing, ripped away to reveal a hollow recess filling with red, an angry trench bisecting his face and ending in a grisly triangle of missing flesh between his eyes. His lower jaw bulged, off-center from the rest of his face.

Dec had been so caught up in the sudden rush of violence before him, that only at that moment did he realize others were fighting as well. Some were trying to pry the woman away from the brutalized boy, while the large man— her husband?—fought them off so she could really go to work.

Pained screams rang out, pleading cries, people begging.

Most of all, though, was the noise of wetness and a squishy tearing. He tried to ignore the savage pummeling of meat, of muscles being flattened beneath concussive blows, but failed miserably. Failed, too, at trying to ignore the sudden squelch of screams cut off too soon.

Dec took to his feet, grabbing the diaper bag and hooking it over his shoulder.

The strap tugged painfully at his neck and collarbone, caught up on something that nearly pulled him off his feet.

He twisted around, in time for his face to greet the bloodied fist of the large man that had been on his right. He skittered back, but didn't fall. Couldn't fall. Instead, he lumbered into a cluster of bodies behind him, and they dragged him into their warring party.

He tripped, and tried to shield Sarah from the kicks and fists raining down upon them.

No, please, no. God no, he thought over and over, not caring a whit about his own survival. Sarah was his top priority, and he tried to shove himself away from the flurry of limbs slapping and punching at his body.

The fat man pushed his way through, his large, pockmarked face leering at Dec with red-rimmed eyes and glistening, hungry lips. The man was drooling as he reached toward Sarah, his fingers grabbing roughly at the infant's shirt, and Dec scrabbled back, or tried to, but there was nowhere to go. All he saw were shoes and legs, bodies towering over him and fighting one another.

Sarah was yanked violently from his arms, and he let loose a hoarse scream.

"No!"

A sticky, warm wetness splashed across his face as the man bit down. Dec squeezed his eyes shut tightly, but there was no way to blot out the pained screams of his baby girl, or the moist, smacking noises of lips around wet meat.

A loud cracking noise silenced his daughter, and a steady stream of blood washed over him and then slowed to a rhythmic drip, drip, drip.

He shuddered and kept his eyes closed, waiting for his own end.

"Oh, God, no," he cried. "No, no, no."

He could hardly hear his plaintive begging beneath the noise of hungry feasts, of jaws snapping shut and gorging on flesh, the stink of blood and ruptured bowels flooding the ER.

A dull thud smacked into the soaked carpet beside him, and he made the mistake of opening his eyes, ever so briefly, wondering if perhaps he would be pardoned from the madness. Maybe they thought him dead already, though he ached with a longing to die. He was a useless failure, deserving of no less. So, when he opened his eyes and saw the fat man, jowls and quavering chins coated in a thick, musky layer of gore that could only have been Sarah, he stilled himself and tamped down on the reflexes to struggle, to defend himself. There would be none of that.

The fat man leaned in, as if to kiss Dec, and bit down on Dec's lower lip and pulled. The frenulum that connected his lip to his gums pulled taut, and then snapped painfully, torn away with his mouth. Dec howled, his gums and teeth exposed, and then the man bent in for another bite.

Dec's hands twisted into the man's hair, pulling that bloody, ugly mug into him for a grisly kiss as he let the fat man dine. His cheek ripped away from the bone, and still he screamed, but he refused to fight, even as a thick, sour tongue pushed through a fresh hole in his face and brushed against his. He gagged against the metallic taste and the rough sensation of the fat man's tongue slathering against his bared teeth, wet chomping sounds deafeningly loud in his ears. A primal instinct told him to fight, but the rational side of his mind resisted, even as a mouth pressed against his eyelid and sucked and chewed. He took it, took it like a man, the way his dad had always told him to when things got rough.

Perversely, Sarah's play mat song still sang in his head, despite the pain, despite his longing to die. The fat man feasted, and the song played on and on.

Head, shoulders, knees and toes, knees and toes…
Head, shoulders, knees and toes, knees and toes…
Eyes and ears, and a mouth and a nose…
Head, shoulders, knees and toes, knees and toes…

12

CRAIG Harbin had killed nearly a dozen endangered animals, and thousands more that were not, during his lifetime of hunting. Both his home and office were crowded with trophies, the heads of elephants, black rhinos, lions, tigers, bears, elk, moose, deer, and buffalo mounted for display.

He lived his life by two guides only—the King James Bible and the Michigan DNR Hunting Season Calendar.

For the last weekend in August, he hunted elk, and again in January if additional thinning was needed to ensure population management goals. During early to late September, he killed bear in the Upper Peninsula. Weekends in October up through mid-November, he killed deer with bow and arrow, and again with firearms in mid-November up till the end of the month, and spent the first half of December using a muzzleloader. In September and October, he liked to mix things up with the occasional goose and pheasant hunt, and mixed in quail hunts with the deer hunts in October and November. Throughout the rest of the year, he hunted bobcat, coyote, and fox.

Over the last decade, he had spent more than five million

90

dollars on African safaris. Some of the animals, like the lions, were protected and lived on game reservations where hunting was illegal. In those instances, he paid extra so that his guides would lure the lions away from the preserve.

In July, he had spent a week in Zimbabwe where his guides managed to lure a lion away from the Hwange National Park. First, they had killed an antelope and tied it to their vehicle and scented an area more than half a kilometer away from the park, drawing the lion toward them.

Harbin had shot the creature with two arrows, but failed to kill him. The animal bolted, and Harbin and his men spent nearly two days tracking the wounded beast. Harbin's heart had raced in excitement, and he'd had an erection almost the entire time.

When they did find the lion, the animal had collapsed and was wheezing, lying in a pool of its own blood. One of the arrow shafts had broken high up, but the three-bladed broadhead had run deep and been buried in the lion's flank. The second arrow was higher up in the beast's ribcage, and had probably pierced a lung.

Harbin had licked his lips, his mouth suddenly dry. His cock throbbed, painful with anticipation, as he raised his rifle and fired into the animal's chest. In his mind's eye, he imagined the lion's massive heart exploding, and again he licked his lips.

"Can you guys give me a few minutes?" he asked his guides. They nodded and ambled back to the Jeep, laughing.

He studied the still beast, a swelling ache of victory riding high in his chest. He felt dizzy, giddy.

He moved to the rear of the corpse and knelt in the bloody mud, setting the rifle beside him. Unable to contain himself any further, he unbuckled his belt and shoved his shorts and underwear down his thighs, the cloth bunching around his knees.

The lion was male, but he didn't care in the least. He withdrew a condom from his shirt pocket and slid it over his engorged member, and slowly pushed into the dead lion's anus, his hips rocking gently at first, gaining steam. He reached and grabbed a fistful of bloody pelt, pulling it hard, damn near yanking the beast's fur out as he drove deeper and faster into the corpse, his balls aching toward release.

Caring not at all about the stench of shit and death, or the buzzing of flies circling him, drawn by his sweat and the fresh body he bucked against, he moaned loudly. His free hand groped for the beast's testicles, and he found himself surprised by the weight of the large scrotum as he cupped the balls in his hand and massaged them. Inching closer to release, the cords on either side of his neck stood out as his desire grew unbearable and uncontainable, the noise of his bare waist slapping against the lion's pelvis filling the jungle.

He let out a vicious shout as he came, slamming his hips against the lion's haunches, suddenly exhausted and spent. He withdrew, gagging on the musky odor of his fecal-stained cock. He'd lost the condom inside the animal's rectum, but he felt too good to care. He could always shower back at his lodge.

Satisfied, his pulse rate slowly returning to normal, he hitched his shorts back up and collected his rifle. Then, he went back to the Jeep and retrieved a machete, which he used to hack off the lion's head, already planning on where to mount his newest trophy.

Harbin loved to hunt. One of his greatest joys in life had been killing anything with four legs, although, eventually, he began to discover the joy in two-legged prey. And whatever he killed, he fucked.

When he was seven, his father had handed him a rifle and helped him kill his first buck. The sensation of taking another life was disquieting, but oddly satisfying. He'd felt a moment's guilt, a slight hesitation, even as his finger wrapped around the trigger and gently pulled. Then he saw the puff of blood and the deer collapsed, and he smiled. He'd felt powerful.

He'd hunted ever since.

When he was younger, a strapping man of twenty-seven, manning the check-in desk of his father's hotel—his father had owned a string of multi-million dollar beachside resorts up and down US 31 and when he finally passed, Craig had inherited them and continued to run them profitably—he spied the long, thin legs of a young girl as she moved with her family toward the bank of elevators. He knew from their guest registry that she was eleven and that her name was Ruby, on the cusp of womanhood, her small breasts barely making a ripple in the fabric of her shirt, her hips narrow but, he found, decidedly inviting. He had licked his dry lips then, too.

He was careful to observe and learn their routine. She and her family would only be in town for a week, but he watched from a distance and they paid him no attention unless it was to ask for dinner recommendations. He always recommended Mabel's, down a ways in Traverse City but before you got into downtown, or Pearl's if they wanted something spicy and didn't mind the drive over to Elk Rapids. Those were his favorites, and he recommended them to anyone that asked. But for them, in particular, there was a certain thrill to the advice, a certain connection between them. He could eat there, knowing that Ruby had been there as well, at his own insistence. And if the end of his shift happened to coincide with their dinnertime, then he could easily and discreetly follow, wait, and watch.

One morning, he watched as the parents left the hotel together, without their daughter. They stopped at the front desk, smiling in recognition.

"Pearl's was great," the father said. "How's Mabel's for breakfast?"

"Mabel's is fantastic any time of the day," Harbin said. "They have great omelets."

The father nodded sagely. "Omelets it is." He rapped his knuckles on the counter, decision made.

"I'll call ahead, make sure they set aside a good table for you. Just the two of you?"

"Yeah. Ruby's not feeling so hot, so we're letting her sleep."

Harbin frowned in commiseration, but inside he was absolutely rapturous. "I'm sorry to hear. You'll have to take her there for supper then."

He made a show of picking up the phone and dialing Mabel's, and the father beamed as he reserved them "the best seat in the house."

Mouth dry, heart racing, Harbin could barely contain himself. He'd been waiting for just this stroke of luck. But, he couldn't rush into it. That was how mistakes were made. Besides, he needed to calm down. Thoughts of the girl's thin, coltish legs ran through his mind's eye, the way her hips swayed as she walked, a little bit clumsily but the bare stretch of skin still enticing.

He had maybe an hour, which was enough time to work with. He had spent days hunting and tracking his prey, and now the animal was cornered and ready to be taken down.

He took the elevator to the third floor and took the maid's laundry cart from storage. If he moved quickly enough, nobody would be any wiser. He didn't even bother knocking at Room 317, using his universal card key to gain entry.

Ruby was asleep in bed, the covers pulled up tightly to her chin.

Harbin approached her silently, savoring the moment. He cupped his hand over her mouth, pinching her nose shut, smiling as her eyes bolted open and flushed with fear. His body pressed against hers, trapping her beneath the bedsheets and comforter.

She tried to scream, but his palm muffled her words. Her arms strained beneath the comforter, pinned to her sides by his knees.

That warm and familiar blossoming heat grew between his legs, straining against the crotch of his khakis. He laughed quietly, keeping her quiet with one hand while his other grabbed her throat and squeezed.

He pinched off the blood flow to her brain, and the lack of oxygen turned her face red, then a deep purple. Her eyes rolled back in her head, but he did not let up on the pressure. She had passed out, but he pressed and squeezed until he was sure she was dead.

He tossed the comforter and sheets aside, then hefted her body off the bed and into the laundry cart, covering her with the clean replacement towels stacked on the cart.

Wheeling her back to the elevators, a mental timer clicked down in his head. He imagined her parents were probably settling in for their first cup of coffee or juice, studying the menu carefully and discussing their plans for the day, one of them perhaps suggesting they take Ruby out for a game of mini-golf if she was feeling up to it. He was unable to suppress the smile that stretched across his face.

The service elevator took him down quickly, and his luck held. Still early in the morning and between shifts, the area was clear. He wheeled the cart out to his truck and loaded the girl into the back, covering her again with the towels. As he unfolded a hotel towel over her legs, he noted the large wet patch staining the crotch of her pajamas, the ammonia stink of fresh urine strong in the enclosed space. He was used to the body's expulsion of waste during death, and was untroubled by a little bit of piss. If anything, it made him hornier. He looked around the parking lot, satisfied that it was empty and nobody had witnessed his movements. The truck's windows were deeply tinted, and he doubted anybody would be able to see inside as they passed by.

He hurried the cart back inside, rode the service elevator back to three, and returned it to the closet. Heart hammering, he licked his lips and unconsciously rubbed at his crotch, squeezing his erection, needing his release. He couldn't wait any longer.

He went back to his vehicle and drove to a secluded spot in the woods, his secret spot, and there he got to know Ruby, and when he was finished he licked his lips, feeling immeasurable relief. His body had been so tense with desire that finishing inside the dead girl had brought him such intense relaxation that he nearly passed out. Instead of sleeping beside her, he got to work. He buried the body and burned the towels and her clothes, then called in sick for the rest of the day.

When the police began snooping around the hotel and questioning his absence, his father's money bought the best team of lawyers possible, and his assuaging conviction that his son was perfectly innocent, to the point that his father lied during questioning to protect his boy, directing the cops elsewhere. Surrounded by lawyers, young Harbin had weathered the questioning, the police stymied by his council's advice of total silence. They had little to go on—the maid's cleaning destroyed much of the forensics that Harbin had left behind, and in the end all the police really had to go on was the thin fact that Harbin had called off sick the afternoon the girl had been reported missing.

The Harbins were well loved in town, and contributed regularly to the policemen's fundraisers and the Kiwanis Club. They went to church regularly and filled the collection plate well, sponsoring St. Francis's potluck lunches and suppers. There were rumors, as there always were, but most suspected that Craig Harbin was completely innocent. He could never have harmed a hair on Ruby's head. Ruby and her family were from downstate, down near Detroit, the whispered voices said with an air of disapproval, and downstate was an entirely different world than the small upstate town of Falls Breath. Those downstate people were savages and trolls, used to murder and pointing the finger elsewhere. Nobody said it, but the implication was clear enough—whatever had happened to Ruby, she'd had it coming. Her disappearance was sad, certainly…but, well, she wasn't from around these parts.

Eventually, Craig was cleared and the case went cold. Ruby was never discovered, nor any trace of her.

After that, he was very, very careful. He saved his two-legged prey for special occasions, and could sometimes go years in between kills. There were seven human deaths by his count, most of them girls, but a few boys, which he enjoyed just as well when the mood struck. Hunting human prey usually took a lot of him emotionally, but left him deeply satisfied. Slaughtering animals was enjoyable enough to satiate him in the cool-down periods, particularly big game like that Zimbabwe lion. While he could go years without murdering a human, he never missed a hunting season, ever.

Harbin's hunting exploits even made him something of a local hero. Much of the local economy was dependent on hunting, and everyone in town knew that Harbin was a splendid sportsman. It was probably that love of hunting, along with his deep roots in the community and the popularity that name recognition brought, that helped him win the mayor's office.

As mayor, he had spent the day watching and listening as the town went to hell around him, a certain bubbly measure of excitation rising in him.

The animals were fighting back.

The *goddamn* animals were fighting back! He laughed giddily to himself, eyeing the woman curled in the corner of the front lobby. He admired the way her crisp uniform shirt wrapped around her torso, even if the real goods were hidden beneath the bulk of her Kevlar vest. He could tell she had rather nice attributes, regardless.

The wolves were at the door, howling. He laughed again, a rush of bloodlust soaking his veins. He thrilled at the prospect of no longer having to hide his ambitions and talents. He was perfectly free to hunt, and would hunt for as long as he could, until a larger, better predator took him down, as was Nature's way, God bless.

Until that moment came, though, it was open season.

⸮ ⸮ ⸮

Shay Hendrix awoke to a painful throbbing in the center of her face. Her skull felt as if barbed wire had been shoved into the hollow recesses and snaked through all the various cavities. Dried blood caked her lips and when she reached for her nose, she gasped, finding the epicenter of her pain. Her nose was broken and puffy, the skin around it aching, that ache bleeding out beneath her eyes.

The back of her head hurt, as well, and the pieces of fractured memory started to fall back into place beneath foggy recollection.

Vaguely, she remembered reaching the glass front doors of City Hall and being yanked inside by Mayor Harbin. Her fingers found wounds dotting her hair, and a small, exposed patch of scalp. He'd pulled hair right out of her head, and then, as she spun around, he'd slammed the butt of his rifle squarely in her face, knocking her out cold.

She wasn't in the lobby, though. She had been moved while unconscious, and found herself in a spacious office that she recognized from newspaper photos and weekly addresses on the public city TV channel.

Harbin's grotesque animal trophies marred the walls, and her eyes passed over the head of a lion that had been much ballyhooed in the local yellow rag, and the source of a number of vocal admonishments online as well as several petitions calling for him to resign. There was a deer, an elk, an antelope. She had always thought Harbin was a small man, a dickless wonder who tried, too hard, to overcompensate for his deficiencies by slaughtering animals. The fact that he literally surrounded himself with the heads of his victims told her all she needed to know about the man.

As her eyes scanned the wall, she pressed her hand into the carpet, readying herself to stand despite her head swimming in pain and the world going all crazy tilt-a-whirl. Her fingers squished against the wet Berber and for the first time, she saw that she was not alone.

Sheriff Tremblay lay nearby, or rather, what was left of him.

The body would have been lying facedown if he still had a head. Instead, there was only a grisly stump, the neck meat savagely hacked at and the white circle of vertebrae unevenly cut through the center.

Without a head, she recognized the sheriff by the stripes on both of his shoulders, and his stocky, well-padded frame was unmistakable.

His pants and underwear were bunched around his ankles.

She covered her mouth, but too late. She had used the hand that had touched the carpet, and the minute her bloodstained fingers touched her mouth, it was all over. She turned to the side and vomit ejected between her fingers and spattered the wall beside her.

"Oh, god," she moaned.

Dizzy, she forced herself to stand, grabbing onto the edge of the large, shiny desk that the mayor used. She nearly pulled the desk blotter off and tumbled back down on her ass, but corrected quickly.

A gentle breeze blew in from the open window, and she saw the street below and the mangled remains of the wolves Harbin had shot down. He had used his office as a shooting perch, and he had a wide, direct view of Old Downtown. Anyone or anything coming down the street was fair game from his chair, which was wheeled right up to the open panes.

The wind carried in an assault of smells, the air itself cobbled together on coppery fumes and loosened bowels. Tremblay had evacuated, and the stench riled her, unable to escape it even by breathing through her mouth.

Standing now, the animal heads circling Harbin's office once again drew her eyes. On the coat hooks screwed into the wall near the door, she noticed a trophy she had not seen from her previous vantage point of the floor behind the desk.

Tremblay's head had been impaled upon a coat hook, his mouth hanging open in a gaping O, eyes wide with—what? Shock, horror, surprise? All of the above? A hole above his right eye had dribbled a line of blood down his face, and the wall around the severed face was splashed with dried, dark red stains.

She shook her head, trying to deny the sights around her. Her hands curled into fists and she beat at the side of her skull, cursing this day, this life, and this total upset in the balance of nature all around her.

Was this the end of the world? she wondered.

Her father had warned her of this day, the day mankind would fall and cease to be, a world gone crazy and upside down, torn apart in a wide, mass hysteria. He had warned her of the devil, and the return of their Lord and Savior Jesus Christ, and the foul demons that would wage war against Heaven with the Earth as their battlefield.

"Have you repented?" she heard her father ask. Her father, who she had not even thought of in years, who she had buried nearly two decades ago. "You foul whore! HAVE. YOU. REPENTED?"

"No, Daddy, I haven't," she whispered to the angry, and oddly soft yet stern voice. "I am a filthy sinner, lost in a filthy world, condemned to hell and hell on Earth. Jesus, forgive me."

Absently, her hands glided over her torso, from navel to forehead, shoulder to shoulder, warding herself with the sign of the cross.

How many times had her father warned of this day? Too many, she knew. Enough to the point of outright dismissal. The boy who cried wolf. She had heard it all her life, and her daddy, he had taken each claim of prophecy seriously.

In 1980, when Leland Jensen, the founder of a Bahá'í sect, predicted a nuclear disaster prior to God's Kingdom being established on Earth. Again, the following year, when Calvary Chapel pastor Chuck Smith said 1981 would be the world's last. And again in 1982, when Pat Robertson predicted the end of the world. Yet again, in 1991 when Louis Farrakhan said the Gulf War would be the final breaking point, the War of Armageddon. In 1993, when another Bahá'í sect leader, Neal Chase, said that the end would come on March 23, 1994. All of the various dates throughout 1994 and 1995, and again in 2011 when all those failed to pass, as heralded by Harold Camping. Her father's deathbed warning to Shay about the years 2000, 2010, 2011, 2012—because the Mayan calendar failed to continue past December of that year—and even 2013 because Daddy had read somewhere that Grigori Rasputin had prophesied it way back when. One of them had to be right. They couldn't all be right, of course, but one of them had to be.

All bunk. All nonsense.

Until now.

Now it was all finally happening. It had to happen eventually, didn't it?

Maybe that was what she saw in Tremblay's empty, dead eyes. A knowledge and the certainty of the inescapable end.

She drifted to the open door on wooden legs. Her hand went to her hip, where her gun was holstered, and met only empty air. She clutched at nothing, and then felt her waist. The Sam Browne belt was gone, as was the radio mic that should have been clipped to her shoulder. No gun, no club, no mace, not even her handcuffs.

Harbin had stripped her of everything except her clothes and boots. She had nothing useful on her. Tremblay's corpse, too, was stripped of weapons and restraints. All he had was a cloud of buzzing flies encircling him.

The office door was open, and beyond was the darkened secretary's office. She slowly walked toward the entrance, keeping close to the wall and poking her head around the corner. One quick look and dodging back, in case crazy Mayor Harbin was waiting around the corner to take her out. When no shots came, she looked around the doorframe again, longer this time, taking it all in.

The blinds over the windows in the outer office were all

drawn tightly shut, which was why it was so much darker there than in the mayor's office. Sunlight came through the blinds well enough to see by, blanketing the room in a murky gray haze, but there was no sign of Harbin. Only an empty workstation, a dead computer, a silent refrigerator in a small kitchen area with cold coffee going stale in the pot, and a quiet corded phone. She recognized the phone as an IP set, and the LCD display was dark. The power was still out, then.

Looking toward the glass door at the other end of the office, she saw the dark—and thankfully empty—corridor beyond.

She pulled at the desk drawers and the filing cabinet drawers, glancing toward the door every few seconds, but everything was locked. On the desk was a hefty three-inch-by-three-inch glass paperweight shaped like a pyramid. The engraving said "Sandy: Congratulations on 5 GREAT years!" and etched beneath that was the city seal. Shay clutched it, the tip of the pyramid jutting from between her thumb and forefinger like a stubby knife.

Walking quietly to the other side of the office, she was careful to stay to the side of the glass door and out of the direct sight line of anyone that might be out there. She ducked into the shadow of the sofa beside the door and studied the hallway on the other side.

The stairs leading to the first floor were a clean shot straight ahead and halfway down. Past the stairs, at the opposite end of the hall, were the useless elevators. There were several darkened offices between her and the stairs, but it was impossible to tell if anyone was inside.

She thought about turning around, heading back into the mayor's office and going out the window. The drop would be steep, and she'd probably break a leg, which would then make her easy pickings for any crazed and wild animals lurking nearby, or a clean target for Harbin.

Had he gone crazy, too, like the animals? Fine until all of a sudden he wasn't? Was the disease spreading? Was she infected, too?

Christ…

She pushed all that out of her head, forgot about going out the window. This door right here, this was the way out.

Shay stood, put her hand on the metal bar, and pushed her way into the dark stretch of hallway. The rush of panic shamed her, brought a red heat to her cheeks, and she broke out into a run, her boots slamming loudly onto the tiled floor.

She hit the first stair and hurried down, nearly losing her balance halfway down, and grabbed onto the railing to keep from tumbling down and breaking her neck.

Glass exploded above her. She looked up and saw Harbin striding through the opening of the office she had passed by only seconds before at the mouth of the stairs. He had an ugly smile on his face and a bulky crossbow in his hands. He raised and fired, not wasting any time at all while Shay fought to process the surprise. She turned to run and a burst of pain blew through her arm as she screamed and fell, rolling sharply down the stairs. The steps kicked at her along the way, bursts of starlight skittering through her vision as her head slammed into the floor.

"Gah!" she cried, her feet kicking at the ground, pushing her forward.

Her uniform blouse was thick and sticky, tight around her biceps. Blood poured down her arm, and as she stood, dizzily, it began dripping from her fingertips.

Footsteps pounded down the stairs behind her, piercing the high-pitched whine that filled her ears.

"Run and hide, you little cunt!" Harbin screamed, his words breaking off into a squealing peal of laughter.

She decided to take his advice, but as soon as she put the weight on one leg, her knee gave out in painful protest. Her spine and ribs ached from where the stairs had punched into her, and the aches bloomed freshly as she fell. She hit the ground hard, jolting her wound and jostling the arrow stuck in her arm. Very briefly, the world went dark, then her eyes snapped into an unfocused blur as a new pain erupted in her scalp as her head was pulled back by her hair.

"Too slow, bitch," Harbin said, pressing the bow into the center of her face. The arrowhead poked into her forehead, scraping at the skin.

Harbin's eyes were wild and red-rimmed, bloodshot all the way through. His face was oddly sallow and greasy with sweat.

He began to carve, dragging the arrow across her forehead, a gush of blood slinking over her left eye, blinding her.

She felt a weight in her hand and realized she was still holding the glass pyramid. Sandy's small consolation prize for being a city employee. She swung with all that she had left and felt Harbin's knees buckle as the cheap award smashed into his face. She brought her other arm, her wounded arm, up and around, knocking the crossbow aside and away from her, wrenching it from his grasp.

She kicked back, then brought her foot up, aiming square for his testicles, kicking his balls back and up into his pelvis. He clutched at his groin and fell, wailing loudly.

Anger flowed through her as she raised the paperweight and brought it crashing it down, again and again, until his hair was matted in a bloody pulp and her face was coated in grisly spatter, her left eye lost behind a curtain of blood flowing from her forehead.

Finally, she collapsed and sank to the floor, one arm throbbing with exhaustion, the other in a blistering heat of pain from the arrow.

Shay couldn't help but laugh, no matter how much it hurt. Her torso was bruised bone-deep, but the laughter still boiled up from deep within her, demanding release. She couldn't say why, but she found all of this suddenly hilarious.

Turning back toward the mayor, she laughed harder. He was out cold, maybe dead. She didn't care because she was still alive, and that was all that mattered.

"You fucking pussy," she said to him in between laughs, and that only propelled the hysteria on even further. "You fucking pussy! YOU. FUCKING. PUSSY!"

She rolled in the blood, a pool of both his and hers, laughing to herself until she grew hoarse and her breathing went ragged, tears running down her face in a torrent. She laughed until her sides ached and she was left clutching her belly in both arms, and then went on laughing through the pain and the tears, exhausted and wondering what the hell had brought all that on.

Eventually, her laughter slowed into stutters and hiccups that left her wheezing. Her abdomen felt like she had just done a thousand crunches.

Once she had herself under control, she got her feet beneath herself again and stood. She'd twisted her knee during the fall down the stairs, and her ankle felt stiff and sore. She hobbled her way to the nearest office, but the door was locked. She tried the next, and then the next.

A dim voice reminded her this was the weekend. Of course, all the offices were locked. Harbin was here only because of Tremblay and the emergency meeting to deal with the fire downtown. The sheriff and the mayor would have been busy trying to muster resources and figure out what was happening. At least until Harbin snapped. Apparently they hadn't gotten very far in calling for support from the neighboring towns before Harbin cracked, or things were equally bad in those other districts.

How widespread was all this? Her flesh prickled into goose pimples at the prospect of this madness being a far-reaching event, her father's voice taunting her with an "I told-you-so."

She tried another door, distractedly, the glass rattling in its frame.

She had been on scene at enough hunting accidents to know not to remove the arrow herself, so she left it alone. She tore loose a strip of material from her blouse and wrapped her wounded arm as best she could. If she could get back to her patrol vehicle, there was a first aid kit in the trunk. Recalling the people she had seen inside the library before her car had died, she thought maybe she could make it there, maybe even find help.

Okay, so that was it then. Time to get moving.

With no clue where Harbin had hidden her and Tremblay's gear, she grabbed his crossbow, keeping the arrow notched and counting three others in reserve.

Good enough.

13

LAUREN'S lips found Jacob's and relief flooded through her, the endorphins kicking in as her brain lit up with simple, pure joy. She held his face between both hands, their kisses growing in urgency.

"God, I was so worried about you," she said between kisses, practically gasping the words out.

She pulled him tighter, wrapping her arms around his neck. Moisture beaded between their cheeks as tears ran freely from his eyes. She wiped them away with her thumb, the feel of his stubble sending an electric thrill through her, and he smiled shyly. She covered his mouth with hers, grinning all the while. He tasted and smelled like beer, but she didn't mind, not at all, because he was with her again, in her arms, safe.

"It's a nightmare out there, isn't it?" he said.

She nodded, tugging at his shirt and working it up over his chest. "Help me," she said, and he pulled it the rest of the way off.

Sometime after their third beer each, after Jeff had dumped more cans into the cooler, the bottles splashing into ice that had mostly melted into a cool pool of water,

107

they had broken free of the radio control room. Lauren led Jacob into the ladies' restroom and let loose with the insatiable desire to cover him in kisses. She'd been keeping herself in check for too long, sitting beside her father and drinking with the boys, trying to tamp down on her top priority of being with Jacob. She'd been so worried about him, and now that she had him back all she wanted to do was keep him wrapped up in her arms.

Her fingers roamed over his chest, following the thin trail of hair that ran down the middle of his torso and disappeared beneath the waistband of his jeans.

"You've got all these cuts and bruises," he whispered. "What happened out there? Are you hurt?"

"Shut up," she said, her words softened by the bright upward curl of her lips. "Talk later."

She worked at the button on his jeans, yanking the zipper down. His worry for her had not put a damper on his desire, and she pulled his face down to hers again, her tongue sliding over his.

He worked a hand up under her tank top, his fingers working beneath the cups of her bikini top to squeeze her small breasts. She moaned into his ear, walking backward, and led him to the long counter of sinks.

She undid her shorts and stepped out of them, while his other hand dove between her legs, pulling aside the bikini bottom. She gasped, dazzling sparks of pleasure dancing through her.

"Yes," she breathed, her mouth at the nape of his neck, biting gently at his shoulder.

She pulled his boxers free, his erection pressing against her belly. She pushed herself up onto the edge of the counter, guiding him into her. She gasped again, her muscles still slightly sore from the previous night—but a good sore, a soreness that she enjoyed and found herself wanting more of. Her hands gripped his ass, holding him there, wanting merely to be filled by him while her tongue slid against his, his hands running through her hair.

"I was so fucking worried about you," she said again, and now she was crying. All the various emotions of the day slammed through her like a tidal wave, exploding for release. All of the fear and panic and anxiety flooded loose.

She had Jacob. She had her father.

For maybe the first time all day, she felt safe.

Lost in their urgent lovemaking, she failed to see the bathroom door open ever so slightly.

۲ ۲ ۲

Scott pressed the wet can of Miller Lite to his forehead, enjoying the slightly cool feel of aluminum against his bare skin. With the power out, the University Center was getting hot quickly, all the still air trapped on the third floor and getting warmer by the minute.

He popped the top on his seventh can and took a long pull. He couldn't remember when Jeff had left, or even Lauren and Jacob for that matter.

He should not have been drinking at all, but the first one had gone down so easily. Just one, he had thought then, taking the can from Jeff, the four of them clinking the cans together in cheers to the impromptu end of the world. Jeff had offered him a second beer, and he shrugged, figuring what the hell. Really, though—where was he going to go? The car was dead, all contact with the outside world was cut off. Was he even on duty anymore? He puzzled over that one briefly, before deciding that no, he was not. Not anymore. He had his daughter, which was really the most important thing.

If the world was ending, did it matter if he enjoyed a few beers before everything else went tits up on him?

By the time he started on his fourth beer, he was thinking about aliens and germs and biological warfare, the thoughts all jumbled around in his head. An alien invasion, was that really what all this boiled down to?

Maybe not little green men, or big *Independence Day* explosions and city-sized spaceships destroying all their shit, but still a form of alien life that had, inadvertently or not, staked a claim.

Microbes, bacteria, maybe a virus. Some kind of space flu.

The one thought that kept recurring, even as he slid into a drunken fog, was a simple question: *How much worse could it get?*

Alone, the three kids run off to do who knows what, he let the anguish free and cried to himself. No matter how much he tried to avoid it, his brain kept pinwheeling back to Hex, and his forearm throbbed from where his dog had bit down and tore him up.

Losing Hex was like losing a kid, he thought. That dog was his little boy, when it came right down to it.

But it wasn't just Hex that had gone mad. It was all the dogs, cats too, if what Dec had said was true. Birds, even. Everything was turned upside down, as if nature itself had turned hinky and become inverted. Everything was a predator now, ultra-aggressive, and all those rules and relationships between hunter and prey had been tossed right out the window. Whatever this disease was, it had changed things rapidly and maybe even for good.

So, how much worse could it get?

Plenty, Scott figured.

If this space bug did all this to the animals, and if it were as widespread as Jacob and Jeff suggested, then things could go only further south. No power, no safe quarters, every man for himself. Getting worse was really only the best-case scenario that his drunken, stumbling mind could fathom.

And if it started infecting people…

Hell, maybe it already has.

The truth was, even with what little Jacob and Jeff had pieced together, neither knew a damn thing about this virus.

How did it transmit? How long did it incubate? Given the time between the meteor shower and the animals' hostility, the bug was clearly fast acting. What were the effects of exposure and what were the symptoms of infection? This stuff with the animals—was it the first stage of infection, or last, or somewhere in between? He didn't know, and Scott reckoned nobody else did either. Not yet, and certainly not with how rapidly the animal kingdom had spiraled out of control and began asserting their dominance in a mad, rabid frenzy.

He thought about the meteorites crashing into Earth all across the globe. Jacob had mentioned Russia and other parts of the US being struck. It hadn't taken long for Falls Breath to fall apart in the face of all this, its resources taxed beyond the breaking point in less than a day. Cops had been killed, firemen trapped, the hospital was overrun, and without power everyone was cut off from one another. Were airplanes falling out of the sky under avian assault all around the world? He shook his head, frustrated by the lack of information. Maybe the big cities were faring better, but he had no way of confirming that. All he could do was drink while his anger simmered to a boil.

When he stood, the radio control room tilted sloppily and he held onto the nearby desk for support, waiting for the world to right itself. Scott had never been a heavy drinker, but even watered-down piss took a toll if he had too many.

After a minute, he felt like he could walk and he lumbered his way to the window. The view was a mix of mundane and special, with the parking lot below and the bay beyond. The sun was starting to descend but had not yet set, the water a crisp, inviting blue.

The water did not concern him, though, not nearly as much as the flashes of movement between the vehicles. Dark blurs darted around the cars, some of them stopping to sniff the ground and chase a scent.

A part of him wanted to think that they were merely

dogs, but he knew how foolish that sentiment was. They were dogs, yes, but whatever bug they had caught had turned them into something far worse, something feral. They had regressed back to a wolf-like state, transformed into constant hunters, killers, and feeders.

He watched them for a time as they weaved through the parked cars. When they got too close to one another the dogs snapped and hunkered down, looking ready to spring until one, invariably, backed off.

He wondered if they would actually fight, if one dog would attempt to assert superiority and become the alpha. He didn't have to wonder long.

A pair of huskies barked, and he could sense the warning in it, one dog telling the other, quite clearly, *Back the fuck off.*

Rather than retreat, the instigating huskie lunged forward, going for the neck and winning a surprised yelp from the other.

They fought for a good long while, to the point of exhaustion and then collapse.

No, that wasn't quite right, Scott realized. One huskie simply gave up, lay down, and bared his belly. Then, the new alpha clamped down on the dog's throat and tore it out, swallowing down the hunk of meat.

Other dogs came forward, circling the new alpha and his fresh victim, each of them watching warily and licking their chops. The alpha indicated something that escaped Scott, and the other dogs came forward, cautiously—perhaps respectfully—and began to eat the body of their fallen pack mate.

For a moment, he watched the dogs tear meat off the bones of an animal they had run with only a short time before. Seeing the strips of bloody flesh, he could not help but salivate and notice how empty his stomach was. Full up on beer, but empty of real food. He couldn't even remember the last time he'd eaten, only that it had been many hours earlier. Breakfast, probably.

Eventually he turned his back on the bloody feasting and

drained what was left in the can he held, putting the grisly sight out of his mind as best he could.

If that was what Hex would have been reduced to, the kind of life he would have had to lead, one in which life itself was a constant war, then maybe he was better off.

He ambled back to the cooler, popped the lid, and enjoyed the brief flash of cool water on his hand and wrist as he snagged a new can of beer. The crinkle of aluminum and the hiss of escaping carbonation was a welcome noise, and he savored the splash of beer against his tongue, feeling surprisingly refreshed by the alcohol.

A scream cut through the building, and he dropped the can, beer exploding out of the mouth of the can as it hit the carpet. He broke into a run, heading toward the direction of the noise.

The pitch and quality of the scream snagged on a primal instinct within him, and he realized that scream was familiar.

It was Lauren.

⚐ ⚐ ⚐

The sex was frantic and brief. Gone was the tenderness of the night before, the gentle touches and soft caresses, him asking her if she was okay, if this felt good, or what about this?

God, had that really only been last night?

Lauren pushed aside the thought, giving herself fully over again to Jacob. Now was not the time for thinking of such things, not while his thumb was between her legs making slow, tight, perfect circles.

"Oh, fuck," she moaned. "Yes!" He brought her body to the precipice's edge…and then shoved her head over heels, a tight contraction of pleasure ripping through her, forceful enough that she nearly blacked out from the exquisite joy, burying her moaning into the crook of his neck before grabbing his face in both hands and suffocating him with intense, grateful kisses.

"Oh my god," she said, his thrusts growing faster as he himself grew close, closer.

His breathing grew ragged and paused momentarily at the height of his release, and she grabbed his ass in both hands, pulling him deeper inside her as he came, feeling on the verge of another orgasm herself, her body responding and clamping tightly around him.

His sweaty forehead pressed against hers, both of them delirious, their panting mixed with laughter and smiles that quickly turned back into kisses.

"God, you're amazing," Jacob whispered.

"Hmmmm," was the only sound she was capable of.

She leaned back into the cold mirror while he stepped away, disengaging his body from hers.

"That was incredible," she said dreamily, her entire body still tingling, flesh covered in goose pimples. She watched him through half-lidded eyes as he pulled his pants up from around his ankles and stood, the waist of his jeans and boxer shorts bunched in both fists, as the bathroom door exploded open, startling them both.

Her eyes shot open in time to see the cricket bat collide with Jacob's face, blood spraying free and smacking against the wall, his body stumbling backward and colliding with the door of a toilet stall. The stall door banged open beneath his weight, followed quickly by a meaty cracking noise as he tripped over his own falling pants and the back of his head slammed into the toilet.

Jeff stood between them, his back to her, raising the cricket bat over his head and hammering it down, over and over. With each lift of the bat over his head, ropes of blood whipped off the end, spattering the mirror beside her, painting the walls of the toilet stall. A pulpy clump of skin smacked onto the countertop beside her, sliding on a slick of gore into the white backsplash. Lauren, paralyzed with fear, choked on a scream that demanded release but was squelched by the impossibly loud sounds of bones fracturing, the sudden stink of raw meat, and a thick, raw metallic odor.

When Jeff turned, she saw the lust in his eyes plain as day. His cock stood free of his unzipped pants, a thin line of pre-cum dripping from the empurpled head. His shaft glistened in its own fluids as he stepped toward her, stroking himself. The slick, meaty noise of his masturbation echoed in her ears as he approached, a wolfish grin splayed across his lips as he jerked off, keenly watching her. He licked his lips like a hungry dog eyeing a savory bowl of beef and gravy chow, muttering to himself. She could not make out the words, but his intent was clear enough.

Before she could move, he lunged forward, pinning her to the counter, and she kept saying, "No, no, no!" over and over. He grabbed at her bikini bottom, roughly pulling the fabric away from her sex as he leaned in and nipped at her neck. His eyes were empty and bloodshot, but his brow was wrinkled in gross determination.

There was only one thing she could do if she wanted to get out of this, get away from him.

She reached between them, taking hold of his wet, sticky cock. His mouth twisted upwards as he practically purred. She pinched him between thumb and forefinger, meeting his gaze and offering a dead smile.

She pinched harder and flicked her wrist hard, snapping his rigid dick in half. While he screamed, before he could get away, she grabbed his balls and squeezed and twisted.

He backhanded her and sent her flying off the sink. She hit the bathroom floor hard, saw Jacob's prone, broken body just a few scant feet away.

Closer was the cricket bat, which Jeff had dropped as she ruined his genitals. She grabbed it, fighting to stand, but she felt dizzy from the blow to her head.

"You fucking cunt!" he screamed, twisting to find her, cradling his junk in both hands, red-faced with tears streaming down his cheeks.

Good, she thought, with more than a bit of vicious satisfaction. "Fuck you!" she screamed, swinging the cricket bat around and clocking him across the face.

The blow was hard enough to spin him around into the countertop, and she hauled the bat around again for a second swing. The wood was stained a muddy crimson, small bulbs of tissue stuck in the grime. Her knees knocked together with the realization that some of this mess was Jacob.

"You motherfucker!" she screamed, slamming the long, thick plank of wood into the back of his skull. There was a sharp crack and a spurt of blood flung across the mirror as his nose shattered against the countertop's edge. He dropped to his knees and tried to turn to face her, blood pouring from his mouth. Teeth were scattered across the counter and along the floor.

"No," he whined, hands raised.

She screamed, loud and primal, some ancient sound of fury rising from her gut, strong enough to force spit from her mouth. She raised the bat, turned it toward its flat edge, drooling as if she were no more than a savage, angry beast. When she brought the bat down, the wood cleaved Jeff's skull in two, the bat lodging in tight just above his caved-in nose. His collapsed in upon himself and toppled forward. Lauren had to step back quickly to avoid him.

The handle of the cricket bat hit the tiled bathroom floor and popped free of Jeff's skull, rolling aside and plopping into the pool of gore.

Lauren stood stock still, chest heaving.

The bathroom door was violently pushed aside again as Scott strode in, overtaken by the shock of what he was seeing, of the stink from the two dead men and the creeping pools of blood on either side of his daughter.

"Lauren, baby," he said, and then she was pressed against his chest, his arms around her.

"Are you," he started, his voice hitching. She knew what he was seeing, how bad it must have looked, even if his presumption was only half-right. These two men, Jacob's pants half-off in the toilet stall. "Did they—"

"No," she said. "No, no. I'm fine. I'm good."

"Christ, Lauren," he said, if only to say *something*.

Eventually she stepped back, turning toward the sink and the corpse that rested there. She stuck to the outskirts of the spilled blood, the pool widening and waving through the white grout and inching toward the drain in the center of the room. Her t-shirt was crumpled in a sink, still wearable despite the freckles of gore, and she self-consciously readjusted the cups of her bikini to cover her breasts. She reached for her shorts, but they were ruined, soaked through in blood and utterly unwearable. She let them fall back to the floor, then hugged herself. Her hands left bloody stains on each bicep, but she barely noticed.

"C'mon, honey," Scott said, nodding toward the door. He held it open, using his free hand to wave her forward, to take her hand so he could guide her out.

Before she took his hand, she reached down for the cricket bat. The plank above the handle was soaked and dripping, but the handle was clean enough. She could wipe off the rest with paper towels, which she grabbed by the handful from the dispenser, doing her best to rid it of all the grime. She let the sodden tissues fall to the tiled floor, not even bothering to throw them away. What would be the point?

"Might need this," she mumbled, and Scott nodded.

"That might be a good idea," he said. "Let's go, hon."

"Go where?"

"Shay was supposed to go down to City Hall. Maybe we can find her."

"Long way to walk." Even to her ears, she sounded distant—entire leagues away, in fact. "Maybe we can take some bikes?"

There were dorms on campus, and she had seen more than a few bike racks positioned outside the front of the various buildings.

"Those'll have to do," he agreed. "We should go to the women's dormitory, see if we can find you some clean clothes."

She nodded dimly. She would need pants, denim preferably. Something to cover her, something that would maybe be tougher for dogs to bite through.

"How are you on ammo?"

They walked down the corridor, back toward the radio station. Scott veered toward the stairs, but she went in the opposite direction.

"Where you going?"

"I need a beer, Dad. Like, desperately."

He looked at her, but she couldn't read his eyes. Eventually, a mirthless laugh escaped his lips, and he said, "Yeah. I guess you do."

"Ammo?" she reminded him.

"We get some bikes, we'll head over to the office, then move on to City Hall."

She nodded. The office. That was what he always called the police station, a sort of private joke.

Inside the broadcast room, she collapsed onto the sofa near the cooler. She found a beer, snapped it open, and took a pull long enough that she had to gasp for air once she unlocked her lips from the can.

"You want to talk about it?" Scott asked.

"No, I don't."

She drank more, noticing the waning daylight. There would only be a few hours of light left, but she pushed aside the thought.

Too close, the dogs howled.

14

SHAY'S back ached, her hips throbbed, and each step sent a jolt of pain through her ankle and knee. Red spots danced across her vision with each stifling movement. Her arm burned, a constant ache where pain blossomed anew with every heartbeat and tunneled through her skull. The arrow was still intact and stuck through, her arm bent across her belly.

She stood at the glass entrance of City Hall and had been watching the street for the last five minutes.

The wolves Mayor Harbin had sniped from his office were still there, of course, but they'd attracted carrion. Black birds had been picking and tearing at the meat, but a pack of three mutts had chased them off. Those mutts then claimed the dead wolves as their own and began eating enthusiastically.

Shay's stomach flopped and she choked down the vomit. A gurgle bubbled in her belly, reminding her of the organ's emptiness. She was starving but pushed the thought of food aside, feeling queasy at the idea of eating. She couldn't stand to watch the obscenity before her, but she had no other choice. She had to know when the path was clear, and then she had to run as fast as she could. The way her head was hammering, and with how faint she felt, she did not think she would be moving very fast.

A long strip of bloody fur and skin tore free from a ribcage, while another mutt nuzzled into the belly meat. A thick pile of intestines spilled out onto the blacktop, and the dogs happily dug in.

Aw, Christ, Shay thought, pressing a clammy hand to her sweaty forehead. She was sweating up a storm, her whole body burning up and feverish. She shut her eyes from the horrors and heard instead a steady *plink, plink, plink* as her blood dripped onto the tile floor.

Breathing deeply, she fought to stay awake. She could not lose consciousness, could not give into the weakness claiming her whole, making every appendage heavy and thick.

Harbin, that sick fuck. The way she was feeling now, that was all his fault. Fucking Harbin.

Harbin.

She turned back toward the atrium and the grand staircase where she had left him.

Where she should have killed him.

He was gone. Nothing where he was but blood, most of it hers she reckoned.

Oh no, nonononono, she mentally screamed, limping back toward the stairs.

A mess of footsteps and slick runners of blood stained the tiles, but the trail was clear enough. He was still on the ground floor.

How the hell did I not hear him? she wondered. Of course, the way her own pulse was clanging in her skull and the constant buzzing in her ears, she should not have been too surprised.

Stupid, Shay. Stupid, stupid, stupid.

She stood still, listening for his noises. He was hurt badly, at the very least. She had clocked him good a few times with that stupid glass paperweight pyramid.

The pyramid was gone, too. Better stay out of arm's reach then, she thought. She had seen firsthand the damage it could cause, and she was fucked up enough as it was.

She couldn't hear him, and could barely hear herself think through the miasma of pain. All she could do was follow the trail, so she put one foot in front of the other, treading slowly and as quietly as possible.

She kept the crossbow at waist-level, her finger off the trigger but within the trigger guard, ready to pull.

In the silence of city hall, her own breathing sounded catastrophically loud. The quiet was eerie, a thick void unto itself.

Shay kept her head on a swivel while following the trail. The line of blood was a jagged mess, but the overall direction was consistent. Still, she made sure to observe her surroundings and to keep a watchful eye.

Harbin was a sick, twisted piece of shit, but clearly a killer of some merit. She could not ignore his hunting exploits, or the possibility that this trail was a ruse meant to lure her and keep her guard down. If he was playing the victim, and she fell for it, that could be her ruin. She tried to put herself two steps ahead mentally, to out-fake his fake out. The truth was he very likely could be hunting her as much as she was hunting him.

She also knew that backing an injured animal into a corner was a very dangerous gambit.

The line of gore twisted around a corner, and she hugged the edge of the wall, peeking around it and seeing only an empty passage. Slowly and carefully, she tread forward.

The hallway terminated at a glass door, an unlit EXIT sign over it. The blood trail stopped before reaching the exit, and instead turned toward a solid wooden door. Shay had been here enough times to know that the room beyond was the public auditorium for City Council meetings, without needing to read the small sign hanging on the wall.

A large red handprint stained the brass push plate, giving her no choice but to follow. She nudged the door open with her boot, her breathing quick and shallow as she limped through the entry.

The smell hit her immediately.

Copper and feces slammed into her nasal passages and she gagged in reflex. The stench of death was overpowering.

She forced herself to breathe slowly through her mouth, forced herself to keep the crossbow steady. Most of all, she forced herself to *look*.

Two rows of wooden benches led to a waist-high wooden railing, a podium centered at the front of the seating area between the benches. Beyond the railing was a curved stage where the council convened, their names displayed at each seat in front of the microphone.

The council had convened one last time, apparently. Perhaps summoned here by the mayor, the councilmembers had been butchered, and then arranged in their assigned seats. The pale flesh and dry, gaping wounds indicated the council had been slaughtered some time ago.

Their heads hung loose on slit throats, tilted back to make it look as if obscenely large smiles had bloomed in the middle of their necks. Each was naked, their torsos opened and gutted. Their innards hung across the council stage like streamers thrown in a perverse sort of celebration.

Harbin stood in the center of the chamber, his back to her. He was naked and covered in filth. When he turned to face her, she saw he was gnawing on a thick lump of meat. As she limped closer, she could tell by the shape that it was a kidney. A kidney from one of the council members. Harbin had twisted a long rope of intestine around his neck and chest, wearing the viscera like a scarf.

His face was swollen in spots, depressed in others. The pyramid must have fractured bone, sunken parts of his face when she had hammered in his skull. One eye was gone, leaving behind a shiny black crater rimmed with oozing sores. His hair was pasted to his lumpy head by blood. He continued to eat, seemingly oblivious.

His eye held hers, even while he noisily bit and sucked at

the kidney; a squelching wet noise and the clicking of his teeth.

"What the fuck," she whispered.

Shay could not even begin to comprehend what was happening. What *had* happened.

Another part of her mind told her not to worry about it. Just shoot the bastard. *Kill him now, and do not fuck it up this time.*

His lone eye wobbled in its socket, but he still held her in his gaze. She limped closer, afraid that if she held her distance she would miss with the crossbow. He made no movements, just stood there, eating and watching her.

This was not quite the same man she had encountered earlier, and that threw her.

He bit into the organ, growling as she drew closer. A primal, animalistic warning sign, but she did not heed it.

Harbin jolted suddenly, lunging toward her.

She fired the arrow. Missed. He leapt over the railing, bolting toward her, and tackled her, his jaws snapping.

She got her hand up between them, holding him back with his chin cupped in her hand, the stink of blood and offal dizzying this close. His drool turned her fingers slick, and his mouth was constantly moving, his teeth snapping loudly.

She brought her knee up for a groin strike, but it didn't faze him. She wondered if he were on drugs, maybe hopped up on something, but quickly dismissed this idea, somehow knowing he wasn't jacked up on anything.

She brought her leg up again, pulling it in between them and tried to roll and heave away from him.

"You son of a bitch!" she screamed.

She fought through the pain of her ruined arm, brought that up and hooked her thumb into his good eye, pressing hard with her nail.

He howled and twisted away from her. The pressure off her chest was an immediate relief, but she had no time to recover. He was fast, too god damn fast, and she was beyond exhausted.

She didn't have any other choice, so she grabbed the arrow shaft jutting from the front of her bicep and snapped it. Her scream ended abruptly as he slammed into her again, but this time she had an arrow at the ready.

Shay slammed the arrowhead into the thin shelf of his temple, the results instantaneous. He went still, slumped atop her.

She wriggled her way out from under him, the awful stench of his gore and the viscera he had garbed himself in embedded in the fabric of her ruined uniform.

She had never felt as tired in her whole life as she felt in that moment, pushed so far beyond the edge of reason and emotionally broken. Her brain could not compute any of this madness, this insane hysteria infecting the world. She wanted to curl into a ball and cry.

But she was also hungry. Incredibly hungry, in fact.

She grabbed onto the arrow haft sticking out of Harbin's skull and pulled it free. Then she jammed the point into his knee, wriggling the arrow beneath the patella and carving it free from the skin and tendons that held it in place. His kneecap came loose with a moist rip, and she brought it to her mouth, gnawing on the ligaments and tissue that had held it into place. Once she had loosened the meat, she slurped it up as if it were an oyster, and then tossed the cap of bone aside to carve heartier serving from his quadriceps.

She ate, but with each bite the hunger grew.

15

AFTER Lauren finished her beer, she retreated into herself. The emptier the can got, the more withdrawn she became.

Her reaction was common enough given the trauma Scott imagined she had experienced. He figured his imaginings were far worse, but the reality was still damn grim. Whatever had happened in that restroom, her boyfriend was dead and she'd had to beat a man to death. Certainly she had no reason to be chipper or raring to go, and if only at the very least, she had earned that beer and plenty more.

He didn't want to push her, but the day was drawing shorter and he didn't want them to be out in the open come nightfall. He also did not want his daughter drinking too much and going outside plastered and lost in an alcohol-induced fog.

She set the can down on a beat-up end table, and he was glad to see she didn't immediately reach for a second. The dogs were howling back and forth. He had looked out the window a few minutes before and didn't like what he'd seen. More mutts fighting each other, snapping and clawing and barking their way into a frenzy of mutually assured destruction.

"We need to get going," he said.

Lauren nodded dimly, and then pushed herself up off the sunken sofa cushion. Walking to the door, he watched to make sure she was walking in a straight line and didn't seem too shaky. He had conducted enough field sobriety tests in his days to feel confident she was sober enough to continue. If she hadn't been, they'd have been bunking down here, an option he was happy to avoid.

"There's a nurse's office on this floor," Scott said, remembering the directory he had seen near the stairwell on their way up. "We'll stop there first."

Lauren only shrugged.

He led her down a brief maze of corridors and administrative offices, following the signs to the nurse's office. His main concern was finding rabies vaccinations for the both of them. He had been vaccinated before, after being bitten by a perp's dog during a drug house raid, but that had been more than a decade ago.

The office was dark and empty. He clicked on his Maglite and began checking drawers and desks. The nurses clearly followed protocol, as everything was locked down. From his pocket, he took out a small black pouch and unzipped it. Inside was a lock pick gun and a tension wrench, which he used on a set of overhead cabinets at the back of the office. The snapping of the gun was extraordinarily loud in the dead quiet of the office, and each pull of the trigger made him wince, expecting the noise to draw unwelcome company.

Given the campus's proximity to the woods and the nature preservation efforts of the student groups, he figured the nurses would keep rabies vaccines on hand, just in case. He found what he was looking for behind the third cabinet door, and studied the label of the glass jar in the beam of his flashlight.

He didn't think Lauren had ever been vaccinated against

rabies before, so he followed the small print instruction for vaccination after exposure. Lauren would need four doses, one today, and then the other three following on the third, seventh, and fourteenth days. She also needed a shot of rabies immune globulin with that first dose. He found this nearby and set it on the counter, then prepared three syringes.

"All right, come on over here," he said. Lauren had been standing in the doorway, watching the outer office and hallway beyond while he rummaged for supplies.

He cleaned a patch of skin on her arm with an alcohol wipe, stuck the needle in her bare biceps, and then pushed down on the plunger. After delivering the vaccine, he injected her with the globulin. During his search, he'd grabbed a handful of Band-Aids and stuck one over the small hole and dot of blood the needle had left behind.

Lauren looked at the small bandage and couldn't help but laugh at the sight of Olaf on her arm. She began humming "Let It Go" to Scott's chagrin.

"Hey, you started it," she said.

Since Scott had been vaccinated before, he was able to skip the globulin shot. According to the tiny directions, he only needed two doses of vaccine, one today and another on the third day. The shot left a hard lump on his arm where the vaccine was deposited and a muscle-deep soreness. He covered the injection site with Princess Elsa.

He pocketed both the bottles of vaccine and globulin since he wasn't sure if Shay had ever been vaccinated. Grimly, he realized how optimistic it was to even think Shay was still alive. He hoped that she was.

"Ready?"

"Yeah," Lauren said. "I guess so."

He figured that was about as positive as either of them were going to feel about leaving this building and heading back outdoors to deal with the bat-shit crazy bitch Mother Nature had become.

The nearest stairwell was at the rear of the building,

opposite the nurse's office. Pushing through the doors, they found themselves overlooking the University Center's food court and the glass-walled atrium. Hustling down to the bottom landing, they saw outside a smattering of brutalized canine remains, dead people, and several dogs sniffing the ground, milling around the lawn and largely ignoring one another until they wandered too close.

Scott wondered if he was witnessing a change in their behaviors, as modified by the virus, or if he'd simply been wrong in the presumption that the animals had been acting on a pack mentality. He had thought the dogs, as well as the other animals he had encountered so far, had been hunting as a unit. Perhaps it had only been their single-minded pursuit of a common target that made them appear unified. Given the lack of any other food sources, they seemed quick to turn on one another. They also seemed insatiable in their hunger, which was worrying.

If they had been pack hunters, somehow shedding their domesticity and rapidly returning to their positions as wolves and conforming to such behaviors, then their rash and vicious to-the-death attacks against one another was a troubling escalation.

"Do you think Jacob was right?" Lauren asked, her voice raw and shaky. "That it's a virus?"

"I think so," he said.

Not taking her eyes off the dogs outside, she said, "It's spreading, then. Getting worse, fast."

For a moment, he wasn't sure if she was referring to the infected animals or to what had happened earlier in the bathroom. Scott was worried about the virus spreading to humans, and if the aftermath he had witnessed between his daughter, Jeff, and Jacob were any indication, it was already too late. He didn't know either of the boys, but he had good instincts and in the limited time he had spent with them over several beers, both had seemed stable enough. Not the type to trap a woman in the bathroom and attack her. Granted, stranger things had happened, and he'd seen plenty of oddities over the years, but given the situation they were in his gut told him the boys had been triggered by something else. The virus was transmitting rapidly, spreading like brushfire as it jumped between animal and human.

"Were Jacob and Jeff infected, do you think?" He practically choked the words out, overcome with emotion from the implications. He had to ask, though. Needed the confirmation, or, even better, the denial that would tell him he was crazy and overreacting.

"Jeff was," Lauren said.

She sounded so sure, so certain, that he didn't argue.

How long until it spreads even further? he wondered. *How much time do either of us have us have left?*

His stomach growled, a new distraction. It had been a long while since he'd eaten anything substantial, outside of beer and whatever snacks had been lying around the radio station. Chips, mostly. He needed something more. A thick cut of meat. His stomach seemed to open wider at the mere thought of a nice big porterhouse.

When he glanced toward Lauren, the craving grew. He could practically see the twitch of a pulse in her carotid, and his gums felt achingly tight, as if his teeth needed to get up out of his jaw and stretch out a bit. He did the only thing he could and looked away, back out the doors ahead of him.

The dogs were avoiding each other, for now. He knew that would change the instant they pushed their way outside and became fresh targets for each of these bloody-muzzled, four-legged freaks. But they had to leave the building, if not now then eventually. He needed to find Shay, find out what was happening outside, and if the mayor and Sheriff Tremblay had been able to mobilize any kind of a response.

His hope was slim, though.

Stay here, and they'd slowly starve to death. Maybe there was enough food in the UC's kitchens, but how long would that last now that the power was out and the refrigerators were dead? He knew the university was in between semesters, so the kitchens likely weren't as fully stocked as they would be during the fall or winter terms when more students were around.

They could have a million hamburger patties and chicken breasts in those freezers and it wouldn't matter. It wasn't the quantity that was an issue, it was the viability. Once those freezers lost their cool and the meat started defrosting and hit room temperature, they would be useless sooner rather than later. They would have to move on, if they didn't die here first. If they didn't turn on one another and murder each other like those dogs.

He tried to push aside the dark thoughts, but it wasn't easy.

They were wasting daylight, standing here watching, waiting, twiddling their thumbs. They had to move.

A bike rack was right outside, just a few paces away. He could make out the chains securing each bike in place, the thick padlocks securing them.

"We're going to have to pick the locks," he said. "It'll take time."

"How do you want to do this?"

"Those dogs are going to come for us, fast and all at once."

He thought about giving her his gun while he worked on the locks, but the nightmare images that followed—her missing and getting swarmed and torn apart—made him reconsider.

"I don't know if we can make it to the dorms," she said. She looked down at her bare legs, the skin covered in goosebumps.

"No. Maybe not."

He took out the black pouch and withdrew the lock pick gun and a tension wrench, handing them to her.

Holding up the slim wrench, he introduced her to the tool. "You put this tension wrench in the lock, and then insert the gun, pull the trigger a few times, and the padlock will pop open. It's going to seem very loud, though."

He said nothing of the pressure they would be under or

how quickly they were going to have to operate.

"I'll deal with the dogs. Maybe they'll get smart and get scared off by the gunshots." He said this, knowing it was nothing more than false hope. The animals were too far gone, past the point of no return, lost in pure mania. Lauren didn't look as if she believed him either.

He gripped the door's push bar, prepared to shove it open. "On three," he said, counting down with his fingers.

"Now!"

He bolted through the door, gun at the ready to cover Lauren. She darted straight for the bike rack and knelt beside it. The dogs were already taking an interest, even before the loud metallic snapping noise of each trigger pull from the lock pick gun.

Scott aimed and fired, the noise of his pistol far louder and booming over the frenetic barking. He killed one dog, then another, the two that were closest. Three more were pounding across the lawn toward them, and he fired off a quick succession of rounds, blood flying along with the ropes of spit hanging from their jowls. Growls turned into pained whines that either turned into shallow death rattles or were abruptly silenced.

A brief quiet descended, and then he heard the snapping of the lock pick gun resume as Lauren went to work on freeing a second bike.

Their backs were to the L-shaped wall of the UC's rear entrance, leaving the ninety-degree arc before them the main worry. He was glad he didn't have to watch both their fronts and backs. Only front and one side.

That exposed side posed the most danger, and he realized just how dangerous and open he was mid-turn as a rushing noise cutting through the grass.

A Great Dane ran forward, opposite Lauren, and leapt over the bicycle rack. The giant dog plowed into Scott, toppling him to the ground. He held onto his gun, even as the Dane bit into his shoulder and wrenched loose cloth and the skin beneath, an intense, hot wave of pressure clamping across his upper chest.

Scott screamed, pressing the muzzle of his sidearm against the Great Dane's skull, and pulled the trigger.

The pressure eased, his torso on fire.

"Dad!" Lauren screamed.

A chocolate Lab was eyeing her with clear intent, stalking her from the other side of the bike rack. She stayed kneeling beside the bike, gave the lock pick gun one last trigger pull, and pulled the padlock free.

The Lab shoved across the narrow bike rack and sprang toward her.

Lauren slung the bike chain out toward the dog, cracking him right across the snout. Before the dog could recover, Scott fired, not bothering to aim carefully, and saw blood spray from the Lab's rib cage as the force of impact plowed him over. The dog lay on its side, whining and growling angrily.

"C'mon!" Lauren shouted, pulling one bike free and toward Scott.

He hopped onto the seat, his movements far slower and labored than his daughter. Blood was sheeting down his chest, his uniform shirt clinging to his sticky skin, uncomfortably tight and sodden. He pedaled as quickly as he could, but he was weak, faint, and already falling behind Lauren.

More dogs were coming, their commotion announcing their presence before they even cleared the side of the building and crossed into the open field before them.

Scott fired, took out one more dog, and then his chamber ran empty.

"Go!" he told her, ejecting the clip and reaching for another, a lightning bolt of pain shooting through his torso and up his neck to remind him of his ruined shoulder. He fought through the agony and slammed a fresh clip in, but reloading the gun had been nothing more than wasted time. "Head for the road. There's no way we can make it to the dorms." The dogs were nearly right on top of them.

One went right for Lauren, but bless her, she still had that damn cricket bat. She brought it up and swung for the fences, as if she were back on the softball field. The side of the dog's head collapsed, an eyeball popping free as he crashed into the ground, screaming in agony and pawing at his ruined face.

Scott shot the other two, but it was too damn close for comfort.

"C'mon!" he shouted, pedaling beside her and keeping his gun ready. "C'mon," he said, softer this time, more to himself. Keeping a grip on the handlebar with his ruined arm hurt like a bitch, and it took some coaxing to get his fingers to work properly. Every jostle and bump sent a fresh blister of agony through him.

*   *   *

Lauren pedaled mindlessly, her entire body quivering from too much adrenaline. Her stomach was twisted up in turmoil and her limbs were jittery, the way she felt when she drank an excessive amount of coffee and not nearly enough food.

Each time she blinked, she could see—too clearly—Jacob's skull, shattered open, his brains bashed into jelly and leaking out of his head out onto the bathroom floor where it mingled with his blood and the filthy tile grout. She saw Jeff's leering eyes and his spit-slick lips as he fondled himself, covered in gore.

She pedaled to put as much distance as she could between their bodies and hers, the devil's own hellions practically nipping at her heels.

She pedaled as if lost in a trance. Eventually, she took notice of her surroundings. Back on US 31, a dead traffic light hung over the intersection. To her right, the three-building strip mall with a restaurant that only served breakfast, and mostly only omelets and pecan rolls at that, a knick-knack shack that catered exclusively to customers looking for doodads like birdfeeders or goofy decorations made entirely of wood, and a Little Caesars. To the left, a tattoo parlor, a 7-11, and a Mexican restaurant that she refused to eat at because it had originally been a funeral home and that kind of creeped her out.

How the hell did we get here? she wondered.

The university was well behind them, and as she turned to look toward the rear she saw a number of animals shot dead. Her father had come to a stop several yards back, and she circled back to pull up beside him.

Scott was slumped forward over the handlebar, one foot on the pavement keeping him upright, if only barely. His injured arm hung limply at his side, blood running down from beneath the torn shirtsleeve and over his forearm, collecting at his fingers and swelling into a steady drip.

"Dad!" she shouted, jumping off the stolen bicycle.

"I need a minute, sweetie, that's all." His breathing was ragged, his skin bleached white.

"Can you make it across the street?" she asked. "To the 7-11?" *They've got to have gauze in there, right, or something at least?*

He tilted his head up, but it clearly took a deal of effort. He was able to nod.

"Jesus, you're pale."

He gasped as he worked his injured arm back into place on the handlebar. Then he decided to holster the gun at his hip and used that to steer instead, letting the wrecked limb fall free.

She hopped back on her bike and easily overtook her dad, who was pedaling much slower. "I can scout ahead," she offered.

"It's not safe."

"And what good are you?" she said, immediately regretting the biting sting her words clearly carried. She didn't even know where those words came from, that upswell of vitriol taking even her by surprise. She swallowed back the inexplicable anger, waiting for him to say something. When he didn't she said, "That came out wrong."

"No, you're right," he said eventually.

Seeing her father so badly wounded jolted her. She had never seen him so frail, so weak. She had always thought him strong, but he clearly was that no longer. Her grip tightened on the cricket bat.

She missed home, her room. Her now-dead and useless Kindle, and the *Spider-Gwen* and *Hack/Slash* comics that were loaded onto it. Her posters of Muse and CCR. All that was history now, a bygone era. That was the old world, she thought. A world of safety and comfort. In this new, mad world, there was no room for the weak.

No room for Jacob. No room for Jeff.

No room for her own father. Not anymore. Not in the state he was in.

What the fuck is wrong with me?

That question brought with it an explosive clarity, and she found herself repulsed by the anger residing somewhere deep inside her. She forced her hand to relax and for her grip to loosen. Forced herself to stop white-knuckling the bat. She shook her head to clear it of the nasty cobwebs that had somehow collected there.

"Come on," she said. "It's right across the street. We'll get you patched up."

She broke away from his gaze, not liking the look that resided in his eyes. He knew, and something primal coiled there, a trace measure of self-protection lurking behind the bloodshot sclera and the wet, puffy rims of his eyelids.

She pushed forward and he followed.

As with the rest of town, the 7-11 was dark. The automatic sliding doors hung twisted at awkward angles, popped out of their frames like loose, barely attached teeth. Beyond was nothing but rows of shelves concealed in the growing darkness of deepening shadows.

She dropped the kickstand and gripped the bat tight,

casting a look over her shoulder toward her father. He licked his lips, his eyes practically lost in their empurpled, swollen orbits. The way he looked at her, his eyes settling on the stretch of her tanned thigh, unsettled her, and she told herself she was imagining it. His lips were shiny with spit and blood. He nodded, then jutted his chin out, urging her forward. He was sweating hard, his skin a chalky white.

She drew a long, deep breath and pushed herself through the jangling door.

The stench was a straight-up obscenity, but one that she was becoming inured to. The convenience store stank of copper and feces, a thick musky stew of odors beneath that. The odor was a mélange of rotting fruit and rotting meat, and an old fish kind of smell. Wet, stinky fur, a smell she remembered from Buckley after he came inside out of the rain and it had been too long between baths.

The wet fur smell drew heavier as she crept further inside.

She spotted the first corpse at the end of the aisle, by refrigerators stocked with bottled water, and quarts and pints and gallons of milk. His face was slashed to ribbons, his neck torn to gristle and gnawed down to the bone.

Lauren moved as silently as she knew how, but worried that her breathing was too loud. The noise of each inhalation and exhalation was like a scream right in her ears, the rapid-fire thudding of her heart a shotgun blast behind her ribcage. Slowly, she put one foot in the front of the other.

Then she heard it.

A wet, meaty smacking noise. Teeth and fluids and tongue slapping against lips and gums. A moist, throaty gurgle, or maybe a drowned growl. Meat being stripped from the bone.

And then a sloppy plopping noise, followed by cautious, padded footsteps.

From around an end cap thick with travel toiletries, a small, furry face poked out. The huskie pup's white muzzle led the way, and the small dog stopped, dead center in the middle of the aisle, directly in front of Lauren.

For a brief moment, the huskie hesitated. His tail gave a small, seemingly confused wag and then stilled as it bared its teeth and a tiny warning came from deep in his chest.

When the huskie barked, it was shrill and small, almost comical. She looked down at the dog, amused. The pup was clearly acting tougher than it really was, and she seriously doubted it had killed the man in the refrigerator aisle, or whatever it was eating down this other aisle.

No, this tiny thing was nothing more than a scavenger. Feasting on something else's kill.

Emboldened by the puppy's immaturity, she took a large step forward, but he stood his ground. The fur all along his back stood, inflating his size but to little effect.

She swung the bat, the flat end of the plank slamming right into the side of the huskie's face. A tooth knocked loose and tittered across the tile floor, pinging against the metal base of an end cap.

The dog was knocked off-balance and tried to regain its footing, but Lauren was on him fast, bringing the bat down in a tight overhanded arc. The flat edge of the wood caromed off the top of the huskie's skull, and she heard an audible crack, accompanied by a thudding bass as the underside of the dog's jaw pounded off the floor, its four legs splaying out beneath him. Clearly dazed, he tried to stand, nearly lost his balance, one eye loose and rolling in his skull.

She swung hard, her aim on the back of the store, as if she were hitting a homer right out of the field.

The pup toppled over, the side of its face crushed and bloodied, scrabbling away from her. His nails fought for purchase on the flat tiles. He couldn't even stand, and she felt disgusted.

Another fucking weakling not fit for this world.

"Fuck you," she said, delivering a swift kick to the dog's side. He snapped at her, but too slow, her leg already retreating.

The huskie shoved itself forward, but there was nowhere for him to go. He was growling now, his barking turning into wheezing, pink, bubbly drool leaking from his jowls.

She fell to her knees beside the puppy and grabbed fistfuls of fur in both hands, twisting savagely as she picked him up. She moved one hand to wrap her fingers around his snapping muzzle, pinning his mouth shut and arcing his head up and away from her. Exposing his neck, pulling the fur away to show his skin.

He squirmed and writhed, his frightened howl a furious cacophony as she bit down, her teeth rending flesh, her mouth filling with hair and the hot, coppery spill of blood. She bit through a thick, ropy vein, the animal's blood ejecting into her mouth and she sucked it down greedily, and what she couldn't swallow poured down her chin, staining her tank top and pasting it to her skin like a thick red blanket, painting her bare legs red. She chewed her way deeper, pulling on the dog's muzzle, opening the wound further, pulling and chewing, pulling and chewing.

The dog fell silent, his body going still.

She ate with a sudden gusto, unaware until this moment that she was badly starved, the taste of pennies a new and constant craving that grew stronger with each new drop of blood she tasted. And the meat! Motherfucker, the meat! Raw and pure, she devoured it, nearly choking in her gusto to consume.

She dropped the dog long enough to let out a deep, throaty burp.

Using her forearm, she wiped at the mess all across her face. The arm slid across her soaked lips, fur caked to her limb and face.

She sat back on her heels, struggling to catch her breath. She had never eaten so much so fast before, and it was a workout in its own right. It felt both heavenly and hellish, and she wanted more. Much, much more.

And then she remembered Scott. That was why she was

here, in this 7-11. She was supposed to be looking for gauze for him, not tearing into this savory meal.

Another metallic belch worked its way loose, and she stood with a pang of regret. She *needed* more, and her stomach felt bottomless and empty. She had to force herself away, and she recovered the cricket bat as she turned down the aisle, scanning the signs for first aid supplies.

* * *

Propped up against the wall, half-slumped off his bicycle, Scott listened to the noises of carnage emanating from the other side of the window. His vision was beginning to blur, the corners darkening, but even this close he could make out the beer posters with their scantily clad bikini beach babes and shirtless, muscled men chasing after them with a six-pack of fresh, relaxing golden lager in hand. Their smiling faces and carefree eyes met his, even as he listened to the growls and the noise of rending meat, and the smack of thick wood against hard bone.

Every time he blinked, the world faded a little bit more, darkened a little further until the world became a grayish vignette.

His shoulder was on fire, the entire length of his arm tacky, his uniform blouse glued to his chest.

He was tired.

He was dying.

That dog had torn up his shoulder something good, worse than he had been willing to let on around Lauren. Those teeth had sank deep, and in the process had nicked something vital, a vein or an artery, and the wound would not congeal and close on its own. The blood wept out of him, slowly but consistently, which made him think that whatever had been cut open was a shallow wound but still deep enough to end him given enough time.

Or he could end it now, and be done with it.

Over the years, he had grown used to the weight of his sidearm, resting there at his hip. There was plenty of ammunition left over to settle his and Lauren's accounts.

She was changing, that much was obvious. He was certain he was changing, too. Maybe even had already changed. Not significantly enough, and not as rapidly as his daughter, but he still possessed enough self-reflection to recognize the sudden outbursts of anger and the flaring, insatiable hunger, and the way the coppery stink boiling off his wounds made his mouth water.

He laughed quietly at the lies he told himself. He knew damn well he would never be able to pull the trigger on his daughter. Would never be able to put the barrel of his gun against her head and murder her. Not even for the best of reasons, not to save her or spare her, and certainly not to save himself.

When Lauren had been born, he had been holding Melisa's hand, and she had been so intent on pushing that she hardly realized their baby had come sliding out and into the doctor's waiting palms. He had turned to look, already nervous, anxious, and worried, and saw his lifeless child, covered in gore, her skin a deep and pure purple, the umbilical cord wrapped around her small body and twisted tightly against her neck. The nurses were fighting to get their fingers in between the skin and the cord.

Scott had lost it then, his knees buckling. Two miscarriages and nine months of anxious excitement to get to this moment, and it was all for naught. Melisa had delivered a corpse. He pulled his hand free from hers and turned, vomiting over the side of a chair, tears stabbing at his eyes, heart stuttering in that moment of pure fear.

And then a choked and foreign cry escaped from Lauren's little mouth. He turned in time to see his baby girl held up as the nurse turned to place her in Mommy's arms.

Lauren was alive, and all that grief flooded straight out of him, replaced with immense joy and a mountain of pride over the pure beauty of his child. She was perfect, all her fingers and toes accounted for, her tiny lower lip trembling as the handful of nurses poked and prodded at her. She was alive, and she was glorious.

So, no, Scott knew, he could never harm her, not even to save her from this world or from herself. He loved her far too much to carry that burden across his soul, even for the short period needed to turn the gun on himself.

He closed his eyes and waited, and the noises inside the store grew softer.

"Dad?"

He slowly stirred, his eyelids heavy. Lauren stood beside him, gore plastered across her whole body. She peered closely at him, and Scott could make out dots of blood in her hair, along with dark tufts of hair fringing her mouth.

He swallowed back the rising gorge and tried to sit up properly on the bike. "I'm here, honey."

She waved a green and white box in front of him, the words printed across it a blur. "I found it," she said. "Now let's get you inside."

"Are you hurt?" he mumbled.

"No," she said. "I'm good. Honest."

Her words sounded hollow in his ears, but he didn't have the energy or desire to argue. Whatever had happened to her, she was still his daughter. He still saw traces of the real her peeking through, and he latched onto the hope that provided.

She helped him get upright, and then helped him get off the bike. Her arms wrapped around him, she led him inside the store.

"The floor's slippery," she cautioned. "But there's a stool behind the counter. Or a chair in the manager's office, if you think you can make it there. It's not far."

"The chair sounds good," he said.

Each blink grew longer, and the convenience store came to him only in brief snatches. He didn't even remember falling into the chair and realized dimly that Lauren must have dragged him there. She was sitting on the desk beside him, opening the box of gauze.

"We need to get this shirt off you," she said.

He grunted a negative and shook his head slightly for added measure. "No, it's okay, honey."

"Dad, c'mon."

"That's not going to help, Lauren. It's bad, I think. I've lost a lot of blood. I think…I think I need more than a little bit of gauze."

He tried to sit up straighter, but habit made him use his bad arm and he could not get a grip on the armrest with his blood-slick hand. *Fuck it,* he decided.

"Now look," he said finally, fighting to free the gun from his holster. "There's maybe ten rounds left in here. You need this."

Jesus, when did this gun get so heavy? he wondered. His hand trembled as he held it out to her.

"You just point and shoot," he said.

He didn't need to tell her much else, really. He'd taught her about guns, had taken her shooting at the police officers' range, made sure she knew about the power of the weapon and respected it. She was not a proficient marksman, but she wasn't too bad. She could handle a gun well enough, and he had little doubt that she would need it.

"Don't do this, Daddy," she said.

"I'm not going to make it." He screwed his eyes shut until the tears receded and his throat stopped burning. "You might be able to, though, if you're careful."

He tried to focus on her face one last time, but all he saw was the dried swatch of red circling her mouth and reaching down her neck, staining her shirt.

Scott pushed the gun toward her, the firearm so damn heavy he had to use every last ounce of strength in him to just hold it. She reached forward and took his hand—and the gun—in hers, her skin warm against his.

"Try to find Shay," he said. "She can help you, maybe."

"Okay," she said, nodding. "I'll do that."

He tried to smile, but could not tell if the muscles were working or not.

"Go to sleep, Dad. Get some rest."

She squeezed his hand, a small measure of comfort that he desperately needed.

Finally, he closed his eyes.

☙ ☙ ☙

Lauren slept on the floor, the door to the manager's office closed, locked, and the desk shoved up against it. She had kept the pistol nearby, and her hand found it easily when she woke.

Her father's ragged breathing and moist gurgling noises had kept her awake for a while, until exhaustion demanded her own body to succumb as she curled up on the tiles and passed out.

Eyes open, she continued to lie still, listening for her father's noises.

The room was silent.

When she rose and turned to face Scott, he was slumped over in the chair. His eyes were open but blank. His mouth hung open and when she held her palm over his lips, she felt no passage of air, saw no rising and falling of his chest. His skin was gray, his body stiff.

She bent over to kiss his cold forehead and said quietly, "I love you, Daddy."

She worked his Sam Browne belt loose and pulled it as tight as it could go across her waist. It hung loosely on her hips, but she considered it good enough. She holstered the gun while she shoved the desk away from the door, then held it tightly while she listened for any signs of trouble outside the office.

Light was creeping in from beneath the door, and the morning light flooding in through the casement windows near the ceiling lighted the room well enough. At least, she thought it was morning.

Unlocking and easing the door open, she peered through the narrow crack. Nobody was out there, so she slowly opened the door further, pausing before stepping out into the store.

The stench of the husky's carcass both repulsed and excited her in equal measure, flies buzzing in and around the matted fur and over the opened cavities she had made with her teeth the previous night. She blanched at the thought, but her salivary glands tingled as her mouth grew moist.

She took a last look at her father, dead in some anonymous 7-11 manager's office, and closed the door. *That should be enough to keep his remains safe*, she thought.

She spent a long few moments watching the street through the clear glass automatic doors, but even the outside was lifeless and still.

That would not last, she knew, straddling her confiscated bicycle and holstering the gun once more.

She put the newly risen sun at her back and pedaled toward City Hall and, she hoped, Shay Hendrix.

16

SHAY awoke in a congealed mess of viscera and entrails, one eye half-stuck together and her hair matted to the side of her head. She had to palm away the gelatinous tar gluing her eye shut, then worked on pulling herself up and out of the tacky mess.

The mayor's remains were nearby, gutted and stinking. Her fingernails had made long tracks across his forearm and chest, from where she had clawed away his fat to expose the meat, tearing away strips of tough, raw protein for fuel. A twisted chimera of reactions pulsed through her, fighting for Alpha position: satisfaction, revulsion, and a craving for more.

She swallowed back a sticky lump, hating herself and the cannibalistic urges that arose deep within her, unbidden and demanding, and consistently unsatisfied regardless of how much she ate. Most of the night had been spent alternating between periods of feeding and sleeping. A long section of one of the mayor's leg, just below the knee, was gnawed down to the bone. Seeing his foot, the skeletal toes jutting up, she remembered growing hysterical over a joke she had told to herself about eating pigs' feet.

Her uniform was sodden, plastered to her skin, and she felt sticky all over. Her self-disgust grew, but as her eyes lingered on the corpse beside her, so too did the hunger.

She had to tightly clamp down the urge to eat yet again, otherwise she might never leave City Hall. Instead, she would gorge herself to death on this fat bastard in this dark auditorium. That was simply not an option.

Her arm burned, but not with only pain. The wound was feverishly hot, and a sweat broke out across her forehead as soon as she began moving again. Regardless, there was a sense of relief at the arrow's absence, even as the channel it had gouged through her ached and throbbed.

The arrowhead, and the finger-length bit of shaft that she had broken loose the previous day, was nearby. She snatched it, her one good hand holding it tight.

Every movement felt leaden, weighted down by the heavy and restrictive uniform. The discomfort ate at her and she weighed her options. She felt sluggish as she moved into the corridor and turned toward the women's restroom.

Sunlight streamed in from the atrium, warm and inviting. Forgetting about the power loss, she flicked the bathroom light switch up and down, irritated. Then the pieces fell back into place and she used a nearby garbage can to prop open the door so she could see what she was doing.

Much of the region used well water, including city services, which she found herself suddenly grateful for. With the water softener out of commission, though, the water gave out a thick rotten-egg smell. Beggars can't be choosers, she reminded herself, her father's voice practically singing the words in her head.

She let the water run, studying herself in the mirror. The sunlight trickling in through the open door gave her enough gray light to see by, and she spent a moment trying to believe her own reflection. Her hair was pasted to her scalp by thick globs of gore, her face practically coated in red. She heaved into the sink, long strings of loose meat freeing themselves from her belly and splashing into the porcelain. Blood laced with yellow strings of mucus followed and she spent a good, long while coughing and spitting, her arms shaking as she held herself up.

"Oh, Jesus," she whispered.

After the sickness passed, her head feeling fuzzy, she set the arrow down on a metal shelf attached to the bottom lip of the mirror and began to strip.

Her uniform blouse was a catastrophe and far beyond salvaging. The fabric peeled away, tugging at the fine hairs across her arms and abdomen, and she let it fall to the floor, kicking it away. The Kevlar vest she wore beneath the shirt was also stained, but seemed to have stopped the gore from ruining the tank top below. Her pants were a total loss, so she worked her way out of her boots and tossed the pants into a corner alongside the discarded shirt. She was soaked right down to her socks and panties, her feet squelching inside the boots. She could live with the discomfort of the bloodstained underwear, but rid herself of the socks. She had always hated going to the beach because of how wet sand felt between her toes, and bloody socks were even worse.

Standing in front of the mirror, she did the best she could to clean herself. The well water was cool against her skin and she had to scrub hard with her hands to free herself of the gore coating her body. She stuffed her head into the sink as best she could, funneling the water across her thick, black hair. Satisfied, she then moved onto washing her face, arms, legs, and feet, then dried herself with handfuls of paper towel.

"Jesus, you're one hot mess," she said, then chuckled.

She toyed with the idea of going back to the council room and seeing if any of the dead officials had clothes worth salvaging, but the grisly scene made that proposition highly unlikely and she dismissed the thought almost as quickly as it had occurred.

If it was really the end of the world, she told herself, who cares how you look?

She pictured herself walking out of City Hall and back onto the street wearing only a thin cotton shirt and underwear that looked like it had been through the period from hell, and tactical combat boots, and couldn't help but laugh. That would surely be one hell of a sight. When she thought of her Bible-thumping, End-of-the-World Daddy and what his reaction to her appearance would have been, she laughed even harder.

Okay then, this is totally worth it just for that thought alone, she thought.

She grabbed the arrow from the shelf and looked in the mirror one last time, mentally prepared herself to head outside.

⚔ ⚔ ⚔

The walk to the library was a short distance, but she took it slow due to her various aches and pains. It gave her time to think, even as she kept a wary eye open for an attack from the dogs or birds or anything else with teeth and claws.

Passing by the cluster of wolves Harbin had dispatched with his rifle, she explored the question that had been hounding her for the past several hours.

The dogs, and even the other animals she had witnessed over the last twenty-four hours, had stayed in packs, hunting together. Harbin, though, had been the only human thus far to attempt to hunt and kill her.

Were humans affected by this…this…whatever it was?

She knew that in animal packs there was also some kind of alpha. Male lions would fight one another for control of their pride, and then the victor would slaughter his adversary's offspring in order to assume total domination and ensure his own bloodline continued.

Was that why Harbin had gone after her? Because she was a rival for his supremacy?

It made sense, she supposed. He was a big game hunter, and a mayor. Clearly, he possessed an alpha streak. She was a police officer—not exactly a career for the passive, beta types. And Tremblay had been the sheriff, a police officer and politician in equal measure, in a position of power not for the faint of heart.

The more she thought on it, the more she thought she was onto something. This infection—or plague, maybe?—brought out something primal and upended the natural order, turned everyone hysterical. Everything and everyone was hyper-aggressive, intent on domineering and eliminating their competition, prone to crazed fits of violence.

For a moment, she was able to look outside herself and examine the issue with a sense of detachment, as if this problem were affecting only others and not her directly. That moment passed almost as soon as it had arrived, her concentration broken by a sharp, loud whistle.

Her eyes fell upon the men at the library entrance, their gazes lingering and intent plain on each of their faces. Both men's eyes moved from her booted feet up her bare calves and muscled thighs, across the thin fabric covering her pubis and up the length of her belly, to her breasts, and finally, her eyes. The leer was unmistakable, and as she approached, a lascivious grin spread across their lips. A plain alpha intent shined in their eyes, and the way their bodies shifted to put a bit more distance between themselves carried a hint of potential violence that she recognized well enough from her years on the force. Men always underestimated her.

She let her eyes drop, forced her body to assume an unchallenging pose as her shoulders slumped and her head tipped down. She made herself look smaller and unassuming, unthreatening. She kept the arrow hidden in her hand, the thin broken shaft tight against the back of her forearm.

While they had been studying her, she had done a quick

assessment of them. They were clearly sentries, guarding the library and whoever was inside. One held a pistol, the barrel pointed toward the ground, and the other a tire iron. As she approached, the man with the tire iron thwacked the steel against his palm.

"Hey there, baby," he said, his eyes locked onto her tits. His tongue peaked out from between glistening lips.

There would be no better opening than this, she knew. She had to strike hard and fast while their raging hormones distracted them.

She lightly pressed her empty palm to Tire Iron's face, his stubble coarse against her soft skin, and forced a coquettish smile as she batted her eyes. Blood still stained the creases of her knuckles. He leaned his face into her hand, his head craning toward hers, already pursing his lips.

She slammed the arrow into his jugular, then tore the tire iron from his grip.

Before the man with the pistol could realize what had happened, she pivoted and brought the tire iron around fast, whipping it into his head. He stumbled back, shocked and wounded, and she pressed the advantage, bringing the tire iron down again over the top of his head, denting his skull, slamming it down once more, skin splitting and his skull breached, blood pouring down his face in a thick, syrupy cascade.

She turned back toward the other man, and swung the tire iron at him as well. He had a hand around his neck, fingers pressed against either side of the arrow jutting from his jugular, and he dimly raised his other hand to ward off the blow. He was too slow, and she caught him across the eyes with the iron. He fell hard on his ass, and she reached down to him, yanking the arrow free. A propulsive stream of crimson fountained out from between his fingers, and she left him to bleed out.

The pistol had wound up in the grass, and she quickly picked it up and tucked into the back of her underwear's waistband. Then, she grabbed a hold of the door handle and stepped into the library.

Rather than be greeted with the peculiar, musty scent of well-worn books and collections of newspapers and magazines, Shay was assaulted by the cloying stench of bodily fluids and waste, and of the unwashed. As she moved from the lobby and into the main collections, following the noises of grunting and panting into the fiction section, the stink only grew stronger. She could very nearly identify the scent of various organ meats as they rotted in the still, hot air. Her nostrils flared as her stomach growled, her mouth watering with anticipation.

Entrails littered the floor, the ropes of intestine and discarded innards practically a roadmap to the main center of debauchery. A corpse, nothing more than an empty, gutted husk of disused flesh and barely concealed bone, was planted beside the shelves of New Fiction, her head cocked at an abstract angle and twisted almost completely around on a broken neck.

Books were strewn everywhere, cast to the floor and flung across the tables. Torn pages turned brown with the dried stains of bodily fluids were scattered around the room, their empty broken-spined shells tossed aside. The room looked as if a tornado had ripped through, and following the excited resonations of moaning around the stacks, she saw why.

A disbelieving laugh nearly escaped her, but she stifled it with her palm. Her skin was still perfumed with a coppery tang that made her gut roil, even as her eyes went wide and a new thrill sent tenterhooks into a deeper, more primal urge buried in her core.

Naked bodies heaved upon one another, their skin stained a delirious crimson and flecked with black chunks, their hair matted and pasted in clumps to their scalps and the sides of their faces.

Her presence did nothing to disturb the animalistic rutting around her, and she waded deeper into the crimson orgy. The room stank of the heavy, musky stink of sex and sweat, of waste and gore. The couplings were erratic and fluid and she briefly watched as men savaged one another, women pleasuring other women, partners swapped in an unending train of thrusting bodies, lost in the throes of their manic fucking.

A creeping wetness moistened her panties and she unconsciously groped at her own breast, her nipple hard in her palm. Her breathing came in hitched gasps as her desire grew, her heart beating faster as an urgent insistence to be filled tensed within her.

She felt insanely tempted to strip out of the thin garments covering her skin and slide into the fray, wanting to taste the bodies of those around her, needing to be tasted in turn. Instead, she waded deeper, past the threesomes and foursomes and moresomes, into the center of the room.

A man stood in the middle of it all, his back pressed against the shelving. His studied the erratic pressing of bodies before him, noting her approach with an upturned smile. Two women knelt before him, passing his cock between their mouths.

Shay's heart quickened at the sight of his rigid, upturned erection. The knob was swollen and empurpled, thick veins lining the shaft and pulsing his hardness. His member was not large, but settled in the smallness of the women's hands, it possessed an undeniable appeal. When he crooked his finger at her, summoning her forward, she felt compelled to proceed. She licked her lips. Her underwear was thoroughly soaked, and a brief glimmer of fantasy ran through her mind in which she pulled aside the crotch of her panties and pressed her backside against him, pulling him inside her. Her fingers squeezed at the arrow cupped in her palm, and she strode forward with a heady confidence.

He was Alpha.

She was the Omega.

Her lips curled at this realization. That curl grew into a wider smile as she realized who the man was. Barret Ward— the fucking mailman, of all people. It had taken her a moment to recognize him. Usually when she saw him he was decked out in his blue postal carrier uniform and a safari hat, half his face hidden behind a pair of sunglasses. Naked, he looked different, older. Although his arms and legs were corded with thick muscle, his old-man tits dropped so that his hairy nipples pointed downward toward his soggy-looking potbelly. His solid cock jutted up from a thick gray thatch of pubic hair, the shaft bent at an upward slope.

Ward was a gruff, no-nonsense sort of man. He did his daily duties with mercurial satisfaction, a disposition that leaned toward abrasive. He was not the type of mailman to nod and say hello. If anything, on those rare occasions that his eyes were bared, his stare carried a cruelness that was razorblade sharp, accompanied by a quick barb that lived perpetually on the tip of his tongue. The Army Ranger tattoo on his forearm had been dulled by the years, but the puckered scars across his abdomen still carried a certain pink shine.

On more than one occasion, Shay had been called out by a parent claiming Ward had struck their child. During a polar snap a few years back, a handful of kids who had been stuck at home due to a school closure were hamming it up with a snowball fight. When Ward passed in their direction, slipping the mail free from his shoulder sling for delivery, they had pelted him with a snowball that was mostly ice. Furious, Ward went after them, surprisingly fast for an old man. He had caught the slowest boy by the hood of his parka and yanked him off his feet, slamming him onto the snow-covered lawn.

Before Ward was able to strike the boy—which by all accounts, was certainly his plan—the storm door sprung open and a mother to one of the kids raced out, grabbing ahold of Ward and pushing him away from the child. Ward flung the mail he had been delivering, letting the letters scatter in the wind, and marched off on his way.

The parents of the boy had decided not to press charges, but it was not the first, nor the last time that Barret Ward had some kind of a run-in with the local youths.

Now here he was, with the matronly seventy-six-year-old retiree who volunteered at the library practically gagging on his spit-shined dick.

His eyes landed on Shay's tits, his gaze pulling her forward. She moved slowly, letting her hips sway in a gentle, exaggerated rhythm, and then knelt and pressed in between the women. The other woman was a ripe and buxom forty-something with a soccer-mom look about her. The geriatric pulled away from Ward's cock, his hard-on clearing her lips with a slick popping noise, and angled the throbbing member toward Shay.

Shay rose up slightly, tilting her head to accommodate the crooked member and took him into her mouth. His pubic hair stank with a heady, fungal aroma, and even through the gore dried against his skin she could pick out the strong scent of menthol he had slathered on his legs for muscle relief.

She cupped his dangling balls in her hand, rolling the testicles in her palm, seeking his eyes with her own and held them while she worked her tongue against the tip of his penis. His fingers sank into her thick hair, holding her head still as he thrust into her face, moaning loudly. With her index finger, she traced the fold of skin behind his balls, the pad of her finger pressing against his anus, circling the clenched opening, teasing him slightly before withdrawing back to his testes.

His mouth fell open, his head slightly nodding.

He liked that, she thought, smiling around his erection. *Let's see how he likes this.*

Still holding his balls in one hand, she reached up slowly between his legs with the other, sliding the arrow point forward. She kept him entranced with her wide eyes, taking his shaft as deep into her mouth as she could, always maintaining eye contact, keeping him engaged and distracted.

To either side of her, she felt the bodies of the other two

women. A soft, wrinkly hand groped at her breast, while the younger woman reached between Shay's thighs, her fingers slipping beneath the sodden panties and circling her opening.

The pleasure was impossible to deny, and she found the excitement building toward a natural crescendo.

She pointed the arrowhead up and thrust quickly, slamming the three-bladed broadhead into the soft knot of his anus. He howled, a barbaric gut-deep bellow, his hands grabbing fistfuls of her hair and pulling, but she refused to relent.

She drove the arrow up further, using the small broken bit of shaft to twist it as she jammed further up, and then quickly yanked it down with all her might. Blood and shit splattered free as his sphincter snared around the broadhead, prolapsed, and tore free of his rectum.

Shay bit down hard on his cock, her teeth snapping through the thin layer of flesh and cutting through the veiny gristle. She twisted her head from side to side, tearing his dick free from its base, squeezing his balls tight between her fingers until they ruptured.

Ward was howling viciously at this point, hyperventilating and breathless from the fresh agony. His grip on her hair loosened and as Shay stood, she stabbed him in the belly with the broadhead. His face twisted into a now-soundless rictus of pain, drool and blood pouring from his mouth, and she freed the arrow, stabbing him repeatedly, holding him up by the shoulder. Finally satisfied, she released him and let him fall, still alive but in enormous pain.

She knew all eyes were on her, and she had to guarantee there was no questioning her claim to this pack. Ward's days as Alpha were over, and they all had to know that. She raised her booted foot up, and then slammed the heel down onto Ward's throat, crushing his neck. She stomped on his face, over and over, until his skull fractured and collapsed into a black and red paste that was swirled with funnels of pulped gray brain matter. Breathless, she smeared the residue onto the tiled floor, the toes of her boot making a waxy scream.

Turning toward her pack, she saw only startled gazes. Then the men rose, a hardness entering their eyes. Shay pulled the gun from her waistband and leveled it, shooting one man after another until four more dead dicks littered the library and the rest willingly lowered their gazes and sank back to their knees. There were no alpha streaks in those boys, she was sure of that much. Not anymore.

I am your queen now, she thought, looking out at them.

Slowly, the tension in the air bled out and her people resumed their day's entertainment, feasting on the corpses or rutting loudly amongst the books.

She turned her eyes on the soccer mom who had been kneeling beside her earlier, and cupped her chin, drawing her closer. She bent to kiss the woman on the forehead, beneath her bangs, and then shoved her face to the sodden panties.

"Lick," Shay said.

17

THE downtown corridor was a miasma of scorched bodies and burnt insulation emanating from the ruined husks of what had once been restaurants and souvenir shops, and the fecund stink of animal fear pheromones.

Lauren's leg muscles burned from pedaling, her whole body a catalog of bone-deep aches and pains. Sheer exhaustion nearly swallowed her whole, but she pressed on.

Although the flames had abated, the heat lingered. The line of abandoned vehicles radiated a ghost of warmth, the paint blistered or burnt away to reveal blackened metal frames. Pedaling past the deserted cars was enough to leave her sweating, a red glow rising across her bare arms.

Small gutters of fire sputtered in the hollows of the collapsed business district, dancing in the windows of the downed aircraft that had buried itself in the street and smashed through storefronts.

Out on the water, a host of boats drifted, encased in black cloaks. She stopped briefly to study the scene, squinting, but unable to make out much. The boats weren't covered, not properly, and not in any way she had seen before. A writhing rhythm shook across the blackness, an

157

inky pulse that wormed through the tarps. With a squawk, one of the black flecks rose and then shoved its way into a nearby gap. The boats were encased in crows, she realized. Whoever had tried to escape land had become fodder for the birds, and now those creatures were feasting on the remains of their catch.

Shuddering, she moved forward again, her legs responding sluggishly but finding the pedals and giving them a slow, tentative turn. She vividly recalled the stinging pokes of beaks on her skin and hoped the birds were properly distracted with their carrion not to pay her much attention.

Scores of ravaged bodies lay in the sand, on the lawn. Whatever animals had felled them must have moved on, and although she did not see any immediate threats, she was more than wary.

Lauren pedaled slowly, made cautious by fear and the worry that the clicking noise of the bike's chains and gears would draw attention.

A loud squawking rang out over the bay, and she shot a nervous glance toward the boats. The crows were writhing, some flying over to another pleasure boat and seeking sustenance. The intrusion sparked a cacophony of shrill, piercing noise, the smacking of feathered bodies loud even from a distance. Soon enough, the crows separated into groupings and the various murders assaulted each other. Feathers burst into the air amid war cries and shrieks of pain, the pulsing black cloud a whirling dervish of angry bloodlust.

She kept to the trail along the shore, unsure what the safest route was. Heat waves shimmered along the central road cutting through downtown, blocked off by a host of emergency vehicles and traffic. The trail at least provided open space and less obstacles to navigate around.

On the beach, she saw a handful of stray mutts chomping at the still bodies. One of the dogs looked up at her, but it was only a passing glance before it returned to its easy meal.

After putting a suitable distance between herself and the ravaged front of downtown, she began looking down the crosswalks to determine if it was safe enough to cross over and cut through toward City Hall. The four-lane break between streets, and the lack of wind, provided enough of a gap to prevent the fire from spreading further down Front Street, so she maneuvered her way through the snaking trail of cars and down the side street past the parking lots on either side.

Finding herself beside the brick front of the Mackinac Brewery brought back memories of beer cheese soup and the walleye sandwich she'd had so often. Every now and then, her dad would even allow her a discreet sip of the seasonal cherry lager or oatmeal stout.

The front doors were unlocked, but the window-facing booths and tables were, of course, empty, the building dark. Her stomach grumbled at the prospect of food—real food this time, and not raw dog meat still covered in fur, although she had eaten that ferociously and without complaint.

Mouth dry, she made her first stop at the bar. Tipping a pint glass beneath a tap of cherry lager, she filled it to the brim, warm beer sloshing over the rim of the glass and over her fingers. She sucked at the foam, then took a long draught, thirsty enough to chug it down.

Halfway down her throat, the muscles in her neck seized and she choked, spitting the beer out onto the black rubber cactus mat lining the floor behind the bar. She coughed, a fist-sized cramp twisting her gut and expelling the liquid she had swallowed. The glass fell, shattering against the bar top and sending shards everywhere.

The spilled beer had a yeasty, fruit smell—entirely ordinary, crisp and fresh, but somehow suddenly malicious. She bent toward the bar, inhaling the beer fumes and shoved away as another gagging fit took over, her nose crinkling in revulsion. Where she had once found the fruity, summery scent pleasant, she was now thoroughly repulsed and sickened.

Her cheeks and tongue felt mealy. She twisted the sink faucet and, rather than fill another glass, stuck her face in sideways, lapping at the running water. She rinsed and spat and then sucked in more water. Satisfied that there were no ill effects from this, she drank more.

Maybe the beer had gone bad, she thought, but was unable to convince herself. The beer smelled exactly as she had remembered it, smelled exactly as it should. The beer had not changed at all, and what *that* signified sent a shudder through her.

She drank more water and tried not to dwell on the implications her mental voice screamed at her. Once her thirst was quenched, she moved deeper into the restaurant, thinking about food more substantial than the abandoned bowls of peanuts and pretzels infrequently dotting the bar top.

She pushed through the swing doors and into the empty kitchen. There were containers of chopped vegetables beneath the steel prep tables, but her stomach kicked at the thought of the wilted greens and dried out, white-veined carrots that had been sitting out since, at least, the prior morning.

She pulled open the refrigerator doors, eyeing the shelves of raw steaks and ground hamburger, the pork cutlets and chicken breasts, and fillets of walleye, perch, cod, and salmon. Although not as cold as it should have been, the fridge had still kept a decent chill and the meat was cool to the touch. She licked her lips, her salivary glands tingling with the expulsion of moisture.

Her nails ripped greedily at the saran wrap covering the ground beef and she grabbed handfuls of meat, stuffing it into her face. Pink fluid gushed over her lips, down her chin, pooling between her neck and the collar of her shirt in a sticky mess. The meat was rubbery, the odor a muscly malodorous stink, but not quite rotten.

She gulped it down, finishing the tray, feeling the animal

part of whatever she was now take over and gorge its bottomless pit of a belly. A cold, disgusting lump filled the void in her stomach, a chilly burp erupting from her mouth.

Satisfied, she let the refrigerator door close on its own accord, dropping the Styrofoam tray and the pink juices it held. Wandering over to the sink, she thrust her head beneath the faucet, scrubbing her face and washing the stickiness away from her mouth and hands.

Gunshots broke the silence, and she fell to her knees, gripping the edge of the washbasin with dripping wet hands.

Men's voices rang out in between the shots, and a slight tremor ran beneath her knees. Closer, booming, explosive grunts, and the heavy pounding of hooves against cement.

Rifle shots broke against the animal noises, followed by loud shouting nearby. A man's voice yelled, "In here!" and the door slammed shut hard enough to rattle the glass.

Keeping low, she edged toward the kitchen doors and peered through the thin gap. She spotted the profile of one of the men, the gun held up with the muzzle pointing toward the ceiling. Fast-moving dark flashes rushed past the window. The man looked afraid, and kept glancing between his companion and out the window at the massive creatures thundering past, his hand worrying against the grip of his rifle.

Quietly, Lauren edged away from the swinging doors, toward the steel door on the opposite side of the kitchen. This door, she knew, would dump her out into the parking lot separating the bar from the bayside road. Once outside, she could work her way toward the opposite end of the block. The bicycle was a lost cause.

Gun in hand, she pushed open the exit, the noises growing louder as she cautiously stepped forward. She peeked around the corner, her mouth dropping open at the sight of what had so scared the two men.

Massive black-haired buffalo stampeded down the street, running as a herd toward the lake. Steam boiled from their large, flared nostrils, their grunting crashing against the air over the clamor of their footfalls. Wicked horns jutted from thick bullet-shaped heads, sheets of muscle rippling beneath their fly-ridden coats.

The kitchen door had sealed flush with the frame, the only means of entry by way of a key. No door handle, no way to open it. No way back inside.

She sidestepped her way down the building's flank, keeping herself pressed close to the brick in order to minimize her profile and, hopefully, make herself less of a target. That herd would tear her apart in an instant, and the pistol she carried would be useless against them.

Her mind struggled to piece together the discordant scene of so many buffalo trampling through downtown before seizing on the answer. There were plenty of farms out on the peninsula. They must have somehow broke free and fled down the thin rail of land, or had been driven down here by whatever hungry masses revolted against them.

Wherever they came from, she was fucked if they got any nearer. She suspected the same was true about the men inside the brewery, as well, and where there were two men, there could be more.

The overhang blocked her view of the roofs, which was okay because she knew that same obstruction would prevent anyone up top from seeing her below. If there was anyone up there, though, by the time she learned of them it would likely be too late. The fire escape winding up the rear of the antique shop was devoid of life, at least.

As she neared the ladder, the fire exit of the brewery banged open, the men tentatively stepping outside. The men met her eyes almost instantly, their eyes going wide and saucer-like.

"There!" one man said.

"I told you I smelled pussy," his companion said.

Lauren turned swiftly and ran, closing the distance between herself and the fire escape ladder, springing up to grab onto a higher rung a few feet off the ground and hauling herself up. Her legs kicked in the air searching for a rung, using her arms to climb. The men were hurrying after her, their feet striking the pavement in loud, heavy percussions.

She gained vital height over them, her ankles out of reach, and clambered onto the metal floor of the lowest level of the fire escape. She looked down in time to see one of the men drawing a bead on her with his rifle, momentarily grateful for the second man, who grabbed onto the barrel and shoved the gun off target.

"Don't shoot her, you idiot! Ward wants 'em alive!"

Sprinting up the steps to the next level, to the topmost floor of the antique shop, she caught flashes of the man slipping the rifle's strap over his shoulder. The window to the shop was stuck, and she had no time to screw around with it. She smashed the glass with the butt of her pistol, using the front sights to clear off the shards so she could slip through. A racket of clattering metal and groaning joints announced the men's ascent toward her.

The shop was dark, but there was enough daylight to see by. A stack of cardboard boxes were lined up against the nearest corner, and beside that an ornate/gaudy end table that looked as if its maker had been inspired by both the Victorian era and ancient Egypt. Atop it was a green shaded office lamp, and an oil painting of a kangaroo hanging on the wall. Small white price tags with too-high prices written in red marker dangled from the corners of everything. Junk, all of it. She began toppling as much of it she could, tossing it in front of the window, hoping to make a hazard out of all the bric-a-brac. All this garbage wouldn't stop them from getting in, but it would at least make it bit more difficult. If she was really lucky, one of them would step wrong, turn their ankle, and maybe bust their head open on the corner of a table.

When the sound of glass shattering reached up from the floor beneath her, she realized how badly she had miscalculated. She had been operating solely on adrenaline and her flight reflexes, her decision-making skills buried in the sheer need to survive, and so she had allowed herself to be trapped. The only way was down, and now they were beneath her.

Stupid, stupid, stupid.

She turned back toward the window, saw the fat, fleshy face of one of her pursuers leering at her. His wide hands gripped each side of the window frame as he levered one thick leg through, then the other, his foot rolling as it landed awkwardly on the leg of the upturned table.

"Shit!" he said, surprised and with a hint of pain. He kicked the table out from under the windowsill and she had to step back out of the way.

No sense waiting for him to get inside, she thought. The antique shop was an open loft-style floor plan. All the junk—"antiquities" was too kind of a word for the garage sale leftovers that found room here—were laid out in neat rows atop scarred card tables, old desks, beat up nightstands, and dining room tables that had gone out of style long before she'd been born. There was no good hiding spot to be had.

I guess I won't hide then, she thought.

The fat man was through the window and striding toward her. His rifle was leveled directly at her, but if his warning about somebody named Ward was right, then she figured he wouldn't shoot.

The green, glowing front sights of her pistol lined up squarely with the center of his face and he stopped and stood stock-still.

"Don't be stupid, miss," he said.

His finger hovered over the trigger of his rifle. Her finger rested on hers, already easing it back oh so slowly. He watched her, and she watched him. For a brief instant, he took his eye off the sights and she completed the trigger pull. A crater opened in his face, snapping his head back. His finger yanked the trigger, his body pulling the rifle up, shooting once into the ceiling. The loud, booming crack of the rifle jolted her and she nearly leapt out of her skin. She stepped back and her shoulders hit something solid.

Hands snaked around her mouth, pulling her off her feet, and she knew then what had distracted the fat man. His companion had come up the stairs quietly and approached her from behind. His hand was enormous, like a bear paw, and it covered her mouth and nose, the flesh of his palm plugging the gap between her lips and she inhaled his odor, a brackish, smoky stink. He pulled her head back, his other arm wrapping around her neck.

"Aw, goddamnit," he said. "You fucking bitch."

She recognized his voice as the one who had claimed to smell her, and now she smelled him all too well. His hand cupped her face so tightly the skin beneath his fingers pinched her nostrils shut. Her chin pushed against his elbow, trying to squirm between the squeezing muscles of his forearm and biceps, to escape his suffocating hand and to create enough breathing room between his other arm and her throat. She couldn't, though, and when she tried to move her foot to kick back at him, she found it stuck, his foot laced around her ankle.

Her nails scrabbled at his forearm, clawing uselessly at the fabric of his coat.

"You're coming with me now, sweetie. Don't matter how. I'll either be dragging you out of here, or you can come on your own. Up to you."

She batted at his arm, and he squeezed tighter, the world going murky around her.

Unconscious, he would be able to do anything to her. Anything. And she wouldn't be able to fight. Awake, she could at least try to resist, put up some measure of opposition no matter how small. Or so she hoped.

She stuck both arms out at her side, like a scarecrow, and forced her body to relax. He kept the squeeze on for a few more seconds, but once it was clear she had given up the fight his arm loosened.

He snatched the gun away from her. The gun she had fucking forgot she had been holding, so caught up in the terror of being choked from behind. The pistol went into his waistband and he gave her an appraising look.

"All right," he said. "Turn around. Get on your knees, keep your arms out to the side."

Oh god, she thought, revulsion sweeping through her, her stomach flipping over at the prospect of this man's intentions, raw beef churning inside her belly and threatening to heave out of her. When she failed to respond quickly enough, he stepped forward and roughly shoved her around, kicking her in the back of her legs.

"Arms out!"

She raised them to the sides and, a moment later, felt the coarseness of rope around one wrist, tight, and he was pulling her arms behind her and binding her hands together. He coiled another loop around her throat and she could feel the pull against her neck as her arms relaxed. Another piece of rope went between her lips and was tied off around the back of her head.

"Get up. Start moving."

He pushed her toward the stairs and they descended. She wondered if she could break her neck by throwing herself down the steps and save herself the agonizing humiliation she expected to follow. As if reading her mind, he took a hold of the rope between her shoulder blades and held on.

He steered her toward the front doors, then reached in front of her to turn the deadbolt before shoving her outside.

Eight other men stood in the street. Between them were three women, each trussed up like Lauren and roped together at the waist. A smattering of children—five of them, she counted—were also tied together in a line. A number of hungry eyes found Lauren, lips glistening.

"We heard shots," one of the men said.

"Bitch killed Alvis."

A quiet murmur spread among the men, but she could not make out any of the words. Not that she needed to. Not that any of what they had to say or think mattered.

She was roughly pulled over to the train of women and

tied off at the end of the line.

"All right," another man spoke up. "Let's get moving."

18

THE rope scratched and bit into Lauren's neck. If she allowed her arms to relax and her wrists to sag, the rope constricted tighter around her throat, choking her.

Nine men surrounded the train of four women, surrounding them and marching them down Front Street. Smoke lingered in the air. More pungent was the reek of the early stages of rot from the mauled animals and their savaged prey, human and animal alike.

The women were spread out more than an arm's distance from one another. Lauren figured it was to prevent them from snapping at one another, noticing that the men, too, kept themselves spaced apart. Not too far, but not too close, either. So far, all had seemed subdued and Lauren noticed that even her constant bloodlust felt quelled since being forced into the group. Yet she knew that, if given an opening, she'd put her teeth to the throat of any one of them and enjoy it.

The men kept them to a slow and steady pace. Cautious but alert, they each kept their eyes wide open and their heads turning in search of potential threats. She watched as they checked down alleys and the dark crevices between buildings, scanning upward to the windows above. How much of it was a defense against tactics they themselves had employed—attacking from the high ground or snatching women off the sidewalk from blind spots—or had borne witness to in the comets' aftermath?

Ultimately, she supposed it made little difference. She could only contend with the here and now, taking things, quite literally, one step at a time. For now, her options were severely limited—hands tied behind her, trying not to choke herself, leashed to a small caravan of bodies ahead of her, and with armed men on either side and behind her. All she could do was put one foot forward, followed by the next, and wait for her opening.

While the men were a threat, they were not an immediate danger in her mind. Clearly they wanted her alive, for whatever reason—reasons she suspected were limited either to fucking or eating—and were intent on delivering her to a man named Ward. The name was dimly familiar, but she couldn't place why. The real threats, the immediate threats, were likely the ones she couldn't yet see. She waited for the stampede of buffalo to find them, for dogs to chase after them from an alleyway, or for birds to launch an aerial assault. She kept her eyes moving, seeking out these threats, the complications and potential game changers.

Slowly, they were led into a turn down Eighth Street and she dimly realized they were heading toward City Hall, her own destination prior to her capture. There was a certain fortitudinous to this, but also an implication that unnerved her. Where was Shay? Would she even be able to find her? What if she had been captured, as well…or worse, had been killed?

No, she thought, interrupting her thoughts. *Don't go down that road.*

They shaved off a few minutes of travel time by cutting through one of the public parking lots. As they passed the drive-thru teller windows of the bank, Lauren noticed a flash of movement across the street, between an Italian restaurant and a photographer's studio. A dark streak slunk low to the ground. She could not discern any other details, and was forced to move past with the rest of the group.

Rather than warn her captors, she kept her mouth shut.

She waited, though, expecting the attack to come at any second. She kept trying to spot the creatures that would come for them, trying her damnedest to not appear nervous, nor overly alert enough to warn those around her.

After five minutes passed and no assault came, she began to relax, but only slightly. She recognized the narrow expanse of road they had been led down, and knew this street terminated outside City Hall.

One of the women ahead of her made to lunge for the corpse of a dachshund as they passed close to a smattering of canines that had appeared to have been shot. The woman behind her was dragged out of line, tripping over her own feet. Panic and excitation soon took over, along with, perhaps, a sudden mouthwatering craving for flesh and muscle. The woman directly ahead of Lauren was pulled off balance, jerking the rope along with her and forcing Lauren to stumble forward. She hit her knees hard, while the woman slammed into the ground, her head bouncing off the pavement.

The men worked to contain them, manhandling them back into place, or at least trying to.

"Get the fuck back!" one of them yelled. "Back in line!"

Several of the women shrieked, their mouths snapping at faces brought too close. Lauren let one of the men drag her back to her feet, while another attempted to corral the woman that had been in front of her.

A throaty growl broke through the commotion. The fine hairs along the back of Lauren's neck stood on end as she turned toward the noise, spotting another flash of movement beside the library, along the stretch of lawn and in the parking lot. A Rottweiler darted around the rear of a Lexus, charging forward toward them.

Lauren stopped counting after twenty dogs.

Before the animals could begin grouping, the men opened fire. The dogs moved faster than most of them could aim, and the shots went wide and high, missing by a mile. A few of the men proved to be capable marksmen, but of the nine, most were losers.

The women were equally disorganized. One darted toward the presumed safety of the library, forgetting her bondage until the ropes halted her. Two of the others lunged toward one of the men, snapping at either side of his neck and falling atop him.

In a slurry of whipping hair and blood, she saw the face of the man who had abducted her from the antique shop. Then his face was lost beneath hungry mouths, his screams inaudible beneath a frenzy of gunfire and vicious barking. As one leg uselessly kicked out, she noticed the hunting knife at his belt. There was enough play in the rope for her to turn and work the knife free of its scabbard, and she hoped she didn't accidentally slit her wrists as she began sawing at the rope.

One of the riflemen saw what was happening, saw his fallen companion and the women gorging on his throat. Saw Lauren. He clubbed her in the head with the butt of his rifle and she stumbled back, dropping the knife. She could feel the flat of the blade against her ass, the knifepoint pressing into the back of her thigh.

In attacking her, the man had taken his eyes off the immediate threat. A Rottweiler leaped onto his back, tackling him to the ground and tearing skin from the back of his neck. As the man thrashed, Lauren caught sight of the exposed knobs of vertebrae before the dog's mouth dug into the opening and attacked the chew toy of the man's spine. Bones popped between the Rottweiler's jaws as its head shook back and forth. A moment later, the man was still.

Lauren kicked her way back, rolling off the knife, and spent a frantic few seconds trying to find the blade once more. Her fingertips danced along the pavement, finding only the edges of tiny stones.

The Rottweiler's eyes were pinned on her. Bloody drool hung from its jowls, and it took a threatening stride forward. Its eyes were home to unbridled savagery and pure hatred.

Midstep, its head exploded, and its thickly muscled body collapsed onto the road with a meaty thud.

Hands hauled Lauren to her feet, and a moment later she felt the ropes fall from her wrists and neck. The shooting had intensified, and a dozen more people came rushing out from the library and onto the street. They attacked the dogs with guns and knives, and some with nothing more than fists and fury. One woman carried a brass stanchion, the kind that were set up for a line to snake through at the circulation desk, the frayed retractable belt dangling off the end. She wielded it like a club, smashing one canine's head with the heavy base. Another woman bludgeoned an animal with the spine of a thick, heavy-looking reference book.

When Lauren turned to see who had freed her, she could not help but smile.

Shay.

Beautiful Shay.

Lauren snatched up the rifle her abductor had dropped and took aim at the nearest dog, then sought her next target. Blood pounded in her ears, and a quiet rumble shook her belly. Her finger found the trigger, and she suddenly felt starved.

Men and women clashed with the beasts, rending one another with tooth and nail, knives and claws. Bullets slammed into canine skulls, leaving behind shards of bone and pulped clumps of brain and gore.

Her heart hammered in her chest, trilling at the heat of war, her blood pumping hot and fast.

When it was finished, it felt like hours had passed, but in truth the violence had resolved in mere minutes. She was left breathless and ragged, and the fog of combat cleared enough that she realized Shay was still there, beside her. They had, apparently, fought together. Shay's lips were close to hers, and slightly parted. Lauren leaned in and mouthed the words "Thank you" as they embraced and kissed each other's cheeks.

"Who did this to you?" Shay asked, gently massaging the raw rope burns around Lauren's wrists.

Lauren spotted the men that had captured her, or what was left of them, at the edges of the crowd. Their numbers had been halved, and those that remained regrouped and strode forward toward the women they had taken prisoner.

They stopped two paces away, their eyes drawn to Shay.

Lauren realized there was something different about the police officer, and that she carried a certain authority now that went far beyond a mere badge. There was a maternal air about her, a sense of strength and leadership, and the men recognized this as well, enough so that it stopped them in their tracks.

"These women were for Ward. Where is he?"

"Ward's dead," Shay said simply, offering them a half-hearted shrug. Then she took Lauren's hand and held it toward them. "You did this to her?"

"She was for Ward," he said again, as if that explained everything.

Shay nodded, and with a slight flicker of her hand the men found themselves surrounded, plainly outnumbered by the women. Looking at the assemblage of bodies, Lauren realized that the majority of Shay's group were female, with only a handful of men.

"Kill them," Shay said. "Do whatever you see fit with their remains."

Shay turned her back on the noise of screams that dissolved into moist gurgles, and the sound of wet, smacking lips and grunts of engorgement. She took Lauren's hand.

"Come."

Lauren turned to follow her into the library, leaving behind the coppery stink of recent death. Inside, she found a barely lit tomb scattered with enough remains to explain what had happened to so many of the men. Gutted corpses were splayed across the floor, purple chunks of organ meat speckling the floor.

"This is a new world, sweetie," Shay said. "This is our world now."

EPILOGUE

NINE MONTHS LATER

LAUREN watched through ice-covered windows as snow fell, glistening in the moonlight. Outside, a pure blanket of white stretched off into the distance, broken only by trees draped in snow. The scene was beatific, but the pain of a contraction wrenched her eyes away from it.

She sat on the corner of the bed, holding her engorged belly between swollen hands. Her eyes pinched shut and she tried to control her breathing. In through her nose, out through her mouth. Repeating until the cramping eased.

"You're doing so well," Shay said, encouraging her through the agony.

The contractions had been coming faster, harder, and longer.

"I'm not ready for this."

"You are," Shay said. "You can do this. You have to do this."

Lauren offered her a lopsided smile, sweeping back sweaty strands of hair and tucking them back behind her ear.

"I guess it's too late go back now, huh?"

After she had missed her period eight months ago, Lauren had found a home pregnancy test in a drugstore while on a reconnaissance run. They had been looking for other survivors, people that they could corral and bring back to the winery. A few weeks prior to the recon, Shay had decided to move the group onto the peninsula, setting up camp at one of the vineyards situated atop a hill that provided them with a panoramic view of the landscape.

The baby was Jacob's. There had been no other men since him, and the last time she had been with him, using protection had been far less important than their primal needs.

She had finally told Shay after the first trimester passed.

Several other women in their group had become pregnant in the intervening months as well. Beyond serving as a food source, reproduction had been the one other thing the men had proved adept at. The rooms of the vineyard's bed and breakfast had become a de facto live storage area, and the men, most of them lone survivors they came across in the wild or on the outskirts of town, were subdued and chained to the bedframes. They were fed as little as possible in order to conserve the camp's rations, and the women were allowed to use them as they saw fit. At least until other priorities demanded the men be dispatched.

Five months ago, they'd had four men subdued. Shay demanded that the group subsist on wildlife as much as possible and hunting parties routinely sought out game. Their hunters returned with deer more often than not, and they had been flush in venison for a good while. Over the last few months, the deer had grown scarce and they had been forced to turn toward their stockpiles.

They were down to two men now. Well, two and a half, really. Six women were pregnant, one with twins if her size was any indication.

Stock and supplies were in need of replenishment. One group of hunters was stalking the city for any signs of life, while another scouted the surrounding woods.

Lauren bent forward, screaming while Shay wrapped both arms around her. She shoved her way out of her friend's embrace, and then turned on the bed, kneeling facedown and grunting into a pillow.

How the hell am I supposed to do this?

"We can fill the bathtub with water," Shay said. "That might help."

"No," Lauren moaned, her face still buried in the pillow. Another contraction hit, twisting her insides into a fist-sized knot.

She'd kill every man, woman, and child in this inn for a simple painkiller. Or better yet, an epidural. She had heard one of the other women talking about how much of a godsend an epidural was. That sow had been pregnant twice before, and was expecting her third any week now. She didn't know which of the captive men was the father, and with only two prisoners left she joked about having a fifty-fifty shot at guessing correctly.

"We'll know once he pops out," the woman had joked. Lauren hadn't laughed then, and it seemed even less funny now.

"Motherfucker!" she screamed as another contraction seized her innards and yanked. "God motherfucking he— gaaahh!"

A part of her dreaded seeing the baby, of seeing Jacob in the baby's features. How much of a resemblance would there be? Would he have the same dusky eyes as his father, or his softly upturned nose?

"Oh, fuuuuuuuuuck!"

Another part of her reasoned that it did not matter, and she was able to close the door on that line of thought. The child could be Jacob's perfect little twin, and it would not change a thing. It did not matter what he, or she, looked like.

The pain of labor was immense, and all she could do was deal with it. There was simply no other choice. She knelt there, her elbows and knees bearing the brunt of her weight, her bare ass sticking up in the air, screaming into her pillow and—after the pain grew so intense she flung the pillow aside—into the mattress.

"You're crowning," Shay shouted over her screams.

"You need to roll over."

"It fucking hurts, goddamnit!"

"You're doing great."

"Fuck you!"

Shay helped her roll over, moved her to the end of the bed, and spread her legs for her.

No painkillers, no doctors. In this room, only her and Shay. Earlier, when the contractions had first started, she had made light of their initially innocuous pings for attention, and joked about how she was doing this delivery old school. The way women did it way back when, before hospitals, before medicine was even a thing. Shay had squeezed her hand and told her, with the pride of a mother, "You've got this." Lauren had nodded, believing that she really, truly did have this.

She had been good and fucking truly wrong. She had been so fucking delusional she would laugh at her earlier self right now if it did not hurt so goddamned much.

"Breathe!" Shay demanded.

Lauren's next scream was belly deep, a primitive and vulgar sound, the pain drawing her torso up. The bed sheet was drenched in her sweat, her whole face slick. She pushed as hard and for as long as she could before collapsing backward.

"That's it, that's it," Shay said excitedly. "Keep pushing, sweetheart!"

Lauren did, the pain increasing even further. She could

feel the muscles stretching painfully inside her as this child forced its way through. Her screams raised a notch as she felt her skin tear, the baby's head prompting a burning sensation in her core, just one more misery to add to the growing catalog of pain she was experiencing.

"Keep going. You're almost there. You're almost there."

Shay's words made zero sense to her. She could barely even hear the woman over the throbbing, hammering drumbeat of her pulse in her skull. She pushed, and a pressure built inside her and then released in a gushing spasm, barely cognizant of the fact that she had just shit the bed. That aching, burning pain grew as her coccyx cracked and her perineum unzipped, and a small human being pushed through her birth canal, cutting her in half like a split log.

She screamed, delirious with pain, and fell back, weary and sore. She felt like she had run a marathon. The longest, most exhausting marathon ever. Her muscles ached right down to the bone, and she shook uncontrollably. It was over. It was over.

The baby screamed, and she caught a glimpse of the child cradled against Shay's chest, the flap of an arm and the turn of a blood-streaked face.

"Oh my god," Lauren said. She could not help but smile, even as her head sank deeper into the thin mattress.

"Oh god."

"I need to get him cleaned up."

Lauren nodded, practically feeling the glow of afterbirth. She was golden. So gold even that the pain was forgotten.

She turned her attention back to the window, to the still-falling snow and the idyllic scene of pure whiteness. She listened to Shay's steps as the woman padded toward the bedroom door and into the hallway beyond.

"Shay!"

A moment later, the woman returned and stood in the doorway, still cradling the screaming infant. She raised an eyebrow curiously.

It did not need saying, maybe, but Lauren felt she had to anyway. Just to be sure. Just so her friend knew.

"Save me a piece."

Shay smiled and nodded. She turned without another word, back into the hallway and to the stairs that descended to the inn's kitchen.

She watched the snowfall for a bit, until fatigue overtook her and her body forced her eyes closed. She needed to rest. Shay would send somebody in to stitch her back together soon enough, but in her exhaustion, Lauren failed to care. She was tired. Beyond tired.

Her baby's cries echoed through the house, and then ended abruptly.

Her eyes fluttered open briefly at the sudden silence, before falling shut once more. Her mouth watered. Yes, she was tired, but she was also hungry. With this last thought, her stomach growled.

A NOTE TO READERS

Thank you for choosing to read my work – it is greatly appreciated and I hope you enjoyed the journey.

If you be willing to spare a minute or two, please leave a brief review of this work and let other readers know what you thought. Reviews are incredibly helpful, particularly for an independent author and publisher such as myself, and can help determine the success of a novel. Reviews do not need to be long – twenty words or so should suffice – but their impact can be enormous.

I look forward to your thoughts, and thank you, once again, for taking the time to read this story.

If you would like to know about upcoming releases, I encourage you to subscribe to my newsletter at http://michaelpatrickhicks.com.

And if you enjoyed this book, please consider joining me on Patreon, where readers receive copies of all my stories and novels every month. Patreon members get all of my work first, before anyone else. For more information, visit: http://www.patreon.com/michaelpatrickhicks

ACKNOWLEDGEMENTS

First and foremost, I must thank my wife for her unending support. Being a writer is so often a solitary profession, and inspiration strikes unannounced, sometimes requiring me to drop everything to jot a note into my phone, or embarking on a long and arduous research trek through Google and the unending web. She puts up with all of it, and that speaks volumes.

Thanks, also, are owed to my fans for their unwavering support. The generosity shown by readers like Kate Martyniouk and KC Santo, as well all of my other wonderful Patreon supporters, help make my work possible with their monthly pledges.

I also owe a great bit of thanks to Stephanie Embry, who beta read this book. Her encouragement and suggestions helped shape this novel at a crucial moment, and her insights were invaluable.

Shay VanZwoll, owner and operator of EV Proofreading, edited this manuscript and cleaned up an awful lot of my errors. Any mistakes that remain are entirely my fault, I assure you!

Making this entire endeavor look absolutely superb is Kealan Patrick Burke, whose beautiful cover art graces this book. In addition to being an awesome artist, Kealan is also a Bram Stoker Award winning horror author, and he's funny as hell to boot. The man is an extraordinarily over-gifted threat to us all. Still, I encourage you to check out his books. *Sour Candy* is a personal favorite and was my first introduction to both his literary chops and his graphic design skills. If you haven't read his work yet, that novella is a mighty fine place to start.

Finally, many, many thanks to you for reading my work. I hope we meet again soon.

ABOUT THE AUTHOR

Michael Patrick Hicks is the author of the science fiction novels *Convergence*, an Amazon Breakthrough Novel Award 2013 Quarter-Finalist, and its sequel, *Emergence*, as well as several horror titles.

His work has appeared in several anthologies, and he has written for the websites Graphic Novel Reporter and Audiobook Reviewer, in addition to work as a freelance journalist.

In between compulsively buying books and adding titles that he does not have time for to his Netflix queue, he is hard at work on his next story.

Website: http://michaelpatrickhicks.com
E-Mail: mphicks@michaelpatrickhicks.com

BONUS STORY

CONSUMPTION

MICHAEL PATRICK HICKS

<h1 style="text-align:center">About Consumption</h1>

You Are

Reclusive chef Heinrich Schauer has invited six guests to a blind twelve-course tasting menu.

What You Eat

While snow blankets the isolated Swiss valley surrounding his estate, the guests feast eagerly, challenging one another to guess at the secret tastes plated before them.

This Meat Is Murder

As they eat, each guest is overtaken by carnal appetites, unaware of their host's savage plans...or of the creature lurking below.

One thing is clear: There is more on the menu than any of them have bargained for.

1

HEINRICH SCHAUER DREW THE blade across the smooth, silky flesh, his face set with concentration. His eyes were narrowed in focus as the knife's tip found thick bone, slicing down at an angle and then across, separating the soft tissue. His fingers pressed into the fatty outer layer, holding the meat still, as his blade sliced with surety and carved free a long strip of meat.

Marveling at the ugly creature lying prone before him, Schauer promised that not a bit of it would go to waste. He had a generous menu planned, the courses incomparable to anything he had ever created.

Setting the meat aside, he turned his attention to the network of tentacles along the beast's flanks. They, too, were smooth, unlike those of, say, an octopus. While it lacked suckers, the heavy musculature was striated into narrow but pronounced gills. Moving away from the base, the flesh tapered to a jagged point, the thick tentacles ending in a jagged, vicious array of stingers.

Again, the knife bit in, piercing the hide and releasing a milky fluid as he separated the stingers from each long appendage. When he was finished, twelve evenly cut stingers stood atop the counter, their gray skin glistening beneath the white lights. While he doubted their digestibility, the stingers would make for a rather dramatic element in the main course's plating.

He took stock of the rest of the monstrosity, formulating plans for each of the evening's dishes, giving new weight to his previously fluid ideas.

The creature was fatty, but well-muscled. Its meat would be nicely marbled, and the back fat would be excellent for pan-frying. Tentacles lent themselves to numerous methods of preparation, and he immediately found himself mentally flicking through dozens of recipes: battered and fried, stewed with saffron and smoked paprika, or perhaps a preparation more classically Asian, with coconut milk and ginger, or stir-fried with scallions and ginger. He smiled as he struck upon the ideal recipe, one that he had always found to be charming with squid. The recipe would work rather nicely, and even provide a bit of levity as the meal got underway.

Yes, that was it, then. Hors d'oeuvres of deviled…devil? He smiled tightly at the small bit of humor as he wiped his hands clean on a dishtowel.

He prepared the broiler and oven, his ingredients neatly arranged, ready to begin.

2

EACH OF THE SIX had received a plain white envelope in the mail, bearing only their name and address, with no return address shown. Each envelope had been sent locally and bore their town's own postmark, with a pre-paid postage rate printed upon it in local currency. Inside, a three-by-four cream cardstock, the typeface simple and unadorned, providing the barest, most pertinent information.

Chef Heinrich Schauer Invites
You To a Twelve-Course Tasting Meal
On the Appointed Date and Time:
Sunday, January 8 @ 8PM
46.559° N, 8.561° E

The guests arrived separately at a Swiss manor situated in a vibrant green field near Lago di San Carlo in the Leventina Valley. To reach the lakeside estate, each of them had navigated through the winding roads of the Gotthard Pass and the Devil's Bridge, named so due to the hazardous River Reuss, which quickly flooded with the spring rains and snow melt from the surrounding Lepontine Alps and led to many drownings between April and May.

Legend said that a Swiss herdsman had found the Reuss so difficult to pass that he wished the devil would build a bridge. The devil agreed, but only in exchange for the soul of the first to cross. The herdsman agreed and sent across one of his goats. This trickery angered the devil, and he drew forth a rock to smash the bridge. Before he could collapse the structure, an old woman drew a cross on the massive stone, preventing the devil from lifting it.

Now, gathered around a great oak dining table, the six sat in silence beneath dimmed, golden light cast from an ornate – bordering on repulsively gaudy – chandelier. In keeping with the evening's dinner theme, each guest had been issued a unique demon's masquerade mask.

One woman wore a red ochre mask with square eyeholes and horn-like hooks on either side that reached down across her cheekbones and, at the top, roped off into a half-dozen points. Another, worn by a male, was the more traditional horned devil disguise.

The third, another woman, wore a leather devil jester mask, while the fourth was adorned by a golden mask with red glittery accents and fat, black, downward-curving tusks.

The fifth's was an odd, earthy bit of macabre: a wooden mask, covered in a shiny black lacquer. The left eye was a smooth triangular cut, whereas the right was more irregular, uneven, lending weight to the shifting imbalance inherent in the mask itself. Above where his left eyebrow would be, the wood was raised into pointy shards. As those rough-hewn bits migrated to the right, the wood roughened further, taking on the appearance of black bark. The bark gave way to raven feathers and thin, stiff roots, and – if one examined it closely, where the bark curved up across his forehead – there, hidden in the coarse folds, was the keen black shine of a raven's eye. On the lower half of the mask, above his lips, were white ornaments that upon closer inspection appeared to be sliced teeth.

The sixth mask was pure white, with giant horns that coiled up, over, and around that man's head, as if he had been fitted with a ram's skull.

A fire warmed the dining room, the occasional loud pop of an exploding knot echoing across the cathedral ceiling. That, and snifters of brandy and glasses of warm, mulled red wine, helped to warm their bones. Silently, they sipped, watching the snow fall beyond the window. Soot-colored sky had given way to inky darkness, the moon hidden by a thick screen of clouds. The wind howled, sending a curlicue of white powder past, the temperature quickly dropping into single digits.

Occasionally, a few of the guests made eye contact and nodded politely, their lips creasing into thin imitations of a smile, but none attempted to raise a conversation or make small talk. Strangers to each other, their faces largely hidden and with only their mouths exposed, several enjoyed the anonymity and escape from the usual. What little could be seen in their eyes made one thing plain – all were outcasts.

A waitress, dressed in a black button-down shirt, a black vest, and black slacks, her face hidden behind a sheer black widow's veil, a raven tricorn mourning hat perched atop her head, circulated around the table, refilling their glasses.

Standing at the head of the table, she said, "If I may have your attention. Thank you. Your first course will be deviled tentacle. The meat was rubbed with a mixture made of Dijon mustard and Worcestershire sauce, coated in bread crumbs and olive oil, and then broiled to perfection.

"Chef Schauer welcomes you with the utmost warmest regards, and hopes that you will enjoy the evening. Your dishes will be ready soon."

Finished, she nodded politely and then presented a crisp turn as she took her exit. The diners nodded expectantly, mouths already watering.

One, the man in the ram's horn, raised an eyebrow, leaning into the group conspiratorially. "Squid?"

The woman seated across from him, wearing the red

ochre mask whose arrangement of horns and hooks made it resemble melting wax, tilted her head, her lips turning downward in thought. "Could be octopus."

"Mmm," he said appreciatively. He recalled a dish of *jjukkumi gui* garnished with cucumber that he'd eaten in Singapore. The baby octopus had been marinated in soy sauce, red chili pepper paste, rice wine, sugar, garlic, ginger, and sesame oil. "Guess we'll soon see."

She returned his smile, the muscles in her face more relaxed this time. Not the prudish affectation of a thin-lipped smile he had received earlier. This one was warmer, and as she sipped her brandy, her face growing warmer, her eyes steadily made more contact with his. When he blushed, she laughed at him, a pleasant sound.

Moments later, small, square white dishes were laid before each diner. The tentacles had been sliced into inch-thick circles of meat, the breading a perfect honey brown, as promised by their waitress. Chopped chives garnished the plate, giving the meal a warm, earthy color.

After she finished chewing, the second woman spoke. "This is…" she began, but paused to seek out the right word.

"Strange," the woman in the melting wax mask said.

"Strange, definitely, but delicious."

"It's not octopus," Ram's Horn said.

"Not squid, either," one of the other men said.

Ram's Horn stabbed at another piece of meat, chewing it slowly. The breading and tentacle separated in his mouth, and he let the pulped flesh rest against his tongue, studying the flavors.

He could pick up the sour-sweet Dijon and the tang of Worcestershire, but beneath that was an odd heated-earth flavor. A certain sour note, an almost dusty taste, but not quite the flavor of mold. Not any type of blue cheese, he was sure. Still, he couldn't quite place it, even as an acidic, peppery taste lingered at the back of his throat.

"I'm stumped," he said.

His dining companions agreed, yet despite the peculiar profile of the starting dish, they found it compulsively intriguing and pressed on.

Chef Schauer was known for his eccentricities in the kitchen. He enjoyed surprising his guests with odd combinations, typically keeping the main ingredient a secret from them until after the final dish had been served.

Schauer had a stable of guests that he enjoyed feeding and sampling recipes on. He was rather proud that no two diners had ever shared a meal, constantly rotating his invitations and ensuring their anonymity. While he could not prevent a bit of table talk, guests were discouraged from speaking too openly of themselves or their affairs. The sole focus, they all knew, was the meal.

As with many of his previous tasting meals, Schauer centered the affair with certain macabre fetishes. Food, he believed, was a celebration of death. Eating was a morbid affair, albeit an ultimately enjoyable one. Meals gave sustenance to the eater, but at the expense of another organism's life. Every dish was a complicit act of murder, regardless of whether or not one's personal view of morality and politics allowed them to view it as such.

Schauer, however, was cognizant of the inherently vicious and violent nature of the cycle of life. He demanded a respectful mourning of that passing, a funereal elegance to the act of consumption.

"That was very good, thank you," the man in the wooden mask said. The waitress gave a small nod as she collected his plate. His eyes followed her as she walked their plates back to the kitchen.

Although none of them knew each other, they had each been invited to previous meals by Schauer in the past. Each time, the location and their company had been different, and while none of them had ever been to this particular property before, a relaxed repose settled across the table. Small talk had begun, food and drinks had been had, and their guards were dropping, slightly.

No one asked after anyone's business, nor did any of them trade information or volunteer details of their lives. Instead, they took turns guessing at what the meat in their first dish had been.

"I don't think it was tentacle at all," the woman in the leather mask said. "I'm Irene, by the way." She did not offer her last name, as that would have been a violation of house rules.

"Noel," Ram's Horn said. "I don't know what that was. I know what it wasn't."

"I'm ruling out any sort of cephalopod. Coraline." She scratched at her cheek, her slender fingers reaching beneath the lines of melting wax.

"A mushroom of some sort? The dish reminded me a bit of chanterelles. And, yeah, I'm Laura." She gave a small wave, then readjusted her mask by grasping the downward-curving tusks.

"Joseph," said the man wearing the standard devil horn's masquerade mask. He clicked his tongue against his upper palate. "And I'm ruling out mushrooms."

"Hi, all. Name's Peter. I don't know what the fuck that was, but I enjoyed it."

"Impeccable," Irene said, turning her head to meet Peter's eyes. He gave her a perfunctory smile, which she quickly dismissed.

"What do you think, Coraline?" Noel asked. "What was it?"

She shrugged her shoulders, shaking her head side to side. "The meat was smooth, no suckers on it, so, definitely not octopus. And I agree, it definitely wasn't mushrooms, although the texture seemed somewhat similar. The flavor was earthy, and the meat was chewy." She puffed her cheeks out, at a loss. "I just don't know."

"We have eleven more dishes to figure it out," Joseph said, a wicked grin plastering his face.

In short order, six bowls of consommé were served. The broth was a luxuriant brown, and a single toasted sesame cracker floated in the center, a sprinkle of grated cheese encircling it.

"Gruyere," Peter said.

"But the broth. I'm getting that same earthy taste. Musky, almost."

"Ashes," Noel said.

The five other diners held the broth in their mouth, their eyes considering.

"Not vegetable ash," Joseph said, taking another spoonful.

"Now that you mention it, it does have an almost sulfurous taste. I can't pinpoint it."

"This is going to drive me nuts," Peter said, his soup nearly gone.

3

A SHARP CRACKLING NOISE filled the kitchen as raw skin hit hot grease and snapped away from the heat. Schauer had taken a strip of back fat off the beast and melted it into a dirty-blonde puddle in a large cast-iron pan. The odor was strong and dangerous, and he inhaled deeply, absorbing the scent of fish, salt, and fat.

In the pot, potatoes boiled, nearly done.

After turning the fish, he began spooning the liquid fat across the pink surface of the salmon. He hummed quietly, completely focused on the task at hand.

Behind him, the creature stirred, a shallow moan burning from its throat. Arms bound to both its sides and the table, torso split wide from chest to waist, it writhed in pain.

In his early studies of the beast, Schauer had found that stress positively impacted the taste of the meat. As such, he deemed it vital to keep the creature alive for as long as possible. In most instances, stress prior to slaughter increased the amount of glycogen and acidity in the meat, making it less tender, less flavorful. Schauer was surprised to find the opposite reaction in the grisly being strapped and splayed across the island counter. Surprised, and overjoyed.

He dumped the water and set the potatoes aside. Although he tended to serve boiled potatoes with boiled fish – not pan fried – he was feeling whimsical. A potato scoop would fashion the meat into small, perfectly round balls. Served with this would be cucumbers dressed with oil and vinegar, a slight callback to Noel's Singapore supper, which he knew the man would appreciate.

Turning to the beast, he ran his hand across the creature's skull, his palm coming away slick. The monster was feverishly hot, no doubt a side effect of Schauer's grueling excavations. He was sure that the beast would be howling if Schauer had not had the foresight to sever its vocal cords. No shared language existed between them, of course, save for the excruciating roars of pain and misery that were common to all.

4

"OH MY GOD, THEY'RE so cute," Laura said. Her blonde head bounced happily as she rolled one of the balled potatoes with her fork. "Sorry, I'm easily amused."

"OK, that's definitely salmon."

"I'm getting ashes, again."

"Yeah, but it's more savory than that. Pork fat, maybe?"

"It does sort of have a bacony component," Joseph said.

"I'm down for anything plus bacon," Peter said.

"That's not surprising," Irene said.

Peter glanced down at his sizeable belly, suddenly self-conscious, his sausage-sized fingers wrapped around the stem of his fork. "What the hell's that supposed to mean?"

Irene blanched, suddenly aware of what she'd said, too late. She stammered, suddenly feeling the alcohol daze. "No, I just mean, you sound like you're from Texas. Isn't everything all about bacon there?"

"We're not supposed to talk about where we're from," Noel said.

"I'm sorry," Irene said, meeting Peter's heated gaze. "Really, I didn't mean anything by it."

Peter was fit to burst, his face burning hot red. He couldn't contain it.

He exploded with laughter, a hearty, gusting noise, his

eyes watering.

Irene suddenly appeared more disgusted than bashful. "You jerk."

"I'm sorry, really. I couldn't help it. You looked so fucking earnest. I just…oh, man. Wow. I had you, huh?"

Irene rolled her eyes, her disgust blunted behind the mask. Then she let out a small smirk, a small chuckle. "You did," she said, stabbing at the fish.

She tried not to laugh, but couldn't help it. Peter was still roaring, infecting the others, until Irene, too, was sucked into the sudden honest joy, laughing until her eyes watered.

5

THE SPOON PROBED THE creature's eye socket, its tip forcing its way into the hollow cavity. The gelatinous membrane folded beneath the metal curvature of the utensil, yielding but not breaking. The creature, its head tied down to the edge of the countertop, writhed in panic and pain, mouth contorting. The spoon eased around the top curve of its eye and across the sides and down the bottom with a slippery squelch, as if Schauer were carving a grapefruit.

He pressed the spoon further down, the metal cupping the underside of the creature's eye as he pushed down on the fulcrum. The eyeball popped loose with a wet burp and a splash of tears running in a rapid current down the side of the creature's skull, flowing in all directions.

A rope of optic nerve came with it, and Schauer had to wonder at how fucked up the beast's visual receptors were at having one of its six eyeballs dislocated and freed from its stationary orbit.

He held the spoon at waist level, a good few inches of optic nerve pulled taut, and took a pair of scissors to the cord. The nerve bundle was tough and he had to press hard several times, rocking the scissors back and forth, sawing through the nerve until it finally snapped.

He spooned the eyeball into an ice cube tray, very carefully. He didn't want to drop the eye or upset its delicate stability. While not as fragile as egg yolk, he treated it as if it were.

Knowing what to expect, he was able to free the five remaining eyes with ease.

6

AS THE GRANDFATHER CLOCK in the foyer struck nine, the waitress promptly presented the plated entrees.

"Before you: a four ounce filet and a cucurbita medley roasted in orange butter."

"Cucurbita?" Laura asked.

"Gourds," Noel answered. He pointed his fork at each cube: "Pumpkin, squash, zucchini."

"Ah, OK. Thanks."

"Ashes, again," Irene said.

"I don't think it's ashes," Joseph replied. "I'm starting to think this meat has a natural sooty flavor."

"Unless Schauer accidentally burnt everything or is just fucking with us."

"I don't think so, Irene. Joe may be on to something."

"Joseph."

"Apologies," Peter said. "Anyway, I concur. It's not ashes."

Noel lifted the filet with his fork and examined the underside. The meat was cut to squared perfection, the size and shape of a deck of cards. Visually, it was unlike anything he'd seen before. Not a white meat, like pork or chicken, but a sickly gray. It had been grilled, and the exterior bore perfect crosshatching, but as he cut into it the tender meat oozed a faint, milky juice, revealing an ugly, bruised center.

True to Schauer's habits, the meat was grilled to medium rare, but, oddly, it lacked any sort of pink coloring. More to the point, Joseph couldn't think of any animal that exhibited such characteristics. He just hoped it was cooked through enough to kill any parasites or bacteria. The last thing he wanted was a case of trichinellosis or brucellosis. Not that he thought Schauer was capable of making such an amateurish mistake. No, more likely it was bit of trickery by way of molecular gastronomy.

"You think he added food coloring?" he asked, noting how intently Noel was studying his food.

"He does enjoy a culinary sleight-of-hand now and then, but this is above and beyond."

"I feel compelled to eat, but a part of me can't get over the strangeness. The taste, and now the appearance, it's all somehow…*off*. I can't think of a better way to explain it," Joseph said, pushing aside thoughts of E. coli and tapeworm and salmonella.

"Me neither," Coraline said, cutting off small piece of filet and running it through the orange butter. The acid cut through the nutty bitterness of the meat nicely.

She chewed slowly, unable to take her eyes off Noel. His hands were strong, but untarnished by hard labor. Short nails, clean. A faint network of scars topped the knuckles of his left hand, and she wondered, briefly, how his flesh would taste against her lips. She felt a sudden desire to suckle the inside of his elbow, to nibble his shoulder and the side of his long neck before taking a plump ear lobe into her mouth, his hands roaming across her body, strong fingers gripping her thighs.

"Are you OK?" he asked her.

"Oh, yes, I'm good."

"You're staring."

"Lost in thought, I suppose."

"Good food can do that," he said.

"It awakens the senses," Joseph added.

She turned to him, mustering up a plastic smile, wanting nothing more than to stab her fork into Joseph's face, over and over. She could imagine the tines piercing his cheeks, ripping the silverware free in a spray of gore, and then hammering it back into his head, his plasma hot and sticky as it splashed across her, his screams drowning the world as he writhed to escape. He couldn't flee, though. She had her free hand wrapped in his hair, her knees squeezing into his hips, and she was stabbing him again, and again, and again.

She forced herself to turn away, afraid that he would register the homicidal intent in her eyes. Noel was as much of a no-go. She stared at her plate, forcing herself to consume even though eating was now the last thing on her mind.

7

FOR THE FIFTH DISH, Schauer planned to serve small, delectable *hachis Parmentier*, arranged in a beautiful, flowery presentation, as if he were serving each guest a corsage.

Standing over the beast, he was absorbed by the creature's inelegant beauty, bordering on pure ugliness. With the spidery arrangement of eyes removed and set into the blast chiller, the head was bifurcated with gory holes.

The cranium was an odd construct, dissimilar from anything he had seen previously and yet strangely recognizable. The skull was warped into multiple layers and planes of bones, an almost hexagonal configuration that was disorienting to study. The dense plates of bone curved and folded back over upon themselves, creating a multistory maze of patchwork lattice.

Its mouth was a brutal affair, hidden behind multiple tusks, some of which reached up across the front of its face while others curved below the reaches of its soft chin. The sharp bones reminded Schauer of a spelunking expedition he had once been on, and he marveled now at the familiarity of stalactites and stalagmites that breached this being's head.

Beneath the gore-stained protrusions was a smeary hole

and a thick plank of forked muscle. A tongue. Getting to it required him to saw through the tusks, and throughout the procedure the beast grunted and undulated beneath the heavy leather straps, its muscles straining.

Removing the cage of bone, he got his first good look at the unadorned mouth. His first thought was of a parasite – a disc-shaped funnel filled with pointed teeth, similar to a lamprey, built for sucking. Yet it possessed a jaw and thick musculature and very long, frighteningly prominent incisors built for tearing and rending.

The bone cage was set to the side, near the severed stingers he had removed prior to butchering the tentacles, a plating design crystalizing in his mind's eye.

He drew a paring knife across the creature's cheeks, its milky blood streaming as the meat was peeled away and set aside atop a sheet of brown butcher's paper.

With the heavier chef's knife, he focused on the creature's abdomen, carving free a thick brisket. After loosening the straps enough to turn the beast over, then retightening and securing it in place, he turned his attention toward the meaty shoulders and butchered a shapely chuck. From the lower back, he removed a sirloin cut.

He took the brisket, chuck, and sirloin and placed them in the blast chiller. Turning his attention back to the creature, he carved away at its ribs and around the curve of its back. He set the rib eye roast aside on another sheet of butcher's paper, and began trimming meat away from the bone, cutting it into a tomahawk steak. This he seasoned with rosemary, thyme, and mint.

Finished, he sat atop a bar stool and poured a glass of white wine. His forehead was slightly glazed with sweat, his once-white chef's coat messed with fresh spatter. He needed a small rest. He sipped and waited, counting down the minutes in his head until the appointed time arrived to remove the meat from the blast chiller. Meat ground better when partially frozen, as the grinding process generated heat. Heat melts fat, and he could not abide losing any of the succulent flavor and juices, or risk making the meat mealy.

One by one, he fed the cuts through a grinder. Working his fingers through the ground mixture to combine them, he was careful not to overwork the meat, for that would make it tough.

He took a good amount of the bluish-gray matter and sautéed it until the color was even and cooked through. While that was cooking, he mashed the baked potato and set the skins aside. When the meat was done, he stirred in the potato mash and poured sauce lyonnaise over it, a compound of the white wine he had opened, and vinegar and onions. He mixed it well, then spooned the mixture into the potato skins he had shaped into cups.

The cheeks were warmed through in a pan with butter and a red wine reduction, thyme, and rosemary. He finished the small cuts with a dash of black peppercorn and Mediterranean Sea salt.

He arranged the cheeks and *hachis Parmentier* on a long wooden board, separating the individual portions with the tusks, cleaned and arranged in a standing crosshatch formation, as if it were a perverse sort of rib cage. Of course, the display stood in mimicry of the creature's mouth, an ode to the cheeks, which he knew would be succulent and tender, perhaps even the best cut from this…*thing*. Schauer was a cheek man. Fish cheeks or beef cheeks were one of his specialties, and always lent themselves toward terrific dishes overflowing with flavor.

This would be no exception.

8

"TUSKS!" LAUREN SAID, SURPRISED and delighted. Childish wonder filled her eyes as the serving board was laid between her and the other guests. She dug in her purse, removing an iPhone.

"Anyone mind?" she asked, waving the phone toward the meal. Before anyone replied, she was already swiping the screen to camera mode. The display told her she had no service, but she thought nothing of it. Schauer was famous for interrupting cellular service during his tastings, wanting his guests to focus solely on the food and texture and tastes, and not on social media or phone calls or the silly apps that occupied much of their daily lives.

"Ah, you're one of those," Joseph said, good-naturedly. When no one else objected, he too began taking photos with his phone.

"One of what?" Lauren asked, clueless.

"A voyeur," Peter said.

"When it comes to food, we're all voyeurs," Noel said.

In her mind's eye, with each click of the shutter, Lauren was already picking out in-app filters, Diptic arrangements, and calculating the number of immediate 'Likes' the image would win her. A cold blue filter, maybe, hash tag foodporn.

"Elephant?" Irene asked, a slice of cheek aloft on the tines of her fork, her gaze naturally turning toward Noel.

"No," he said immediately. "Elephant meat is a very dark red, and it's very lean. Not nearly as fatty as the dishes we've been served. It's also quite a bit more gamey, sort of like elk."

"He could be using pork fat. It's certainly tasty enough," Peter suggested.

"I think it's seal," Coraline said.

Joseph shook his head. "Seal meat's pretty dark, too. And sort of fishy tasting. It's definitely got the fat component, though."

"What else has tusks?" Lauren asked.

"Hippos," Peter said.

"Hippo meat's purple," Irene said. All eyes turned to her. "What?"

"Hippos are endangered," Laura said. "And besides, hippos don't have tusks."

"They do," Peter said. "Their incisors are ivory. Big, too, but not as big as these."

A small lull settled over them, as they thought about what the meat was. Eventually, their eyes migrated toward Noel.

"I've never had hippo," he said with a shrug.

9

NORMALLY SCHAUER BLANCHED AT food photography during a meal, and found it obscene. Watching his guests on the monitor, the video feed piped in from a closed-circuit camera in the chandelier over the dining table, he found himself surprisingly pleased. The photos would never make their way into the world, but the obvious admiration of his efforts buoyed his spirits. The snapshots, perhaps, were their way of memorializing the food, and in effect, the creature itself.

He abhorred social media and the instant documentation of one's life without any pause for reflection. After one gentlemen – Frederick Hansworth – took to Twitter to broadcast his location and alternately praised and condemned Schauer's dishes based on some backwards system of rating that only Hansworth truly understood, Schauer had been forced to install cellular signal dampeners. He hated the false publicity those damned tweets and fucking status updates brought his dinners as they made weak-kneed efforts at capturing his glow within their own pathetic radius, as if they were somehow equal to him. Or, worse still, that he was somehow subservient to them.

Hansworth! Fucking Hansworth.

The name stabbed at his brain, an invective vulgarity.

The first and last time he had ever allowed the man into his private domain; afterwards, he had banned the oaf from his restaurants worldwide.

Of course, he had kept tabs on Hansworth. At this very moment, if he so chose, he could learn the location of Hansworth in a heartbeat. Enough time had passed, the dust settled, that anyone who proposed a correlation between Hansworth's disappearance and Schauer's rage would be seen as a mad conspirator, or tabloid gossiper.

Temptation lingered, though, and Schauer's mind turned toward formulating a tasting meal around long pig, his long-simmering hatred for vile Hansworth returning.

He forced the thoughts away. Now was not the time to have tonight's vision clouded by such pettiness. Besides, Hansworth would not be long for this world, with or without Schauer's direct intervention. He took some solace in that, at least, and it sent a small ripple of pleasure through his core.

10

"GOD, I'M GETTING STUFFED," Irene said, patting her prominent belly.

"Only seven more courses to go," Peter said, a wide, wicked grin spreading across his face. He seemed to take great joy in Irene's dramatic eye-rolling.

"No time to cop out on us," Noel said.

He had spent several days consuming an enormous amount of water to stretch his stomach and limited his food intake to a few low-calorie dishes. His wife thought he'd gone vegetarian based on the number of salads and celery stalks he'd eaten.

His lie was only slightly less than the truth: telling her he would be dining with multiple potential business partners in Asia and that they enjoyed their large, multi-course meals. Copping out early would be a sign of weakness. She'd grudgingly accepted the excuse. On the drive here, he'd removed his wedding band and tucked it into the pocket of his sport coat, disconnecting himself from that life in accordance to Schauer's demands of complete anonymity. Ditching the ring felt good, and he allowed himself to slip into the role of some other, better version of himself.

Unfortunately, all that water had expanded more than just his stomach. "If you'll excuse me," he said, pushing his chair away.

The waitress approached as he was halfway out of the dining room, asking him if he needed any assistance and then providing him with detailed directions to the bathroom. The interior of the manor was expansive, and appeared far larger once inside than it had from outside.

Clearly Schauer had not inhabited the manor for long, and seemed to have little intention of staying. As he wound his way through the long stretches of corridor, he peeked inside the rooms he passed and noted that the pieces of furniture in the dining room, sitting room, and foyer were the only ones not covered in white drop sheets.

The noisy clacking of high heels stamping against the wooden floor drew his attention. Turning, he watched Coraline approach. Her figure was even more gracious than he had surmised. She appeared pleasant enough while sitting across from him and largely hidden by the massive slab of oak as they dined. But standing, her long, toned legs stretching the hem of her svelte black dress as she strode toward him…she was magnificent. While he'd certainly noticed her finely-muscled arms and long, elegant neck, and a rather eye-catching bust line, he hadn't realized until now how incredible her figure really was.

"The waitress said the bathrooms were this way," she said, slipping up beside him with an endearing amount of familiarity.

It took him a moment to remember how to form words, the shape of them clumsy in his mouth. He managed to creak out a, "Right. Yeah," before mentally kicking himself.

She smiled, her brilliant teeth shining in the dim accent lighting. Somehow – neither of them was quite sure how – their hands found one another as they slowly walked to the corridor's end.

By the time they reached the bathroom door, a heat had generated between them, and Noel's concerns for his bladder were replaced with a sudden impulse and an utter lack of control.

He pulled her to him, finding her lips with his own, his hands urgently exploring and taking note of the garments beneath her dress. Fingers roamed over a thin line of fabric across her hips, tracing along the warm skin beneath, neatly plucking at the thread and mentally cataloging it as a thong.

Coraline could hardly believe what was happening, but she lost herself to the sudden rapture. Her earlier fantasies crumbled under this new reality as she reached between his legs and cupped him through his slacks, measuring his hardness. A throaty purr escaped her as he gasped in her ear, and she twisted her mouth away from his, finding his neck. She could feel his plasma coursing through the thick cord of subtle blue beneath his flesh as she sucked and licked, wending her way down to the crook of his shoulder, lapping at the hollow of his collarbone as his buttons pulled away.

She was intensely aware of the hand pressing between her legs, reaching fingers brushing at the smooth hint of cotton that covered her mound, tugging the cloth to the side. She moaned, "Yes," encouraging him deeper, her hips rocking against his palm as she rode his strong fingers.

"I've been thinking of this all through dinner," she whispered, tasting the salt of his skin against her lips.

She nuzzled back up the opposite side of his neck, feeling the veins pulsing in his throat as she bit.

Surprised by the sharp, piercing pain, he clenched her hair in his fist. Rather than try to pull her away, he pressed her mouth harder against his neck, her tongue sliding against his skin as his blood ran over her lips.

She sucked at the wound, the fluid salty and coppery, his cologne providing a sandalwood aromatic. He shuddered, the fingers of one hand weaving through her thick black hair, the fingers of the other folding into a pleasant hook as he penetrated her deeper. A flash of warmth rocketed through her core.

A chill brushed her skin as he found the zipper of her dress, the rending of metal teeth loud in the hallway. He fumbled at the door, then finally opened it and pulled her through, pressing her against the sink counter. She twisted free of the top half of her dress, hiking the hem over her hips, and he tore her bra loose.

Another moan ripped out of her as his hands grabbed at her breasts, and she watched the slow, dark trickle of red sliding down the open front of his shirt, a lazy river wending down his chest. Fumbling with the buttons of his pants, she freed him, pulling him inside her.

She lapped at the minor pool of fluid collected in the hollow of his collarbone and at the base of his throat, feeling the first faint tremors of orgasm approaching. She pulled at his hair, roughly, tearing small clumps free.

His tongue circled her nipple, and she demanded, "Bite me."

He took the raised nub of flesh between his teeth and bit down, gently at first, but her grunts demanded more, and he knew that she needed to bleed. He needed to taste her fully.

Grabbing the fleshy bulb of her breast between his fingers, he squeezed and bit down, the nipple almost chewy as his front teeth punched through skin, a bloody welt raising against his tongue. He bit harder and pulled, the pink tip popping free.

She screamed in pain, a delightful howl in his ears. Her nails raked away strips of flesh from his back as their mouths rediscovered one another, blood pooling between their half-naked bodies, gluing them together.

He took a fistful of her hair and rammed her head back against the mirror, his reflection cracking into a hundred new dimensions.

Reaching for a shard of glass, she dug the pointy area into his cheek, stabbing the mirror clean through, into his mouth. He spat in her face, and her tongue darted out in reflex, tasting the coppery, red emulsion against her lips.

Tearing the dagger loose, the skin of her own hand sliced open around it, she stabbed him in the chest, again and again and again.

He grunted loudly in her ear, his hips bucking. She peppered his bleeding cheek with kisses, working her way down to the rhythmic pulsing in his neck, to the slow trickle she had begun. Her lips clamped over the bite marks, her teeth making fresh ruptures, and she bit down, hard and deep, opening his throat wide. He couldn't contain himself against the spasm of contractions as she came, and he drove himself deeper, gasping, until he was spent.

Emptied, he fell free of her grasp and crashed to the floor, lightheaded. The pain was beginning to register, and he noticed for the first time the odd reflection of himself at his chest. Dazed, Noel pulled the shard free, minor glints and reflections surrounding him on the floor. Coraline was sitting on the counter, licking the gore off her fingers from her ruined breast.

He watched as her rosy tongue curled around her slender index finger, their eyes meeting briefly before he fell into a pit of darkness.

Coraline pushed herself off the counter, her hand sliding across more broken glass, her palm opening with an acute pain as tendons in her fingers were destroyed. She studied herself in the mirror, a length of glass in hand, suddenly starved. The blade at her throat, cool against her skin, she pressed against the vein and opened it, drawing it full across. A smile bloomed below her chin, breaking open wide with a shower of red.

11

"THIS NEXT COURSE IS a vegetable dish. Chef Schauer has prepared a kale casserole, roasted cauliflower with grapes, and Brussels sprout gratin. Enjoy."

Four dishes were plated as eyes turned toward the empty seats.

"Where are Noel and Coraline?" Peter asked.

"Bathroom, I thought," Joseph said.

"I wouldn't be surprised if Coraline is purging herself," Irene said, spearing a Brussels sprout. The dish was creamy and she nodded appreciatively at the taste of nutmeg and butter.

"Well, their loss," Joseph said, enjoying the cauliflower. The grapes added a nice, springy bite of freshness, the capers and lemon balancing the dish with a hint of tartness and acidity.

Although Peter avoided green bean casserole, he found the substitution of kale to be a particularly wonderful modification of such a tired and trite standby.

Casserole dishes reminded him of shitty Thanksgiving dinners with many of the same family members he diligently

219

avoided the rest of the year. The noticeably canned flavors of gloppy mushroom soup always recalled past arguments over gay rights and liberal politics as he was dragged into the fray of heated shouting matches from the older, far-right religious conservatives of his clan. Most of the men he found himself annually surrounded by were dolts who considered him an abomination.

Biting into a crispy leaf of kale, he vowed to never attend another Thanksgiving dinner with his family ever again. The news would break his mother's heart, but heartache was a constant in life. He saw no reason to willingly inflict that…that *bullshit*…upon himself yet again. Truthfully, he'd let that annual charade play out for far too long.

Anyway, Aunt Muriel's casserole didn't stand a chance against Schauer's dish. The mushrooms were fresh and buttery, and the notes of garlic, salt, and allspice wove through the greens in symphonic harmony. Even the fried onions, battered with buttermilk and yogurt, seasoned with ancho chile powder, were crafted with precision, not that premade, store-bought crap in a plastic box.

Muriel's husband, Frank, was an especially atrocious sort. Rotund and big-mouthed, a bigot to the core. For the last six years, he'd begun every Thanksgiving dinner by praying to God that Obama's Kenyan birth certificate would be found and that the Good Lord would strike down that antichrist in a hail of brimstone and restore America's glory. Rather than bow his head as he delivered his micro-sermon, he would glare directly at Peter, an outspoken and registered Democrat, locking eyes with him, as if he were taunting him. He knew that Frank would love it just as much, if not more, if God would strike down Peter with a rain of fire and ash. The man was rotten with hate.

As he ate, Peter daydreamed of carving up Frank, as if he were one of Mom's predictably dry, dull turkeys. He would take a large butcher's knife to each of his joints, removing his legs and slicing open the flesh on either side of his breastbone, peeling away the meat.

He simmered in his rage, his face reddening.

"You all right?" Joseph asked him.

Peter blinked, as if he were awakening from a long, troubled sleep. He hadn't realized he was slouching and scooted himself up in the chair.

"Distracted, I guess."

"You were shaking," Irene said.

Laura leaned across the table, pressing the back of her hand against his forehead. "Shit, you're burning up. You sure you're OK?"

"No. I mean, yeah, I'm fine."

Joseph nodded, letting it rest. Each of them knew the false bravado was a lie, recognizing their own burgeoning wickedness with each passing course, a hidden undercurrent of rage that the food helped to fuel. But they pressed on in feeding their inner demons, and let the matter drop.

12

SCHAUER WATCHED THE SAVAGE copulation, marveling at the gruesome affirmation of life as it bled out into death.

Noel and Coraline were fine dining companions, and he was struck by their loss. This he brushed aside, with the knowledge that they would be immortal soon. Their deaths would give way to ancient life, and their souls would be enraptured in a higher plane. The Old Gods would see to that.

Towering over the still-breathing, diminished husk of Baen'sollogotgartha, he squeezed the being's fleshy chest and promised him the world.

The Old God had been lost to antiquity, nearly entirely forgotten by mankind, but Earth would soon be reminded.

Rumors had persisted, as they often do. Back-alley gossip amongst certain types of collectors, the believers of the outlandish, hunters of the unknown. Mysticists, occultists, cult members, fetishists of paranormal Nazi experiments, whispering and wondering, each of them.

The seizure of this beast had not been cheap. Most of the rumors he'd followed had led to dead-ends. After an arctic research team met a mysterious and violent end, he had begun to wonder. With that wonder came an enormous amount of private funding for further explorations and excavations. Of the one hundred and twenty-seven people he had hired, all but four had lived to bring him this beast. The greatest hunt of mankind, conducted entirely in secret.

And this evening, a meal unlike anything ever known in the history of human consumption.

This was his sacrifice.

13

AFTER CLEARING AWAY THEIR vegetable dishes, the waitress returned with four overly large saucer plates garnished with chopped mint. Standing in the center of the plate was a large, heavy, metal tumbler filled with a slushy white liquid. Beside the glass of frozen punch was a chilled coffee spoon.

Joseph dipped the spoon into the glass, taking a small sample. He immediately went back for more with a guilty rush, his endorphins singing.

The frozen drink was made of milk, bourbon, and vanilla, then dusted with freshly ground nutmeg. Heavy, but unabashedly appealing, the milk punch was the perfect cleanser after the earlier meals.

Unbidden, he thought of his mother lying on her deathbed, kept alive by the whiny susurration of a breathing machine. She'd been a violent alcoholic and a large part of the reason why Joseph rarely drank.

One summer day – he must have been seven or eight – he'd gone outside to play following a heavy rain. When he returned, his shoes caked in mud, he'd made one hell of a mess of the carpeting as he ran through the house. She'd been furious, and, at the end of a lengthy sermon that found him on the receiving end of a leather belt, he'd been dutiful in cleaning things as best he could.

That night, when he was sleeping on his belly, his mother came into his room, tottering on shaky, drunk legs, and pressed a hot iron against his left shoulder, ending his pleasant dreams with a painful burning, pressing hard despite his screams and the rubbery stink of searing flesh invading both their nostrils.

Spooning the punch into his mouth, he could almost feel the tight contraction of his scolded skin beneath the hot soleplate.

Pulling the cord on her life support was his fondest memory of dear old mother, watching as her thin chest deflated and stilled. Burning down the home he'd been raised in later that week was a very close second.

He smiled around the spoonful of punch, the bourbon heavy and warm against the back of his palate.

"It's good, huh?" Laura said, clearly pleased.

"Very," Joseph said, listening to the wheeze of the breathing machine whispering its last gasp.

What little of Laura's face that was unhidden by the demon's mask indicated a pretty woman. She was petite, small-breasted, and he had admired the curve of her shoulders and the line of her spine through the open-backed blouse when she turned away from him. He enjoyed her apparently good-natured and easily amused personality, her vivacious smile. Despite her being half his age, he wondered what it would be like to fuck her, her body writhing beneath his as he held an iron to her belly.

She ran her spoon across the top of the punch, skimming the frozen concoction away from the glass. With the spoon halfway to her mouth, she looked down and, her curiosity plain, asked, "What the hell is that?"

"Let's see," Joseph said.

Laura tilted the cup toward him, and he saw immediately what her concern was. Buried in the punch was a gleaming, black object, perfectly round.

He dug around in his own cup, unburying a similar object, and hoisted it up. Bringing it closer to study, he could make out the features better. The blackness came in varying shades, and he saw the imprint of multiple hexagonal shapes beneath the icy casing.

"I think it's an eye."

Laura went pale, her spoon clattering against the plate and table before shaking itself to the floor. She pushed the plate away, unable to hide her disgust.

"It sorta resembles a bug's eye," Peter said, having found the decorative eye in his tumbler. "But way too big for that, right?"

"Oh yeah," Joseph said, "way, way too big."

"I don't think I can have any more either," Irene said, pushing her plate away.

Joseph and Peter looked expectantly at one another, the same playful question in each of their eyes. "Well?"

With a small chuckle, Peter stared directly at Irene as he shoved the spoon in his mouth. Her face scrunched in disgust as she turned away, an audible, liquid pop coming from both men's mouths as they bit down.

Peter's mouth screwed up around the taste, his lips curving downward. His throat bobbed as he forced it down.

Joseph spat his out into the cup with a groan. He took the freezing tumbler and twisted to the side, spitting several more times. The taste was similar to bleach, but much saltier, and a thick sheet of the eye's jelly clung to his taste buds. He spent another minute half-gagging and spitting, then reached for his wine, hoping to drown away the putrescence.

"Maybe you weren't supposed to eat that," Laura said, looking for all the world as if she were seasick.

"I think I'll go join Coraline in her purging efforts," Peter joked.

"Where are they, anyway?" Laura asked, turning to Irene.

"Probably they discovered some other earthly delights to take part in," Joseph said, refilling his wine glass.

Surprised, Laura let out a quick laugh. "You think? Oh my god."

Joseph shrugged half-heartedly, kicking off his shoes beneath the table. His socked foot found her ankle and brushed against the bare skin, stroking upwards. She shot him a small smile, apparently not minding, and drew her chair closer.

14

THE EIGHTH DISH WAS joint meat with an arugula salad. The roast was herbaceous, the salad hitting a sweeter note with its honey and balsamic vinegar dressing, and topped with goat cheese and an egg.

"OK," Laura began, "what has horns, fucked-up bug eyes, and a shit brown egg yolk?"

Her stomach still roiled from the earlier eyeball incident, and the food was no longer sitting right with her. She felt bloated and gassy, the contents of her stomach shifting painfully, and an acidic burn lingered at the back of her throat. She picked at the food with her fork, moving it around the plate but unable to eat anything.

The egg appeared rotten and its odor was cloying. The brackishness made her belly lurch, but Irene, still feeling somewhat adventurous despite an upset stomach, and being unfamiliar with such an odd egg, sliced into half of it with her fork, spilling the brown yolk across the greens, and stabbed into the arugula. The bite was nutty and creamy, but held an unctuous flavor that she could not quite pinpoint. Greasy, certainly, and bitter, like lye.

As the treacly yolk slid down her throat, she placed the flavors with an unexpected connection. The taste reminded her of an abortion when she was two days shy of becoming a teenager.

The food carried with it a proprietary invasiveness, and she felt a too-familiar pinch in her cervix, a cramping deep in her core that she blotted her eyes shut against. A gorge rose in her throat, stuffing her esophagus, the muscles in her neck collapsing around this reaching otherness as it crawled up and up, stretching into her skull.

Gagging, she dropped her fork, a painful twitch in her eye. Something was pressing against the back of her orbital bone, and she could feel her right eye pushing up against the eyelid as that thing tried to shove it out of the way.

Gritting her teeth against the pain, she backhanded her fork to the hardwood floor, where it rang out with a metallic crash.

Startled, the other guests stared at her with concern. Blood was leaking from a tightly pinched eye, pooling against the inside of her mask. A sharp cracking noise echoed across the table as the suture that fused her maxilla and zygomatic bones fractured, and she let out a wretched, agonizing cry.

Peter shot up, his chair falling behind him, and bent to try to help Irene. He had no idea what he could do or what could be happening to her, but he was driven by the instinctual need to assist. His first thought was that she was choking, but that didn't make any sense. As far as he knew, choking people didn't bleed from their eye.

Irene's mask was askew, the shattered bones of her orbit punching through the skin and upsetting the balance of her leather mask as the geography of her face quaked and ruptured.

Her eye twisted through the mask's eyehole, dangling by the optic nerve across the side of her face.

Laura screamed, shoving herself away from the table, not knowing what the fuck was happening. In seconds Irene had gone from bad to worse and she could feel the electric hum of chaos as everything unraveled around her.

Joseph yelled a warning to Peter. "Get back," he said

several times, but the words were lost. Either Peter was ignoring him or couldn't hear him over the increasing din of Irene's screaming.

Peter bent closer, seeing something writhing in the red-black hollow of her eye socket. A thin, bluish muscle was expanding, inchworming its way forward along the raw rope of optic nerve, its bulbous, multi-eyed face seeking the air, sniffing its way out of her skull.

"What the fuck," Laura shouted, now standing and rushing backward, away from the table. In her panic, she didn't realize she was going the wrong way until her shoulders slammed against the heavy panes of the window. Frost nipped at her, surprising her as her bare back pressed against cold glass. The doorway was now at the opposite end of the room, past the horror show Irene was inexplicably birthing.

Peter couldn't get away fast enough. The creature exploded free of Irene's face, her jagged bones opening long slits in its sides as it pushed free. He had time to see a disc-shaped mouth as it opened, springing at him, biting down on his large, fleshy cheek. He tried to tear it away, but the fucker was clamped on too tightly, and he could feel it sucking against his flesh, inhaling him.

Its tail grew larger, its body stretching as it wrapped around his neck. He pulled, but the tail cinched tighter, the skin slimy. His fingers slid off the damn thing, unable to find any purchase.

Joseph stabbed at it with a fork, sure that he could hear the abomination squealing in pain, even under Irene's tortured moans. Peter's face was going purple, and Joseph found himself surprised at how strong, and how much bigger, the creature was. Fucker's like a python, he thought.

He screamed loudly, forgetting about Peter's predicament in a flash of pain as Irene drove a steak knife into his shoulder blade and ripped it free. He turned toward his assailant, her cratered face unbearably close, and managed to dodge out of the way as she thrust the knife toward his belly. She howled in anger, and with her mouth open, he saw this waking nightmare expand even further.

They were small and multi-legged. No, not legs. Tentacles. They reached and grasped at the sides of her unhinged jaw, their bodies snaking across her tongue and teeth, seeking escape. Beneath her blouse, he could see something roiling in her large belly, pouches of fat rippling against the fabric.

He stabbed at her with the fork, burying the utensil in the side of her face, but it didn't even faze her. Irene was running strictly on autopilot, he realized, nothing more than a vessel for these monsters excavating their way free.

He stepped back as she threw a half-hearted swing his way, then doubled over with pain, a wretched tearing noise sounding from her abdominal cavity. Fluids slapped at the floor, and her blouse and slacks were immediately drenched. Paralyzed by fear, he watched as her intestines unraveled between her legs, slopping against the floor with a wet staccato as more of those tentacled, spidery creatures crawled free. Her body went slack and collapsed upon itself on the floor.

He felt faint, a wave of nausea sweeping over him as his stomach cramped. He fought back the urge to vomit, but could taste the knot of bile at the back of his palate.

Joseph glanced back, toward where Laura had been seated, but she was gone. He heard her scream and stared over his shoulder, finding her by the window, batting at her hair. Some of the spiders had reached her, were crawling on her. She managed to fling several off, their bodies sailing into the fireplace and exploding in the flames. He hurried her way, smacking away as many as he could and taking her hand, pulling her away from the window.

"Up," he said, leaping atop the table and pulling her with him. He kicked aside the dishes, rushing to the opposite end, flailing at the creatures as they tried to jump on him.

Peter fell to his knees, his fingers uselessly trying to pull at the thing coiled around his throat. He couldn't breathe, and the world was turning black at the edges of his vision, the dining room growing dimmer. His face throbbed, and he could feel hundreds of teeth grinding against his cheekbone. It had sucked away the flesh and fat and muscles and still buried itself deeper and deeper, consuming him, growing larger and stronger.

Small appendages tickled his ear, and he swiped at them. He was lethargic, but still cogent enough to realize that whatever was on the side of his head had bit him. Was still biting him, nipping at his ear. He wanted to scream at the unpleasant feeling of tiny legs stepping across the folds of his ear, dipping inside the ear canal. He tried to wave it away again and a searing pain flushed through his hand. Holding his arm before him, he saw that two fingers had been torn away, the small bones of his first knuckles exposed around ragged clumps of pale flesh. His eardrum ruptured as the creature burrowed deeper, a painful, fuzzy feeling as it rutted around inside his skull.

The snake constricted further, the mouth hinging open wider and darting through his eye with the horrible, wet burst of an exploding water balloon.

When the darkness came, he welcomed it.

15

PULLING LAURA ALONG, JOSEPH shoved through the first door they came to, off the right side of the dining room. He suspected the kitchen lay beyond, and had noticed their mourning-veiled waitress coming and going from there. He decided the time had come to speak to Schauer.

Rather than a kitchen, he found a large, empty room. The waitress was there, and if the cigarette butts at the base of the stool she sat on were any indication, she had been chain-smoking through much of the evening. A dumbwaiter stood open on the opposite wall behind her; the kitchen appliances were clearly unused. Dirty dishes were towered atop the counter, beside a disused, dusty sink.

"Where is he?" Joseph asked. He stifled a belch. The waitress stubbed out her cigarette on the countertop, and that was when he noticed the gun. She held the revolver in her lap, pointed at him.

She raised it and fired, but he was already moving, slamming the door shut behind him. Two more rounds found their way into the door, the wood splintering and sending tiny shards at his face.

Laura was screaming, and he moved her farther away from the door, briefly taking her in his arms. The bugs, or whatever they were, were preoccupied with the easy pickings in the dining room.

"We need to get out of here," he said.

"What about Noel and Cora? We should find them."

"They could be like Irene. Maybe what happened to her happened to them and that's why we haven't seen them."

She stopped dead in her tracks, pulling at his arm. "We all had the same food. What if that happens to us?"

The thought had lurked in the back of his mind, but he'd forcefully sent it to the side, ignoring it. There were enough problems to deal with.

"It won't," he said, but the words lacked the weight of assurance or conviction.

"I don't feel good," she said.

"C'mon," he said, dragging her forcefully along the corridor before she could protest or ask more questions.

"I overheard the waitress say the bathrooms were at the end of the hall."

"Forget them. We need to go."

"No, we can't. We can't do that. Are you crazy, we can't leave them here."

Nearly shouting at him, her voice went shrill. He hated the way women's voices took on that whiny, high-pitched tonal quality when they were upset, expecting the rest of the world to cave to their pathetic needs.

"Fine," he snapped, cheeks burning. He shook his head, but went along with it. If more of those things were waiting for them, it would be her fault, and he'd have no problem shoving her into the heart of the horror and running away. She was thin and small, not much meat on her, but enough to be a distraction. Easy pickings.

"Cora," Laura called. "Coraline!"

"Would you shut up, at least?" he snapped. "You're going to bring those things right down on top of us."

She rushed past him, peeking into the open doorways and finding empty rooms and sheeted furniture. "Noel?" she tried, moving on when he failed to respond.

Joseph took the next door, and she rushed past to check

the one after that. Every few seconds he stared over his shoulder, worried he would find those bug things scrabbling against the walls, coming for him, fully expecting the waitress to pop around a corner and shoot him to death. He could hear the creatures wheezing in the air, the gasp of a dying old woman, the stink of bleach and ash hanging in the corridor.

The two bathrooms were on opposite sides of the hall. Instinct drove them together, Joseph opening one door while Laura, who he now noticed was awfully pale, her eyes glassy beneath the mask, crowded next to him. He closed the door on inky darkness and turned toward door number two, heart racing.

His slick palm grasped the knob, turning it. His brain spent a long moment absorbing the sight of blood-slicked floors and shattered mirrors. Laura gasped in his ear.

They were everywhere, hundreds of them, and much, much larger than their dining room kin. The largest of them fought one another, feasting on falling brethren, their massive tusks goring soft bellies, boney cages parting as their round, tubular mouths suckled at seeping, bluish-gray flesh.

He could barely make out the remains of Noel and Coraline, the latter splayed open and dismembered, thick, gory streaks trailing away from her body on the white ceramic tiles. The smaller spiders gnawed on her innards, while a larger beast tucked its snout into Noel's waist, clumps of his skin and plasma sheeting its enormous, abstract cranium, wet smacking noises echoing through the chamber of Noel's chest.

Laura bumped into him, her body flailing and shoving him forward. He turned to cuss at her, but saw the bathroom door being pulled shut, barely catching sight of black fabric before the lock clicked into place. He ran to the door, searching for a way to unlock it, but found no more than a solid brass plate. No lock. Not even a handle. The door could only be opened from outside the bathroom.

Sensing their presence, the beast kneeling before the dead diners looked up, gore trickling across the boney cages that hid much of its face, crouched on thickly plated knees, its arms like thick tree trunks, terminating in three long, ropey fingers that curved into serrated talons. Tentacles swam through the air, seeking them. The walls shook under the deeply resonant grunts, the bass of its guttural cries quaking through the floor and up the skeletons of Laura and Joseph.

They stood stock still, not even breathing, hoping they would somehow be ignored.

Joseph doubled over with a pained wince, his arm curving around his belly. A wad of phlegm lodged in his throat, and he tried to clear it. His other hand groped at Laura, and she bent to help, concerned.

"I'm sorry," he said, knowing that his death was imminent. Knowing that Laura's was, too. Still, even a few more moments of life were better than none.

He forced himself to stand upright, despite the agony. Grabbing Laura by both arms, he pushed her forward, toward the giant beast crouched before them. Tentacles snapped around her, and he heard bone crunch beneath their grasp. She was dead before she had time to scream, her head hanging at an unnatural angle, neck broken. The tentacles twisted and pulled, her head coming free, the rest of her body dragged toward those massive, parting tusks.

His stomach clenched and roiled as the muscles cramped and constricted. A sharp, stabbing pain shot through his core as his innards calved. He flung his mask off, then pulled free of his sweater and tore the button-down shirt beneath it open, buttons clinking against the slippery tiles.

In the mirror, he watched in horror as the skin of his torso rippled, as if a strong ocean current shifted through him. His flesh was nearly transparent, thin, and shot through with black piping. He pressed his fingers to his greasy belly, punching through the too-thin screen, and stretched it open. With a dazed sense of curiosity, Joseph watched a host of tentacles unravel and spill out of the ruined cavity.

The massive beast stopped eating, bits of Laura dangling from the ivory cage across its mouth. It stared at him, watching him with keen interest, waiting.

A slick wad, thick and heavy, climbed up Joseph's esophagus. Pinpricks of pain tickled the back of his mouth as the creature rose, entrenching its stingers in the soft tissue lining the inside of his neck as it dragged itself higher and higher.

Collapsing to his knees, he screamed in pain, his mouth full of blood and a repulsive, oily liquid.

Joseph had noted the taste in the previous dishes and was familiar with it now. He could finally pinpoint what, exactly, that particular flavor was. Bitter and ashy, unusually greasy, with the sliminess of okra. He tried to swallow it away, but that was of no use.

The taste of death flourished in his mouth.

16

BAEN'SOLLOGOTGARTHA AND THE OLD Gods of
its realm promised immortality to those they consumed.
Not on earth, but elsewhere, on another plane. A plane
where mankind would be seen as gods in their own right,
where their power over existence would be immeasurably
strong.

Schauer craved no power, and cared little for the weight
of life and death in his hands. As with any number of
magnificent chefs, though, he sought the power of
transformation.

Footfalls sounded against the stone steps as the waitress
descended into the manor's basement, gun in hand.

"It's time," he told her.

She nodded mutely, removing the tricorn hat and veil,
setting them neatly on the counter. She undressed and
quickly folded her clothes, placing them beside the
mourning wear. Schauer took her hand and gave it a gentle
squeeze.

Opening her mouth, she put the gun barrel to the back
of her upper palate and pulled the trigger with no hesitation.
Matter exploded out of the back of her skull, smacking

against the creature's face. Its ruined mouth opened and contracted, its forked tongue seeking sustenance.

If time allowed, he would prepare a meal of long pig for his final guest, here in this kitchen.

Good food did wonders for a soul, Schauer knew, and the mingling of a particular blend of flavors could bring tears to one's eyes. In the best instances, they helped another individual experience something communal, to share in the stories and cultures of another. Meals could inspire and lift a man.

In the best cases, ingredients were used in unusual ways to elevate an otherwise common dish to something extraordinary. With that sense of respect and endearment, those meals became transformative in nature.

For years, he had sought the perfect guests. Those with palates of depth and subtlety, and a breadth of experience, who could appreciate mysterious, experimental meals and allow themselves to be consumed by the heady flavors of the dish plated before them. It had taken time, but Schauer was patient.

His patience had been rewarded. His skill had aided him well, and his dreams had been realized. With little more than his culinary know-how, Schauer had transformed his guests, elevated them.

Bending over the beast, he rested his hands flat against the shiny, sweat-slick cranium, and licked at the open wounds. The white sheen was coppery and burnt tasting, highly metallic and acidic, sulfurous almost. He ran his long tongue across the side of a fractured plane, and up to the hollow of an eye hole, allowing the cloying flavors to meld along his sophisticated palate. In return, the beast's own tongue sought and probed, longing for a taste. He dared not get close, though. Not yet.

For these beasts, consumption was a sex act. Their reproduction was predicated entirely on cannibalism and ruinous parasitical acts with other creatures. They were a driven species, their methods of satiation distilled into the simple act of eating, of devouring, the cycle of life reduced to a system no more complex than the rending and tearing of flesh and muscle with gnashing teeth and swallowing throats, followed by an engorged birthing.

He surveyed the husk of the creature. Plenty left, yet, for a feast. A knot bloomed and twisted in his belly, wrenching his guts in a violent twist. He doubled over in pain, gasping in agony. Still, he smiled, and thought for the last time of his assembled guests and the arctic surveyors before them.

Through the simple act of consumption, he had made each of them gods.

Soon, he would join them, and the world would change in their wake.

www.ingramcontent.com/pod-product-compliance
Lightning Source LLC
Chambersburg PA
CBHW050610190726
48283CB00007B/2352